Y049089

The item should be returned or renewed by the last date stamped below.

Dylid dychwelyd neu adnewyddu'r eitem erbyn y dyddiad olaf sydd wedi'i stampio isod.

PILLGWENLLY

30 /5/29

−7 JUN 2024

WFS

To renew visit / Adnewyddwch ar
www.newport.gov.uk/libraries

D1334257

RUBY

Heather Burnside

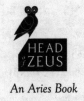

An Aries Book

First published in the UK in 2019 by Head of Zeus Ltd
This paperback edition first published in the UK in 2022 by Head of Zeus Ltd,
part of Bloomsbury Publishing Plc

Copyright © Heather Burnside, 2019

The moral right of Heather Burnside to be identified as the author of this work
has been asserted in accordance with the Copyright,
Designs and Patents Act of 1988.

All rights reserved. No part of this publication may be reproduced,
stored in a retrieval system, or transmitted, in any form or by any
means, electronic, mechanical, photocopying, recording, or otherwise,
without the prior permission of both the copyright owner
and the above publisher of this book.

This is a work of fiction. All characters, organizations, and events
portrayed in this novel are either products of the author's
imagination or are used fictitiously.

9 7 5 3 1 2 4 6 8

A CIP catalogue record for this book is available from the British Library.

ISBN (PB): 9781803282916
ISBN (E): 9781789542080

Typeset by Silicon Chips
Cover Design © Heike Schüssler

Printed and bound in Great Britain by
CPI Group (UK) Ltd, Croydon CR0 4YY

Head of Zeus
5–8 Hardwick Street
London EC1R 4RG

www.headofzeus.com

For Dave

Prologue

Kyle was soon standing at the reception desk ready for his pre-arranged meeting with Ruby. As she looked at him, she felt a tug of repulsion. There was no way she could go through with this, and the meeting with her cousins had given her the courage to put him off even though she was still fearful of his reaction.

'I'm not doing it,' said Ruby.

'You what?' he asked, glaring at her.

'I can't. I thought I could, but I can't.'

'What the fuck's wrong with you? You're not some innocent fuckin' virgin, y'know. I know for a fact you've had plenty of customers in the past; I've been asking around. And now, just cos you're the fuckin' madam, you think you're too good for the customers.'

Ruby could feel her heart racing and her hands were sweating as she saw the look of fury on his face, but she tried to keep her voice even. 'It's up to me whether I take customers or not, so if I say I don't want to do it then I won't do it.'

Kyle swiped angrily at her, catching the attention of two of her girls and a customer who were in the waiting area, but she dodged away quickly. He then leaned over the reception counter, his head poking forward.

'If it wasn't for the fact that that lot might call the cops, I'd drag you into one of those fuckin' rooms now!' he threatened. 'I'm having no fuckin' tart thinking she's too good for me. You're lucky to get a decent looking bloke after some of the fuckin' weirdos you're used to shaggin' so you'd better have a rethink and fuckin' quick if you know what's good for you. I'll be in touch.'

Then he was gone and Ruby felt her shoulders slump in relief. She saw one of the girls in the waiting area look across at her but she quickly raised her hand palm outwards to stop her coming over. 'It's OK,' she said. 'Just a troublesome customer, nothing to worry about.'

Ruby looked down at her computer screen, refusing to maintain eye contact with the girl. She'd tried her best to play it down, but was worried that if her staff saw the fearful expression on her face they would realise the threat that Kyle really posed.

I

August 1991

Nine-year-old Trina was helping her mother, Daisy, with the housework. As they worked, they both sang along to Tracy Chapman while two of Trina's younger brothers were playing noisily, drowning out the sound of the stereo.

'Shut up your noise!' shouted Daisy, her Jamaican accent still pronounced after more than twenty years in the UK. 'I can't hear meself think.'

The two boys stopped their play-fighting, looked at each other and giggled.

'Get up the stairs,' said Daisy, clicking her tongue in annoyance.

'No, we want to play out,' said Ellis, the older of the two boys.

'Go on, and take Tyler with you,' said Daisy.

Trina looked across at her youngest brother, Tyler, quietly playing with his battered toy cars in a corner of the room. He was so different from the other two, Ellis and Jarell, who could be such a handful.

'Go on, hurry up,' said Daisy. 'Let me get me work done.'

Trina put down the duster she was using and walked over to Tyler, ready to take him by the hand.

'No! Not you, Trina,' said her mother. 'I need your help.'

'But who's gonna look after him?' asked Trina.

'Them two can,' said Daisy.

Catching the expression on her mother's face, Trina knew she wasn't in the mood for arguments. She picked her duster back up and carried on with what she was doing, despite her qualms about the ability of Ellis and Jarell to look after Tyler, who was only three.

Usually the responsibility fell on Trina to look out for her three younger brothers – Ellis, aged seven, six-year-old Jarell, and Tyler – when her mother was busy cooking, shopping or washing. But today was cleaning day and Daisy often asked Trina for help. It seemed to Trina that her mother was overwhelmed with the amount of work involved in looking after a three-bedroomed house and four children. Nevertheless, she undertook her tasks every Saturday without failure, not happy till every surface was dusted, hoovered and cleaned.

Daisy was a respectable woman who took pride in having a clean home. Despite her status as a single parent on benefits, she did her best to maintain her high standards and set a good example to her children. She was an attractive woman in her thirties, of average height and with a womanly figure. Trina took after her mother in looks, but not in height for she was very tall for her age, something she had gained from her absent father.

Trina looked up from her dusting as the boys dashed excitedly to the front door. She was envious of them. It didn't seem fair that she should have to stay and help her mother while the boys got to play outside. But that's the way it was and she had long ago come to accept her status as the oldest child. Not only was she the oldest but she was also a girl, which made a difference as far as her mother was concerned. Girls helped with the housework; boys did not.

'And keep a tight hold on him!' Daisy shouted to her two eldest boys as they fled out through the front door.

They were no sooner outside than there was a knock on the door. Daisy clicked her tongue again.

'What on earth's the matter!' she called, trying to ignore it.

There was a second knock. Trina said, 'I'll get it, Mam,' happy to put down her duster again.

But before she got the chance, they heard a man's voice outside. 'Daisy! I know you're in there so answer the door,' he shouted.

Trina continued making her way towards the front door till she felt her mother's sharp pull on her shoulder.

'No,' she whispered. 'Get behind the curtain. Don't let him see you or there'll be hell to pay.'

Alarmed, Trina quickly took her place with her mother, standing to one side of the open curtains so they couldn't be seen through the window. Daisy was busy peering through a gap at the edge of the curtains. A shadow fell across the window and the man's voice came closer.

'Open the door, Daisy! I know you're in there. I've just seen the children leave,' shouted the man.

A look of concern flashed across Trina's face as she picked up on the grave tone of the man's voice.

'I think it's Mr Dodds. Shouldn't we let him in, Mam?' she whispered.

'Shush,' said Daisy, adding a stern, 'No! The man can wait.'

Something about Mr Dodds' tone and her mother's gruff manner set Trina on edge. As they waited for him to go away, Trina could feel her heart beating so rapidly that she thought it would burst through her chest.

'He's gone,' Daisy finally announced, releasing her grip on the curtain and striding away from the window. 'Thank the Lord for that,' she added, stopping to touch herself in the sign of the cross.

For a few moments the sound of the hoover drowned out all other noise so it wasn't until Mr Dodds stepped into their living room and sidled up to Daisy that she saw him. Trina noticed her mother's startled reaction when she caught sight of his tall, lean frame hovering over her.

'What on earth are you doing in here?' she demanded, switching off the hoover.

'You forgot to lock your back door,' he said, a self-satisfied smirk playing across his thin lips. 'So now I'll have the rent I've come for.'

Trina continued with the dusting, her body half turned towards her mother and Mr Dodds as she watched what was happening. She hated Mr Dodds. He was creepy with his lopsided features and the dirty, unwashed smell that came off him. She often saw him calling at other houses in the area, wearing one of the two creased and greasy suits that he rotated each week.

Trina noticed the way her mother nervously patted down her already tidy hair and shuffled uncomfortably from one foot to the other. 'I haven't got it,' she mumbled.

'I beg your pardon?' Mr Dodds shouted so loud that

Trina turned fully round, dropping the can of bargain-brand spray polish that she had been holding. As she bent to retrieve it, she heard her mother repeat herself.

'I said I haven't got it. Not this month. The kids needed new clothes.'

'Well I'm afraid that's not good enough,' said Mr Dodds, adopting a frown and pursed lips, full of self-righteous indignation. 'You shouldn't be spending the rent money on clothes or anything else.'

'I couldn't let them go without,' said Daisy.

Mr Dodds sidled even closer to Daisy and Trina saw her mother recoil as she caught a whiff of his malodorous breath. Then he hissed into her ear, but Trina couldn't quite catch all the words. Something about, 'other ways to pay'.

'Not over my dead body!' yelled Daisy, backing away from him. 'How dare you suggest such a thing! And in front of the child as well. Now, get out of me house before I do some damage.'

She lifted the metal piping of the hoover and held it menacingly towards Mr Dodds who squirmed.

'Very well,' he said. 'But don't think this is the end of it. You owe me two months now and I'll see to it that I get it, whatever it takes. By the time I've finished with you, you'll be begging me to take you in payment.'

'I'll rot in hell first!' shouted Daisy, waving the hoover at him till he dashed from the house.

Trina knew what was coming next. It was time for one of her mother's rants. Mr Dodds had got Daisy's hackles up, and it would be a while before she calmed down. She switched the hoover back on, sweeping it angrily along the carpets as she let out a stream of invective.

'How dare he! What does he think I am? Damn him and all men like him. He should go to hell for saying such a thing. Him and all his kind. And look how he's got me cursing… Damn you, Isaac, for leaving me in this state. Shaming me good name, and hardly a penny to spare. Dirty, good-for-nothing man. I should have known better than to marry you. Me mother warned me, but I wouldn't listen.'

She clicked her tongue in that familiar way of hers when she was displeased or angry about something. 'Young and foolish, that's what I was. But I'm paying the price now.'

On and on went her diatribe. Trina had known that it would inevitably lead back to her father. It always did. It was rare that Daisy had a good word to say about him. Trina wasn't surprised; her recollections of her father weren't good ones, but it didn't help to be constantly reminded of his failings. Still, she knew better than to say anything while her mother was in full flow.

Trina was glad when she'd finished her chores. She managed to get out of the house on the pretext of looking after Tyler, knowing that her mother didn't fully trust her other two brothers to take care of him. She quickly slipped out of the front door and found her youngest brother alone, running one of two wrecked toy cars up and down a dirt pile on the unadopted path at the end of their street. Her other two brothers were nowhere to be seen.

'Come on, Tyler,' she said, holding out her hand to him. 'You can't play there.' Tyler paused in his play and looked up at her. His bottom lip stuck out and Trina could tell he was about to cry but she stopped him. 'Look, your cars are getting dirty. You can play up there on the pavement.'

Then she took him by the hand, picked up his cars and

headed towards a group of girls who she had seen at the other end of the dirt path. Tyler began to whine.

'You can have them in a bit, once we're off the path,' said Trina, squeezing his hand to make sure he'd got the message.

She pulled him forcefully along, ignoring his squeals till they reached the other end of the path. Then she set the cars down on the pavement. 'Now play there, and shut it!' she ordered, drawing the attention of the girls who were huddled in a group.

Tyler went quiet, staring at her with big, sad eyes before he knelt down on the pavement and carried on playing. Trina looked across at the girls; her so-called friends. They had been deep in conversation until Trina came along, but now they were silent.

Jessica and Laura were a similar age to Trina but Trina was a head taller. Holly was also shorter than Trina and was a year younger. Out of the three girls, Jessica was the most outspoken and, as Trina approached them, she greeted her obsequiously.

'Hi, Trina,' she said, but Trina wasn't fooled. She knew the greeting was disingenuous. The other two girls followed Jessica's lead, competing to see who could be the most ingratiating.

Trina responded with characteristic hostility. 'How come you didn't call for me?' she asked, with a sneer on her face.

Jessica and Laura both answered at once, eager not to upset Trina, but their answers differed. 'Ellis and Jarrell said you were busy,' offered Jessica, while Laura said, 'We were just coming.'

'Liars!' said Trina, scowling at the girls. 'No way were

you coming to my house, Laura, and I'm gonna ask my brothers about you, Jessica.' She switched her glare from Laura to Jessica. 'If they say they haven't told you owt, then you'll be for it.'

Jessica flushed before lowering her head and for a moment all the girls stood in silence, Trina basking in their discomfort. Then she asked Laura, 'What've you got?'

Laura eagerly passed her the magazine she had been holding.

'There's a picture of New Kids on the Block inside,' she said. 'Do you want it?'

'I thought you were putting it on your bedroom wall?' said Jessica.

'No, it's OK. Trina can have it. I'll get another,' said Laura.

Trina flicked through the magazine while Jessica chatted to the other two girls about her latest ballet class. Then she found the poster she had been looking for. Taking care not to damage it, she removed it, but left the rest of the magazine ripped and incomplete before passing it back to Laura. Then she turned to Jessica.

'Ballet's for snobs,' she snarled. 'How come you go there?'

'My mam wants me to go,' said Jessica.

'Well your mam's a snob then,' said Trina who would have loved to have gone to ballet classes but knew her mother couldn't afford it.

For a few minutes more she baited the girls until she grew bored and decided to return home to search for something with which to stick the poster onto her bedroom wall.

'Come on, Tyler. We're going home now,' she said. 'And don't you dare start crying again!'

Tyler saw the expression on Trina's face and obediently let her lead him home.

Trina wasn't a bad person, but she did derive a certain satisfaction from seeing the girls squirm, especially knowing that they only pretended to like her out of fear. She had found a way to exert power over others and, in a life where things were otherwise out of her control, it gave her a kick. It also helped her to deal with all the festering resentment that bubbled away inside her.

All these girls had more than her and they all had better lives. She might not be able to boast about her nice life like they could but at least she knew how to command some respect from those who secretly thought they were better than her. It was Trina's first step in learning how to use her strength of character and imposing physique to her advantage. And that knowledge would stand her in good stead in the future.

2

August 1991

It was Sunday morning. Trina groaned when she heard her mother shout from her bedroom doorway.

'Come on, you as well. We can't afford to be idle on the Lord's Day.'

Trina looked at the time on the old alarm clock sitting on top of her chest of drawers. Eight o'clock. Why couldn't her mother let her lie in on a Sunday just for once? All the other local girls got a lie in on a Sunday. In fact, some of them didn't get up till eleven, and Trina didn't see why she should be forced out of bed. She turned over and shut her eyes. Just as she felt herself drifting off, she heard her mother shouting again.

'What on earth do you think you're doing, Trina? Come on, up. Now!'

As she shouted, Daisy pulled back the bedclothes.

'Aw, Mam,' Trina pleaded. 'It's Sunday.'

'I'm well aware of what day it is, my girl. That's why we've got to be up. Now, come on. And don't you dare take that tone with me if you know what's good for you.'

Trina looked up at her mother who was staring intently back, her tense body language letting her daughter know that she wouldn't stand for any arguing. When Daisy said you had to be up, you had to be up and that was that. Trina sat up in the bed and stretched till her mother left the room, satisfied that she had made a move.

When Trina got downstairs her mother was busy in the kitchen making breakfast while her brothers were in the living room getting ready.

'Go and help Tyler with his clothes then you can get yourself dressed and eat your food,' said Daisy.

Trina sighed and walked back towards the living room.

'And don't come that attitude with me,' said Daisy.

Another hour and they were all fed and dressed, and the boys had been given a brisk wash before they were allowed to leave the house. Daisy had swapped her everyday jeans for a smart skirt and jacket, and her hair was neatly plaited. Likewise, Trina's hair was in plaits and she wore her best dress.

The boys were also kitted out in their best clothes although the trousers were now too short for the older two and Tyler's jacket was a bit too tight. Unfortunately, the children outgrew their clothes before Daisy could afford replacements, and the few new clothes she'd bought were in the wash. Her own clothes were old but she kept them looking good.

They caught the 192 bus near to home and within no time they had arrived at the Bethshan Tabernacle, a popular local church, with Daisy's dire warnings to behave still ringing in the children's ears. Trina had already picked up on the fact that it was important to her mother to create a good impression.

Daisy and her children sat amongst her group of regular friends and relatives. Trina noticed her grandmother in a tweed jacket and skirt with a matching hat, and two of her aunties and uncles. Her older cousins weren't there, and Trina felt a touch of resentment that they always seemed to get out of going to church. She, on the other hand, had to attend every Sunday. Maybe when she was a bit older, she'd be able to get out of going to church too.

As they took their seats in the pews, Ellis and Jarell argued over who sat where and Tyler pushed noisily past people, trying to get to his grandparents. Trina noticed some of Daisy's friends tutting and whispering amongst themselves. Her mother scolded her sons for making a noise, and Trina's grandparents tried to calm Tyler down. She could tell her mother was stressed, glancing anxiously around as though she was bothered about the impression people had of her children.

Daisy was a single mother to four young children, alone and on benefits, and would therefore never be fully accepted by the churchgoers. Even at nine years of age, Trina was aware that these people had been far more accepting of her mother when she was still with her womanising, bully of an ex-husband. For some reason he seemed to command respect, and Trina wondered if it was because people were frightened of him. She knew that people treated her mother differently now, but she couldn't quite understand why.

Trina also wondered about the need to go to church every Sunday. When she had asked her mother why, Daisy had grown quite cross and said, 'May God strike you down for your blasphemy, child.' Her words and the tone she'd used to convey them struck such fear into Trina that she hadn't bothered asking again.

As she sat there fiddling with her hands, Trina willed the sermon to be over. The words of the sermon went straight over her head. She couldn't relate to anything being said and her mind began to wander. Trina looked forward to the singing, especially when they had a group performing on the stage. When that happened, everyone usually danced along to the music and it was good fun. But this bit was boring. What she really looked forward to was going back home. As it was Sunday, all the chores for the week were done and she could spend the rest of the day doing what she wanted, content in the knowledge that her soul had been cleansed for the week.

It was the following day and Trina was keeping an eye on her brothers after school while her mother was in the kitchen at the back of the house doing some washing. When Trina heard a knock on the door she rushed to answer it, eager to alleviate her boredom.

As Trina opened the door she spotted two strange men, both burly, one with red hair and a beard, and the other dark with crooked teeth. Behind them a large white van was parked. By the time Trina's mother ran into the hallway, her hands still full of suds, shouting, 'Don't let them in!' it was too late.

The men barged roughly past Trina who stood looking at them, bewildered as her mother grabbed hold of one of them and tried to stop him from going into the living room.

'Get out of me house! Get out of me house!' she yelled. 'You're not having me things. It's all I've got.'

But the men ignored her anguished cries and marched straight into the living room. Daisy soon caught up with them and there was a heated discussion. Red Beard took a piece of paper from his clipboard and handed it to Trina's mother asking if she was able to pay.

'Not today, but I'll have the money next week,' said Daisy.

'Sorry, but it's not good enough,' said the man who then instructed his colleague to start collecting goods in payment.

Daisy ran in front of Crooked Teeth and tried to block his way. 'No, not me stereo,' she pleaded. 'Please don't take me stereo.'

'Madam, could you please step out of the way?' said Red Beard, but Daisy stayed put, blocking his colleague's path.

'Very well,' said Red Beard, putting his clipboard down on the sideboard and stepping towards the TV.

Daisy switched her attention to him. 'No!' she yelled. 'You can't take the TV. Me kids are watching it. You cruel, cruel man!'

Tyler picked up on his mother's distress and began wailing while Ellis and Jarell tugged at the man's clothing to try and stop him getting to the TV. Trina noticed the other man lift the stereo while all the commotion was going on. But she didn't try to stop him. Something about the officiousness of the two men unsettled her, and she was wary of going against them.

Daisy swung round, looking from one man to the other, unsure who to deal with first. In the midst of her confusion Red Beard unplugged the TV and barged past her carrying it. Ellis and Jarell chased after him, screaming and tugging at his jacket to try to stop him. He set the TV down in the hallway while his partner carried the stereo outside to the van.

Daisy pursued Red Beard through to the kitchen and Trina could hear her mother remonstrating with him over the seizure of more goods. 'Quick,' Trina said to her brothers. 'Let's get the TV back while it's still in the hall.'

But by the time the children had gone through to the hall, Crooked Teeth had returned and was already carrying the TV out of the house. Now Ellis and Jarell also began to cry, and Trina felt unshed tears of anguish pricking her eyes.

'He's got the TV, Mam!' she shouted, and Daisy came dashing into the hallway.

'No!' shrieked Daisy. 'How can you do this? Me poor kids.'

By now Daisy seemed to have accepted there was nothing she could do to stop the men. So, instead, she reached out to her two oldest boys, putting an arm round each of them to offer them comfort. But their howling continued. Unsure what else to do, Trina took Tyler into her arms and tried to cuddle him while he struggled to break free and wailed down her ear.

Trina couldn't understand why her mother had given up the battle to hold onto their things. But she didn't realise that her mother was far too proud to go out into the street and give the neighbours something to gossip about. Trina felt upset and indecisive. Tyler's wailing and her other brothers' crying and screaming was becoming too much. She looked to her mother for guidance but Daisy seemed as defeated as the rest of them, standing there with a solemn frown on her face.

When Daisy eventually snapped and screamed at the boys to shut up, Trina was relieved in a way. She could see the men had almost finished as the pile of things in the hall had now gone. Both of the men were still outside but then Red Beard came back into the hallway and handed Daisy a piece of paper.

'Here's a list of the goods we've taken in payment,' he said.

'They're not goods!' screamed Daisy. 'They're our things. What are me kids supposed to watch now?'

'Sorry, love. Just doing my job,' said the man as he casually walked away.

'You wicked, wicked men!' shouted Daisy.

The front door was open, but Daisy seemed past caring about the neighbours or anyone else as she waved furiously at the men and shouted, 'Bastards!'

Trina heard the sound of the van's engine starting up. When the vehicle had roared off down the road. Daisy slammed the door shut and pushed her sons away from her.

'Get out of me sight!' she yelled.

The boys ran, frightened, down the hallway and up the stairs, with little Tyler trotting clumsily behind. But Trina stayed in the hallway, concerned for her mother. It was the first time she had ever heard her mother use bad language, and it unsettled her.

She looked at her mother who had now stopped shouting. Daisy's eyes were moist and as the tears slid down her face, she dropped to the floor, covering her face with her hands and bawling. Then Trina's own tears came and she knelt on the ground, her child's arms encircling her mother in a futile attempt at comfort.

After a while Trina asked, 'Why did they take our things, Mam?'

She braced herself for another angry reaction from her mother. But Daisy didn't shout. Instead, she raised her head and looked at her daughter, her expression one of defeat and humble resignation as she said, 'Because we don't have any money, Trina.'

When Daisy slowly walked back towards the kitchen, Trina was hit by a deep sadness. She recognised that this was a bad day for the family, not just because of the things they'd lost, but because of Daisy's response. It wasn't often that Trina saw her mother so wretched that she was reduced to tears and foul language. Trina felt helpless and she wondered not only how her family would cope, but just how much worse things were going to get.

3

August 1991

It was only a day later when Trina dawdled in from school to find her father occupying their worn old sofa with a scowl on his face. Isaac was a big man, both in height and frame. He was good-looking and muscular too, and it was easy to see why women found him difficult to resist despite his bullying ways. It was also easy to see why men found him so menacing; he had a reputation locally as a ruthless fighter who spared no pity for anyone who crossed him.

Trina watched her mother setting a cup of tea down on the coffee table in front of her father, muttering as she did so.

'I never thought I'd see the day when I had bailiffs turning up at me home.'

'Alright, Daisy. No need to keep saying it. I told you, it'll be sorted,' he said. 'And if I'd have been here, they wouldn't have fuckin' got away with it!'

Daisy didn't say anything about his bad language, a sure sign to Trina that she was treading lightly with him for some reason. Once she had put the cup down, Daisy turned round and addressed her daughter.

'Where you been till this time, child? Your father's been waiting to see you.'

Trina very much doubted that. When he had lived at home it had seemed to her that he couldn't stand the sight of his children. Now, however, he was sitting there with Tyler on his knee running a toy car along the length of his father's muscular arms.

'Well?' said Daisy. 'Aren't you going to say anything to your father?'

Trina looked across at her father whose face broke out into a fake smile. 'Hi, Dad,' she muttered.

'How's my girl? Come and sit next to your dad for a bit,' he said, patting the cushion next to him and grinning widely as though he was enjoying her discomfort.

Trina walked across the room and sat down awkwardly beside him. 'Where are Ellis and Jarell?' she asked her mother.

'I've sent them to the shop. They'll be back soon,' said Daisy.

'Yes, then we can all be one big, happy family again,' said Isaac, laughing.

Daisy joined in with his gaiety, but to Trina it seemed as though her mother's laughter was forced. When the merriment stopped, Daisy asked, 'Well, child, aren't you going to tell your father about your day? I'm sure he'll want to know what you've been up to at school.'

To Trina it was like penance, having to make conversation with her uncaring father while he feigned interest. As she sat there talking to him, she willed her brothers to get back soon. Perhaps they would take some of the pressure off her.

Eventually they did come back and her mother went into the kitchen to finish making the tea, leaving Isaac with his four children. Once the boys were there Trina tried to excuse herself by saying she was going to help her mother. As she stood up her father pulled her back down onto the sofa.

'Leave it,' he growled. 'Your mother can make the tea herself. I want my kids here with me. I haven't seen you in ages. I thought you'd have wanted to see your dad too.'

His last sentence was spoken like a question and Trina felt pressured to respond.

'Well, yeah,' she said, frightened of saying the wrong thing and making him angry. 'Course I do. I just wondered if my mam needed some help, that's all.'

'Well she doesn't,' he snapped.

Isaac stayed and had dinner with them before he left. Trina was relieved when he had gone, although she didn't say that to her mother who seemed in a better mood than the previous day. Daisy wasn't exactly happy but she seemed more at ease, as though some of her worries had been alleviated.

When she got into bed that night, Trina said her prayers as she did every night; she was too afraid of the wrath of God otherwise. But this time she didn't just say her bedtime prayers, she added a prayer of her own; *please God don't let him come back*.

Once she had finished praying, Trina dwelled for some time on bad memories of when her father had been at home. His perpetual anger. The rows. The put downs. The smacks. The rare outings. Him flirting in the park. Suddenly pleasant and likeable. Then disappearing for days. And the peace offerings whenever he came back. Toys that she never played with; contaminated by his deceit.

When she eventually drifted off, she was playing the same words over and over inside her head, *please don't let him come back, please don't let him come back, please don't let him come back…*

4

September 1991

Trina's prayers went unanswered as Isaac moved back into the family home a few days later bringing with him a TV, stereo and various kitchen utensils. As Trina eyed the household items lined up in the hallway, it reminded her of some sick kind of TV quiz show with her father as the booby prize. Trina knew that the replacement goods were some sort of deal her mother had struck with him, but she was just glad that at least they were getting something in exchange for having to put up with her father.

For a few weeks everything seemed fine between her parents although Isaac never accompanied the family to church. He was good to his kids though, in those early weeks, treating them whenever the ice cream van came round and giving them money for sweets from the corner shop, just like the other kids in the street. Sometimes they even had cake after tea, and Trina dared to dream that perhaps they could be just like normal families.

But then the rows started again. At first they were out of sight of the children, but Trina could hear them when she lay in bed at night. Her father's angry voice carried up the stairs, his use of expletives countered by her mother's disapproving tones. She couldn't fully understand what the problems were, but she thought it had a lot to do with her father's compulsion for chasing other women. She grew to dread coming home from school, feeling as though she was walking into a battlefield.

Then, one night, it was the final row. They had just eaten their evening meal when Isaac announced that he was going out, and he turned towards the hallway. The other children were upstairs playing.

'No, not again!' said Daisy. 'And I suppose there'll be strange women ringing the house again too.'

'Go to hell, woman! I'm only going out with me friends. Aren't I allowed some kind of life?'

'Not when you're chasing other women.'

'I'm not chasing any fuckin' women! I just want a break, that's all.'

'You think I believe that, Isaac, when some strange woman is ringing asking for you? And what about my break? I'm the one stuck in this house all day.'

'How many times do I have to tell you, woman? She was nothing to worry about.'

'Well why did she have your number then?'

'She just wanted to buy some stuff that I took round the pub, that's all. I gotta make me fuckin' living somehow. Have you any idea what it costs to keep you lot?'

'Yes, Isaac, I know too well, because I have to manage on my own every time you leave.'

'Cos you fuckin' drive me out!' he yelled. 'With all your moaning and cursing.'

'What do you expect me to do, Isaac? Just let you go out the door not knowing when you'll be back? And me with four children to look after.'

'Get off me case, woman,' he said, storming out of the room and into the hallway.

Daisy chased after him with Trina close on her tail, watching nervously from the living room door and wondering what would happen next. She saw her mother grab his arm.

'Come back, Isaac, or I swear God will strike you down.'

'There you go again with your cursing. Fuck your God and get your hands off me, woman!' he raged.

But Daisy wasn't prepared to let go. She clung onto his arm, trying to pull him back as he made for the front door. To Trina it was as though the scene was being played out in slow motion. She could anticipate her father's reaction, but she was powerless to stop it. She willed her mother to let go of him, but she didn't speak. It didn't pay to get involved when her parents were both angry.

'How dare you speak to me like that, Isaac! And in front of me daughter, too. You've no right to leave me to manage on me own. You need to face your responsibilities and stop chasing after other women.'

'Do you think I'm fuckin' stupid, Daisy? I know you only want me for me money. You've even turned me kids against me.'

'You did that all by yourself,' she shouted, flinging herself in front of him to block his way to the front door. 'Don't you dare leave this house, Isaac!'

His voice became a low growl and Trina could tell his anger was escalating. 'I'm telling you one more time, woman. Now get out of me fuckin' way or there'll be trouble!'

'No, I won't!' shouted Daisy.

She didn't get the chance to say anything else before Isaac raised his mighty fist and brought it down hard, striking an angry blow to her face. Daisy squealed and bent forward, clutching her face in her hands. But she was still barring his way to the door. He grabbed hold of her arms, crushing them between his powerful hands before lifting her, and flinging her down onto the hallway floor behind him.

Trina heard a loud thud and spotted the blood on her mother's face. But Daisy wasn't beaten yet. She quickly raised herself from the ground and sped after him, pulling his arms back once more as he struggled to open the front door. Isaac swung his arm back till his elbow impacted painfully with Daisy's chin. She let out a yell, then he turned back and viciously rained punches down on her face and body.

Forgetting her fear, Trina screamed for him to stop, but he didn't let up till Daisy lay crumpled on the floor. Then he was back at the door again. As he pulled the front door open and stormed from the house, Daisy remained slumped on the ground, shocked and yelling after him.

'You've hit me. I can't believe you've hit me! Don't you ever dare to come back here, Isaac Henry.'

Isaac ignored her yells and slammed the door shut after him. As soon as he was on the other side of the door, Trina ran over to her mother, distraught.

'Mam, Mam. Are you OK?' she asked, kneeling down beside her, unsure what to do.

She caught sight of her two oldest brothers coming down

the stairs, just as her mother heard them approach. 'Get back up those stairs!' she yelled. 'Trina, make them go to their room then you can come and help me,' she ordered.

Trina did as she was told, racing up the stairs to intercept her brothers. It wasn't easy. 'What's happened to her? And why can't we come downstairs?' asked Ellis.

It only took one word for Trina to explain what had happened. 'Dad,' she said.

'Has he gone?' asked Ellis.

'Yes, he's gone.'

'Well why can't we come downstairs then?' Ellis persisted.

'Mam doesn't want you to,' said Trina and as she looked at her brothers, she saw a look of defiance on Ellis's face. 'I swear, Ellis, you're not to come down. Our mam is really angry and she'll go mad if you come down.'

Ellis didn't say anything more; he just turned round and walked back to his room with his shoulders slumped and his two younger brothers following despondently behind.

'I'll let you know when it's alright to come down,' said Trina.

By the time she went back downstairs her mother was already at the kitchen sink trying to clean herself up. Trina helped her by holding a cold compress to her busted nose and wiping away her tears.

Eventually her mother was calm enough to speak to her. 'That's the end of it now, Trina. I won't put up with it no more.'

Trina nodded solemnly but didn't react except to ask, 'Can the boys come downstairs now?'

'Yes,' said Daisy. 'You can tell them I fell over and banged me face by accident. And not a word of this to anyone else, do you hear?'

Trina nodded again and went to speak to her brothers.

Isaac did call at the house again but only to collect the things he had brought with him. Trina watched, her stomach growling with fear and annoyance as he lifted the TV, stereo and various other items and walked out of the house without saying another word.

It was the last time Trina saw her father, just a few weeks before her tenth birthday. But she didn't miss him and the endless rows that accompanied him whenever he returned home. If anything, she was relieved to see him go. In fact, the whole family were much sorrier to lose their TV and stereo than they were to see the back of their bullying husband and father.

5

February 2005

Ruby was sitting in the public gallery at Manchester Crown Court surrounded by the clientele of the Rose and Crown. Prostitutes, pimps, drug dealers and conmen; they were all there. Next to her was her friend, Crystal, who had been tense throughout the trial of her former pimp and lover, Gilly.

As Ruby tried to concentrate on the judge's summing up of the case, she heard a sniffle and looked over at Crystal. Her friend often looked bedraggled; Ruby put it down to the fact that she worked long hours as well as taking care of her four-year-old daughter, Candice. But today she looked worse than ever.

Crystal's eyes were red-rimmed through crying, the small pupils and dark rings underneath them demonstrating a lack of sleep. Ruby could see fresh tears, which had smudged Crystal's mascara and eyeliner, leaving black streaks on top of the dark circles.

Her body language also spoke of her sorrow; her shoulders were hunched, her features strained, and she rung her hands as she waited for the judge to finish speaking so the jury could announce the verdict.

By contrast, Ruby was a woman who looked after herself; that was apparent from her taut muscles and radiant complexion with chestnut-coloured skin as soft and smooth as velvet. Her face was crowned with neat cornrows whose plaits spilt out enticingly onto her broad, honed shoulders. She was clean-living in relation to her diet, having given up the drugs long ago, unlike Crystal who seemed to rely on a cocktail of toxic substances to get her through the day.

Despite her physical appeal, Ruby was anything but sweet. Her face was beautiful but harsh, her strained features accompanied by a subconscious snarl, sparked by painful memories that haunted her. She appeared formidable, invincible and had a mood to match. But, although Ruby was feisty and sharp-tongued, she was extremely loyal to the people she cared about.

Ruby tutted as she looked at Crystal and whispered, 'What the fuck you snivelling for? You're better off without him.'

Ruby's eyes drifted across to the man in the dock. Gilly. He too looked tense, but he was trying to hide his disquiet behind a look that spoke of pure arrogance; chin jutting forward, eyes narrowed and a painted-on sneer.

For a few seconds Ruby studied him. Today he was smartly dressed for court in a shirt, tie and jacket, an obvious attempt to impress the jury. His hair had also been freshly washed and combed, his natural blond tone shining under the lights of the courtroom.

But Ruby saw through his innocent disguise. She knew the real Gilly. The scruffy one. The nasty one. The violent pimp and drug addict. And his smart appearance couldn't hide the badness that she knew was within him. Neither could it hide his pale, scabby face, a result of his drug abuse, which Ruby assumed had increased since he'd been charged with GBH the previous year. Although he'd been held on remand ever since, Ruby guessed that he was having no difficulty getting hold of drugs on the inside.

He caught her eye and she quickly shifted her gaze – not that she was afraid of him, but she didn't want him to think he merited more than a fleeting glance. As she looked away her mind drifted back to that day when she'd found Crystal, almost a year before.

Ruby had known there was something amiss. She'd seen Gilly and Crystal leave the Rose and Crown and it was obvious to her, and the other girls she was sitting with, that he was angry with Crystal about something. When he'd told Crystal he wanted a word, Ruby suspected he might be having more than a word with her.

She'd left it ten minutes, but when they still didn't come back to the pub she grew concerned and went to find out what had happened. There was no sign of Crystal or Gilly outside the Rose and Crown or in the street that led down the side of the pub, so Ruby had carried on along the street on her way to work.

But something had stopped her. She'd spotted somebody slumped against a bin in an alleyway and was ready to dismiss it as another of Manchester's down and outs. Until she saw the blood trail. Then she realised that that person was her friend, Crystal.

Ruby panicked when she first reached Crystal. There was no sign of movement and she'd thought she was dead, especially when she noticed all the blood. Crystal's face was a mess and it was obvious she'd been battered. Ruby instinctively knew who was responsible. *That bastard Gilly!*

Ruby still recalled the surge of emotion on seeing her friend in that state. But she'd managed to hold it together while she'd dialled 999 and asked the operator to get someone there as quickly as possible. Thank God she had found her when she did or who knew what might have happened.

Prior to the attack on Crystal, Ruby had also been one of his girls, working as a prostitute on the streets of Manchester. But after he had done that, she had vowed to go it alone, and had done so for the past year. She'd never liked working for him in the first place and didn't want another pimp pocketing a big share of her earnings. Anyway, Ruby knew she no longer needed a pimp's protection; she was more than capable of handling any problems herself.

Ruby had become so immersed in her own thoughts that she almost missed the verdict coming in. She felt a sharp nudge from Crystal who nodded towards the jury. Ruby looked across the courtroom and noticed that the judge had finished his summing up and the foreman of the jury was now on his feet ready to give the verdict.

The judge asked, 'Foreman of the jury, do you find the defendant guilty or not guilty of grievous bodily harm?' to which the foreman responded straightaway.

'Guilty!'

'Yay!' shouted Ruby, standing up and waving her fist in the air.

She caught Gilly's eye as he was led from court and he glowered at her. It was a look so full of hatred that it sent a chill right through her. Despite Ruby's relief that he had been found guilty she was already dreading the day he was released. Ruby didn't scare easily but she knew Gilly was a dangerous man. Nevertheless, she had stood her ground in helping to bring him to trial. There was no way she was going to let him get away with what he had done to Crystal. But she knew that once he was released, he would want his revenge.

There were mixed reactions around the rest of the courtroom and Ruby noticed that most of the public gallery didn't share her jubilation. Like Crystal, many of the other girls were afraid of crossing Gilly and even the male customers of the Rose and Crown were wary of him.

But by far the worst reaction came from Crystal who had broken down, wailing and sobbing his name. Ruby was about to say something, but she knew many of Gilly's cohorts were watching her so she took Crystal's arm and pulled her gently from her seat.

'Come on, let's get you out of here,' she said.

Crystal's unwavering love and respect for Gilly both baffled and incensed Ruby. Crystal should have been as glad to see the back of him as she was. But Ruby wasn't going to share her thoughts in front of this lot. No, she had to get Crystal alone first. Then she'd really let her know what she thought.

6

February 2005

Ruby and Crystal were sitting inside the Rose and Crown, a run-down pub behind Piccadilly, on the other side of the city centre from the courts. It was their regular, which they had frequented since their early days of prostitution when they were both still teenagers. There weren't many customers in the pub at the moment and Ruby guessed that most of the regulars had gone to one of the pubs near to the Crown Court after Gilly's trial.

Ruby was becoming exasperated with Crystal's whining. It seemed that no matter what she said, she just couldn't get through to her. 'What the fuck have I just told you, Crystal? I've been working on my own ever since Gilly was arrested for doing that to you, and it's working out fine for me.'

'I know that, Ruby, but I'll still miss him. It felt better somehow knowing he was there to step in if I had any trouble.'

'But he wasn't always there though, was he, even before he went inside? When you get in a car with a stranger, you're on your fuckin' own, girl. A pimp might be able to

35

give a client a good beating after he's abused you, but it's too fuckin' late by then, isn't it? The damage has already been done. And talk about trouble, he was worse than the fuckin' clients. He treated you like shit so I don't know why you're so upset about him. He got what he deserved.'

'How can you be so horrible about the man I loved, Ruby?' said Crystal who was once again on the verge of tears. 'Don't forget, he's not only my lover, but he's Candice's father too.'

When Ruby saw how upset Crystal was, she regretted being so hard on her. She was also sympathetic about the fact that Gilly was the father of Crystal's child as it was something he'd always vehemently denied. But she knew she was right about Crystal. She had to learn to stand on her own two feet instead of keep letting men take advantage.

'OK, sorry I was a bit over the top, but you should think about things seriously, Crystal. Don't go rushing into anything with another pimp. Think about how much better off you've been since Gilly was arrested.'

'I know. But I just felt safer knowing he was around, that's all.'

'Listen, girl, there's ways of keeping yourself safe, y'know.'

'What? You mean…?' Ruby nodded, knowing Crystal was referring to the knife she carried. 'Jesus, Ruby! I couldn't do that. I'd be frightened to death of using it.'

'You'd be amazed what you can do when it comes to the crunch, Crystal. You don't have to do any major damage. Just the sight of the blade is enough to send some of the cowardly fuckers running.'

Crystal didn't say anything more, but Ruby noticed her shiver slightly when she mentioned the blade. Maybe she had been a bit tough on her, especially considering her so-called lover had just been sentenced to ten years imprisonment. She and Crystal were two different people and Ruby appreciated that she couldn't always expect her friend to see things from her point of view. Forcing a smile, she picked up her glass and finished her drink.

'Look, it's time for me to go, Crystal. But, whatever you decide to do, just remember that I'll always have your back.'

Crystal smiled, tears still in her eyes, and Ruby leant over and gave her a hug before leaving with a few parting words, 'Don't forget, I'm always at the end of the phone.'

Then she patted Crystal affectionately on the back and was gone.

Ruby drew up in the car park of the large Victorian house where her flat was located, and stepped out of her gleaming silver BMW. She was glad to get home. The meeting with Crystal had been emotionally draining. But, at the end of the day, she was a good friend, and Ruby cared about her. She hoped that eventually Crystal would get Gilly out of her system. It was a strange relationship and Ruby knew that it wasn't just about being lovers; as well as sharing a daughter they had also indulged in drugs together.

When Ruby got inside her flat her mood soon lifted. She loved the way she had transformed the place over the years, making the most of the building's original features; the ornate ceiling roses, decorative cornices and fireplaces. Every room had benefitted from her style and enthusiasm with oak doors, polished natural wood flooring, and expensive rugs forming a centrepiece in the lounge and bedroom. She had also had a modern bathroom and kitchen installed. The décor was tasteful throughout with colours carefully selected and complemented by plush furnishings.

But her change of mood was also partly due to the enthusiastic greeting she received from her live-in lover, Tiffany. Ruby was still living in the same flat she had moved into when she first left home at sixteen. Since her first flatmate had left, Ruby had been through a few others including Crystal, who had lived with her for a while until she had become pregnant with Gilly's daughter and decided she needed a place of her own. Then Ruby had met Tiffany and it just felt right. So, when her latest flatmate left, she stopped looking for flatmates and moved her lover in instead.

As soon as Ruby walked into her living room Tiffany was up out of her seat and ready to embrace her. Ruby looked affectionately at her girlfriend, then across at the TV on which Tiffany had been indulging in the latest trashy series, and she smiled.

Tiffany was tall, blonde and willowy and, although her relationship with Tiffany wasn't the first one Ruby had had with a woman, it was the most intense. Tiffany wasn't the best looking girl around, but she had a certain attraction that drew people in. Her prominent cheekbones and sultry eyes more than compensated for her slightly misshapen nose and thin lips, and she had a friendly, chatty way about her that made her popular.

But what Ruby really loved about Tiffany was her unconditional love and support. They had been together almost a year now and had met in a trendy bar in the gay village. The attraction was instant. As soon as Ruby saw those sultry eyes, she was drawn in by them and it wasn't long till Tiffany came over for a chat. Ruby loved her confidence and the easy, relaxed way she acted. The chemistry between them was so powerful that Ruby hadn't been able to resist her attentions and she was soon falling into bed with her.

In the weeks that followed, the more they chatted, the more Ruby realised what a straightforward, upfront person Tiffany was, and she liked that. She was also a good listener, and someone Ruby felt she could confide in. Since then it seemed to Ruby that their love was becoming stronger each day. Unlike most of the men Ruby had encountered in her life, like landlords and pimps, Tiffany didn't have any ulterior motive. She just wanted to love and be loved, and she had always treated Ruby with respect and devotion.

Like Ruby, Tiffany was on the game but she had never worked for Gilly. Instead she had worked alone at Ruby's insistence ever since her former pimp had been locked up for drug dealing.

'Sorry I couldn't be with you, babe. How did it go?' asked Tiffany as she slung her arms around Ruby and kissed her fully on the lips.

Ruby responded to her embrace then stepped back slightly when Tiffany spoke, her hands still cradling her lover's elbows. 'The bastard got ten years, thank God!'

'Great!' said Tiffany. 'I bet you're relieved, aren't you?'

'Yeah, but he probably won't serve all of that, unfortunately, and Crystal's been a pain in the arse. She's not stopped bleedin' whinging since the verdict came in.'

'Jesus! You'd think she'd have been glad to see him put away after what he did to her, wouldn't you?'

'My feelings exactly,' said Ruby. 'But you know what Crystal's like. No matter how he treated her, she still kept going back for more.'

'Weird, isn't it?'

'Dead right. I've told her not to bother visiting him, but whether she'll take any fuckin' notice, we'll just have to wait and see. Anyway, how did you get on?'

'OK. The clinic gave me the all clear.'

'Thank Christ for that!' said Ruby.

They were referring to Tiffany's urgent visit to the sexual health clinic to get checked out after a condom had burst during sex with a client. They had both been worried about the outcome ever since the incident so it was a big relief to Ruby on hearing that Tiffany had been given the all clear.

Tiffany grinned salaciously at her. 'Looks like we've got some celebrating to do then,' she said, leaning in to Ruby for another kiss.

After such a stressful day Ruby was more interested in having a sit down and a cup of tea, but as Tiffany began kissing her passionately, then moving her hand around to cup Ruby's breast, she found herself responding. For precious seconds they carried on kissing, their hands caressing each other's bodies.

Ruby relaxed and lost herself to the power of Tiffany's touch, her nerve-endings coming alive with the thrill of it. Then she felt Tiffany's hand slip down her jeans, her fingers searching. Ruby let out a groan as Tiffany slipped her fingers inside her, moving them to and fro until she found her G spot.

'Jesus!' Ruby sighed, thrusting her hips in rhythm with Tiffany's finger action.

Tiffany removed her fingers and grinned again at Ruby. 'Bedroom?' she asked.

Ruby may have been the dominant one in the relationship but when it came to lovemaking Tiffany knew exactly how to play her. Without speaking, Ruby followed her through to the bedroom, debilitated by the strength of her desire.

Afterwards, they both lay in bed, feeling the warm afterglow of their lovemaking, Ruby's designer clothing scattered on the floor and her precious jewellery carefully placed on her dressing table. Ruby felt that she had never been happier. She had the most wonderful girlfriend in the world as well as her own stylish pad. She also earnt plenty so she was able to treat herself to whatever she desired; designer clothing, jewellery and a high-performance car.

The only negative about her life was what she had to do to earn her money. But for Ruby that was a small price to pay when she considered the gains, and she was well able to protect herself from any problem clients.

Ruby finally had the lifestyle she had craved from being a young child when she had seen her cousins with their designer gear and flash jewellery. When she reflected back on her life, she remembered how much she'd had to go through to get this far. It hadn't always been easy but she hoped all her troubles were behind her and that nothing would destroy the happiness she'd found.

7

October 1991

Trina was hanging out with a group of local girls; Jessica and some others. Jessica had a packet of sweets that she was sharing with her friends. Once she had passed them around the group, she took one for herself without offering any to Trina.

'How come you're not giving me one?' asked Trina, with defiance in her voice.

'Well, you haven't brought any sweets to share with us for ages and my mam says I should only share with people who share with me. It's only fair,' she said.

Trina saw the sly look on Jessica's face and became annoyed at her peevish attitude. But her rage was superseded by the other emotions that engulfed her; shame and inadequacy, knowing it was rare that anyone bought sweets for her and her brothers since their father had left. She felt sure Jessica knew that too, and was deliberately trying to humiliate her. Trina also felt resentment at her father because he didn't provide for her and her brothers like other fathers did.

She was tempted to lash out at Jessica. A swift slap would

soon wipe that smug look off her face. But Trina's shame was overpowering, and hitting Jessica would only emphasise it. So, instead, she used words to deal with Jessica.

'I don't like them anyway. I've got some better sweets at home; they're chocolate. I'm going back to eat them, but I won't be sharing them with any of you.'

Then she stomped angrily back home.

It was Saturday and Trina and her brothers were on the way back home from their grandparents' house. It was unusual for Daisy not to go with them and Trina had felt a little put out at first. But then her mother had told her she was too busy and insisted that, at almost ten years of age, she was old enough to visit without her.

Trina was clutching a plastic carrier bag containing an assortment of food items that her grandmother had sent home with her. It had become a habit of her grandmother's ever since Trina's father had left. As they made their way down their street, Trina was looking forward to the smile on her mother's face when she handed over the bag and Daisy eagerly looked inside.

Trina and her brothers bustled excitedly through the front door but Trina's mood soon changed when she saw the lopsided features of Mr Dodds staring back at her from the bottom of the stairs. He winked saucily at her while straightening his tie, making Trina feel uncomfortable. She looked further up the stairs to find her mother on her way down, self-consciously flattening her skirt and tidying her hair.

Something about the scene didn't seem right to Trina

and, for a moment, she forgot about her eagerness to show her mother the bag of goodies. But the boys were oblivious. They dashed down the hall, hugging their mother and all talking at once.

Daisy hugged them and smiled stiffly then addressed Mr Dodds. 'I'll see you again next month for the rent.'

He leered at her, which made his face look even more lopsided, and said, 'Yes, we can keep to the same arrangement if you like.'

Trina could sense his change of attitude towards her mother. He was usually nasty but this time, although he wasn't exactly nasty, there was something not quite right about the way he was acting. Trina also noticed the way her mother tensed and flashed a warning look from him to the children as if forbidding him to say anything further. Then Daisy brushed her children aside and rushed to the front door, holding it wide open for Mr Dodds to pass through.

'Goodbye, Mr Dodds,' she said, her tone full of mock formality.

His grin remained fixed as he walked through the door, his face passing within inches of Daisy's, and Trina saw her mother flinch as he drew up close. She was glad when her mother had shut the door and Mr Dodds was on the outside.

'He's creepy,' she said to her mother.

Daisy had a look of consternation on her face as she bit back. 'Yes, well, he might be creepy, child, but he puts a roof over our heads so it's something we have to put up with.'

Trina picked up on her mother's hostile tone and didn't say anything further. Instead she walked over to Daisy and handed her the bag. 'Look what Grandma sent,' she said, hoping to please her mother.

Daisy grabbed the bag and peered inside it, drawing her breath when she spotted the large slab of cake, and pulled it out. 'Oh, she didn't need to do that,' she said, her eyes moistening. 'I hope you said thank you.'

'Yeah, course I did,' said Trina.

She watched her mother riffle through the other items in the bag and could almost picture her mind mulling over what she would cook them for their evening meal. 'OK, you can go out to play now while I put these away and do some cleaning,' she said, her head still lowered over the bag.

The boys raced back up the hallway and Trina was about to follow them when her mother stopped her. 'Not you, Trina. We need to have a talk,' she said.

Trina's face fell. Seeing the look on her mother's face, she wasn't looking forward to this talk, whatever it might be, but she obeyed and followed her through to the kitchen once the boys had gone out to play.

Inside the kitchen, Daisy unloaded the bag of goodies while Trina stood awkwardly, awaiting instruction. Her mother put some veg into the bowl and gave them a wash, then she passed Trina a knife and a chopping board and asked her to prepare them. Trina did as she was told, aware that this must be a serious talk if her mother was prevaricating so much.

Daisy then stepped towards the fridge and busied herself with sorting out some ingredients from around the kitchen. As she worked, she began speaking to her daughter, all the time occupying herself with food preparation and failing to make eye contact. Once she finally started speaking, it was a while before she stopped.

'You're growing up child and it's about time you knew about the world. It pains me to say it, but men can't always be trusted. They'll want to do things to you, but you mustn't let them. Do you understand what I'm saying, child?'

She gazed up from her food preparation for just a moment until Trina nodded her head. Then she returned to what she was doing and carried on speaking.

'Never let anyone touch you where they shouldn't. You don't want to end up pregnant like I did. I was only a young girl, a teenager. I wish I'd listened to my mother, but I didn't and now look at the mess I'm in. I shouldn't have let your father win me over, but I was young and foolish and I don't want you to make the same mistakes.'

She paused and then took a deep breath as though she was having difficulty holding herself together. Then she continued, her tone now becoming angry and embittered.

'You can't trust a one of them. Not a single one! They're all after the same thing and once they get it, well… And that's not to mention the diseases they can give you. Terrible, terrible.'

She tutted, then added, 'Do you understand what I'm saying, Trina?'

Trina nodded again. It was obvious that her mother was upset and she didn't really want to add to her suffering. But Trina was confused. Daisy had misrepresented her words as a lesson in the facts of life even though they were delivered as a diatribe. And at the end of her mother's speech, Trina wasn't really any the wiser. The only lesson she had learnt was that men were not to be trusted.

After that day Daisy intensified her bad-mouthing of Isaac and all other men, her voice often sad and resentful. This cemented the idea in Trina's mind that all men were bad.

Witnessing the family's reduced circumstances, the attitude of Mr Dodds and the change in her mother, on top of the awful memories of her father, Trina thought that Daisy's words rang true. Her reaction was to build a barrier around herself. Each time her mother called her father it added another layer of reinforcement to that barrier, like hammering in poisoned nails, which strengthened Trina's lifelong resolve to never trust a man.

8

December 1991

Trina's tenth birthday would always stay in her memory, but for all the wrong reasons. Her mother couldn't afford a party so Trina's grandmother had kindly offered to host one instead.

'You should be grateful, child,' said Daisy when she saw Trina's reaction to the news. 'If it wasn't for your grandparents you wouldn't be having a party at all.'

'Can I take some friends with me?' she asked, thinking about how impressed the local girls would be.

'No, I can't just turn up with a lot of strange children; it wouldn't be fair to your grandparents.'

'Aw, Mam. It won't be the same without my friends.'

'Stop your moaning, Trina. You'll have your brothers and your cousins.'

'But that's not the same, Mam.'

'Enough, child,' said Daisy. 'Or I'll ring your grandmother and tell her not to bother at all.'

She had that familiar harsh expression on her face, which

told Trina it was the end of the conversation, and she didn't dare push things further.

On the day of the party Trina arrived with her mother and brothers to birthday greetings from her grandparents. Inside the kitchen-diner they had pulled out the dated dining table from its usual place tucked away in the corner and extended it to its full size. Trina noticed there were already several dishes laid out on the table, which was covered in a flowery plastic table cloth. Daisy walked over and added a plate full of sandwiches she had brought with her. 'Oh, you didn't need to,' said Trina's grandmother. 'I told you we'd take care of everything.'

'It's the least I could do, when you've done all this for my Trina,' said Daisy.

She looked across at her daughter, and Trina knew what was expected of her. 'Thanks, Grandma, thanks, Grandad,' she said, walking over to them and hugging each of them in turn.

'It's no problem, child,' said her grandmother. 'Come on through and you can open your presents before the others get here.'

Trina and the rest of her family followed her grandparents through to the lounge where her grandmother passed her two presents, adding, 'Happy tenth birthday, Trina.'

'Aw thanks, Grandma,' said Trina, smiling.

She rushed to open the two presents, starting with the smaller one first. It was a bag of toffees. She thanked her grandparents and put the sweets to one side then opened the larger present. She grew excited as she felt material beneath her hands, hoping it was a new outfit she could show off to her friends. But then she saw the lurid pink material beneath the wrapping paper.

She slowly pulled it out and held up the garment to examine. It was a dress, an old-fashioned dress in bright pink, made of a horrible material and full of frills in a lighter shade of pink. It was revolting but she had to pretend she liked it.

After a few minutes there was a knock at the front door and her brothers rushed to answer it, growing excited when their Aunty Tamara and Uncle Josh arrived. Trina was pleased to see them until she saw her mean older cousins, Josh and Calvin, hovering in the background. Aged thirteen and fourteen, Trina would have thought the boys too old to go to her party and had secretly hoped they wouldn't be there.

Although Aunty Tamara was loud and lively, she was a good soul and she walked straight over to Trina, holding her tight and planting kisses on top of her head.

'My you've grown, child,' she announced. 'Just look at you.' She released Trina from her tight grip then held her at arms' length while she looked her up and down. 'You're so tall, child, and a good looker too. You'll break a few hearts, my girl.'

'Not if I've got anything to do with it,' muttered Daisy. 'She'll stay well away from men if she knows what's good for her.'

'Oh, leave her be. A girl's got to use what nature gave her,' said Aunty Tamara who then laughed raucously.

While this discourse was taking place, Aunty Tamara still held Trina at arm's length. Trina could feel herself blush and she saw her two older cousins snigger at her discomfort.

Meanwhile, her younger brothers were tearing around her grandparents' living room, playing a game of tag.

'Anyway, we've brought you a present,' said Aunty Tamara. 'I hope it fits.'

Trina hastily tore off the wrapping paper. Knowing that Aunty Tamara was fashionable and had good taste in clothes, Trina was eager to have a look. She pulled out the garment and held it up to examine. It was a nice top but then she realised it was too small.

'There, I told you it would be too small,' said Aunty Tamara, addressing her husband. 'But you wouldn't have it, would you?'

'Never mind, we can always return it for a bigger size,' said Daisy.

'No, we can't,' said Aunty Tamara, 'because Joshua here tore the label off and put the receipt in the bin.'

'Get off my case, woman!' cursed Uncle Josh.

Trina found it hard to hide her disappointment. She thanked them anyway, knowing that it was what her mother would have expected.

The first half hour of the party carried on in a similar vein with various relatives and adult friends arriving. There were no more presents but each of them brought Trina a birthday card and a dish of food to be added to the others.

By the time they had all arrived there was an assortment of West Indian food laid out on the table: jerk chicken and lots of other traditional Jamaican dishes including beef patty, a fish dish that Trina wasn't familiar with, a spicy chicken stew, rice and peas, banana bread and various other sweets. To her consternation Trina noticed that there wasn't any jelly or trifle or little sticks with sausages and cheese on like she had eaten at her friends' birthday parties.

The adults chatted in loud, excited voices, keen to catch up with each other, and laughing boisterously as they shared jokes. Trina walked through to the living room where the other children had gathered; her brothers and her two cousins, Josh and Calvin, were the only youngsters there. She noticed Josh nudging Calvin as she walked into the room, a sly grin on his face.

'This party's shit,' he said, eyeballing Trina as she made her way towards them. Then he turned from his brother and addressed Trina. 'How come you're not having it at your house anyway?' he asked.

Trina knew that her cousins would only ridicule her if she told them the real reason; that her mother couldn't afford it, so she just shrugged and said, 'Dunno.'

'What you got for your birthday?' asked Calvin.

'Clothes,' said Trina.

'That some of 'em?' he asked, referring to what Trina was wearing and squealing in amusement. 'Fuckin' hell, man, that's a state,' he continued. 'You wanna get some cool gear like mine, all top notch fuckin' designer labels these.'

Trina wasn't bothered about designer labels but she was bothered that he was deriding the new clothes her mother had struggled to buy for her. A few mean words from her cousins made her feel suddenly self-conscious and inadequate.

She looked up to her older cousins as they always seemed so cool and switched on. But the flip side of that was that they also made her feel inferior because she would never be as smart or as cool as them. And Trina couldn't understand how Aunty Tamara and Uncle Josh managed to afford all the designer gear as Aunty Tamara was always complaining that she wasn't well off.

'There's not even any fuckin' music,' said Josh.

'Put some on then,' said Calvin.

'No chance, my dad'll go fuckin' spare.'

The lack of music was soon remedied when Aunty Tamara bounded into the living room. 'Get some lively music on that stereo, Josh,' she ordered, pointing to a pile of CDs which she had left nearby. 'It's like a graveyard in here.'

Aunty Tamara started off the dancing, her moves lively and provocative. The alcohol was now flowing and the adults gradually came into the living room and joined in while the youngsters looked on, bored.

'Come and have a dance,' Aunty Tamara shouted over to Trina and her cousins.

The boys resisted, but Trina was dragged onto the dance floor. She felt embarrassed as her aunty gyrated close to her and she could hear her two cousins laughing in the background.

Eventually she managed to escape and found that her two cousins had now disappeared. She had a look round the house, but they seemed to have left. Despite their ridicule and insults, at least they had provided some company for Trina. Now there was no one left to talk to, so she busied herself by keeping an eye on her younger brothers while her mother joined in the dancing and drinking.

Trina was willing the party to come to an end when she became aware of a fracas. It seemed to be coming from outside the front door and she strained to hear what was being said. The loudest voice was one she recognised and it sent a cold chill down her spine. It was her father.

9

Trina could hear her father yelling even though he was still outside. 'I told you, I'm not leaving here till I've seen my fuckin' daughter. I've got a present for her birthday.'

'No, Isaac. You're not coming in. You've got a drink inside you and you'll only cause trouble.'

'No, I fuckin' won't!' shouted Isaac, and Trina could tell he was already becoming angry.

'You stay where you are, child,' warned Trina's grandmother while some of the men rushed to the door to sort out her troublesome father.

She could hear various angry words being exchanged, and lots of bad language, then a scream, which she thought came from her mother.

'Just give me the present and I'll take it to her,' said Trina's grandfather. 'I swear, Isaac, if you don't go now, I'm calling the police.'

Then all went quiet and the adults trudged back into the room. While Daisy went over to her sister, Tamara, who consoled her, Trina's grandfather handed her the present. The wrapping paper was torn and creased and some material was poking out.

Trina opened the present tentatively while her mother looked on. It was a shell suit. She almost squealed with delight when she pulled it out of the wrapping paper, and caught sight of the popular sports label. If only her cousins had stayed to see this! It was the best present of the day and Trina had wanted one for ages. She looked up with a smile until she caught the scornful expression on her mother's face and quickly put the present back down.

'It's alright when you can afford them sorts of gifts,' her mother muttered.

'That's supposing he did buy it,' said Aunty Tamara.

Trina's grandma tutted. 'Tamara, that's not a nice thing to say. He might have his faults, but at least he brought something for the child.'

As she spoke, she looked at Trina with kindness in her eyes, and Trina knew the words had been spoken for her benefit so that she wouldn't feel any worse about the fact that her father had gate-crashed the party and caused a load of bother.

Her grandmother's words also acted as a warning to the other adults to stay quiet on the subject. Daisy responded by tutting and leaving the room. While she was gone, Trina took another surreptitious look at the shell suit. She couldn't help but feel a shiver of delight when she imagined herself parading around in it and getting admiring glances and comments from the local girls.

It wasn't long before Daisy came back into the room, carrying their coats. 'Thank you for everything,' she said to Trina's grandparents, 'but I'm afraid it's time for us to go now.'

'Aw! You sure?' asked Aunty Tamara.

'Yes, I think the children have had enough excitement for one day,' she said. Then she turned to Trina. 'Come on, child. Collect your presents while I round the boys up.'

Trina gathered up the other presents first, eager to take the present from her father but apprehensive about her mother's reaction when she did so. While she dithered, her mother walked back into the room with her younger brothers.

'Come on now, Trina. We're all ready,' she said, gravely.

Trina picked up on her tone and ignored her father's present. She was just about to walk out the door with the rest of her family when her grandmother rushed over to her carrying it.

'Don't forget this one, child,' she said, smiling at Trina then flashing a knowing look at Daisy.

Trina returned her smile and took the present. But as she trudged through the streets with the rest of her family, she had mixed feelings about it. She was delighted to have received just what she wanted but, at the same time, she couldn't help but feel that the present was somehow tainted by the way in which it had been delivered and by whom.

Daisy stayed quiet for most of the journey home. Despite the present from her father, Trina felt that it had been one of the most miserable days of her life so far. It was one thing having the present you wanted, but another thing not being able to show any joy at receiving it. Her tenth birthday somehow summed up the state of their current existence as a family, and Trina couldn't help but wonder if things would ever get any better.

The following day when her brother, Jarell, came into the house after playing outside, Trina stared at him in dismay. His knees were bloody and he was crying inconsolably, his eyes red and a stream of mucus trailing from his nostrils. Ellis tripped into the house after him.

'It was that Shaun Gallagher again,' said Ellis. 'Him and his friends started picking on Jarell for nothing. They were going to get me as well but they couldn't catch me. When I turned round I saw Shaun pushing Jarell over, and he cut his knees on the floor.'

'Why didn't you hit him back?' asked Trina, but she didn't get a reply from Jarell who was too busy sobbing. So she turned to Ellis, 'And why did you run off and leave him?'

She was incensed. This was the second time this had happened this week, and for weeks prior to that her brothers had put up with racist taunts from Shaun and his friends.

Ellis answered her questions in a roundabout way. 'There were three of them,' he said. 'And they're all bigger than us.'

'Well they're not bigger than me,' said Trina, knowing which boys Shaun Gallagher hung about with.

She was becoming increasingly annoyed as she took in the state of Jarell and decided it was about time she did something about it.

'Come and show me where they are,' she said to Ellis, putting her shoes on, but before she had chance to walk out of the house, she saw her mother approach and stand just inside the living room door, blocking Trina's exit.

'Oh no you don't, my girl!' she said, her arms folded beneath her breasts and her head shaking slowly from side to side.

'Why not? Are you going to see Shaun's mam and dad instead?' Trina asked.

'No, I'm not, and I want you all to stay away too. I have enough troubles of my own without getting involved with that sort of family. Just look at what they've done to my boy's knees. Come into the kitchen, Jarell, and let me get you cleaned up. And I don't want to hear another word about it, Trina. You stay away, do you hear?'

Daisy fixed Trina with a steely gaze and Trina knew she wouldn't accept any arguments. She nodded but stayed silent, despite feeling a strong sense of injustice.

It was some time later when Trina walked through to the kitchen to find her mother chunnering away to herself. She was cutting vegetables on the work surface, with her back to Trina, and didn't hear her approach. On hearing her mother, Trina stood still, listening to the bitter words that were pouring from her mouth.

'Damn you, Isaac! You should be here to sort things out instead of me having to put up with my children being picked on. You've got more than your share of faults, that's for sure, but those nasty boys would never have picked on my children if you were around.'

Then she chuckled ironically to herself. 'Eeh, everybody knows not to mess with you, Isaac, especially when you're in a bad mood. You'd even frighten the devil out of his den.'

Then she sighed before reaching for another potato. Trina

fled quietly from the room, before her mother could catch sight of her and realise she had been eavesdropping. Her mother's words echoed her own thoughts. Trina might not have got along with her father but there were advantages to having a father with a hard man reputation. And now that he wasn't around she had no choice but to stand back and let the Gallaghers get away with picking on her brothers. She was so tempted to step in, but she'd do her best to heed her mother's warning.

10

October 2006

These days it was rare for Ruby to work the streets. She'd built up a regular clientele and allowed those who she trusted to come back to her flat. Not all of the girls liked to take clients back to their homes but Ruby wasn't interested in their rules; it was her flat and she'd do as she pleased. But there were some clients who preferred her to visit them at home or in a hotel room.

On this particular occasion she didn't have any work booked for the night so she'd made one of her rare outings to Aytoun Street. She was pleased when a client had pulled up and asked her to come to a five-star hotel in the city centre; it meant she wouldn't have to hang about all night waiting for other clients to arrive. Although she was a bit apprehensive at spending the night with a new client, he was willing to pay a lot of money for the privilege so she took the chance.

Ruby was a little nervous when she entered the hotel room with him. Despite having been on the game for a number of years, she still felt daunted when going into a situation she knew nothing about. She was therefore relieved when the client seemed what she would have termed 'normal'. In fact, he was quite the gentleman, smiling warmly as he took her jacket and offered to pour her a glass of champagne.

While Ruby sipped at her champagne they made small talk. The man was in his late thirties and above average looking, although a little overweight. He had a confident air about him and she wondered, as she did with many clients, why he had resorted to using prostitutes. Surely he wouldn't have too much of a problem attracting women. But then, clients met prostitutes for all sorts of reasons and she guessed from his chat that he travelled a lot on business and sometimes got a bit lonely when he was in a strange city.

Eventually the inevitable happened. Ruby kept to her usual routine, carefully undressing and laying her clothes on the floor by the side of the bed where she could reach them easily. It was while he was taking her from behind that he grabbed hold of her hair and yanked it hard whilst slapping her repeatedly on her backside.

'Take your hands off me!' said Ruby, trying to stay calm although she could feel anger firing up inside her.

The man ignored her and continued to thrust himself deep inside her while slapping Ruby's backside and pulling her hair. The stinging pain in her scalp brought tears to her eyes and Ruby yelled at him to stop. But her distress seemed to heighten his vigour and he continued thrusting while continuing to yank on her hair and slapping her so hard that her backside felt raw.

'I said get your fuckin' hands off me!' she roared, drawing back her arm and using all her strength to elbow him in the stomach.

The man yelped in pain and instinctively reared up and gripped his stomach. Within nanoseconds Ruby was off the bed and had reached for the knife she kept concealed inside her jacket. She swung round and pointed it at him.

'Do you want a fuckin' taste of it?' she shrieked, jabbing the knife into the tender flesh of his throat but stopping short of drawing blood.

To her surprise the man looked up and grinned, despite the pain in his stomach and the menacing presence of the blade, which Ruby kept tight against his throat.

'Ha, so you like to dominate, do you?' he asked while Ruby stared at him nonplussed. 'Pardon me. I assumed you like to be the submissive one like a lot of the girls. But, if domination's what you're into then let's go for it. I've got some cable ties in my case. You can tie me to the bed if you like.'

'Are you fuckin' serious?' asked Ruby. 'My arse is stinging like hell and you're asking me to carry on? Not a fuckin' chance!'

She stood back, pulling the knife away but still holding it at arms' length to ward off any further danger.

'My apologies for misreading the situation,' said the man, managing to maintain a cool façade despite his obvious pain and, Ruby assumed, apprehension at the sight of the knife.

'Yeah well, next time you should fuckin' check first,' she said, pulling her clothes away from the side of the bed while still holding onto the knife.

When she had moved a good distance from him, she scooped up her clothing, dashed to the bathroom and locked the door so she could put her clothes back on. Once she was fully dressed, she emerged from the bathroom, still pointing the knife at the man in case he should try anything else.

'I take it we're finished for tonight then?' he asked, unfazed.

'Too fuckin' right we are!' said Ruby, throwing him a look that would cut through steel.

'In that case I'm afraid I won't be paying you.'

'Stick your dodgy money up your fuckin' arse,' raged Ruby before striding through the room and out the door.

When Ruby arrived home, Tiffany was letting a bald, middle-aged man out of the flat. She raised her eyebrows inquisitively at Ruby as she walked past her while Tiffany said goodbye to the client and locked the door.

'I didn't expect you back so soon,' said Tiffany as soon as she found Ruby in the lounge.

'I've had enough for tonight. I've just picked up a right fuckin' weirdo who thought I was having a bit of S&M,' said Ruby.

'Really? Did you tell him where to go?'

'What do you think?' asked Ruby, cynically.

'Umm. I hope he didn't hurt you.'

'Not too much but my bloody arse is still stinging.'

'Really? The cheeky bastard!'

'Dead right!' said Ruby. She then sniffed, her demeanour displaying an air of nonchalance. 'Was that client your last for tonight?'

'Yeah, that's me all done,' said Tiffany, flashing a wad of notes at Ruby.

'At least *you* got paid for tonight.'

'Aw, you mean the bastard didn't pay you either?'

'No but, to be honest, I just wanted to get out of there as soon as possible. I can't be doing with clients who think they can start roughing you up. You would never have thought it to look at him either. He seemed a real gentleman.'

'It just shows, you never know what you're dealing with in this business,' said Tiffany, sitting next to Ruby on the sofa and giving her arm a sympathetic stroke. 'Why don't I pour us both a nice glass of wine and we can relax for the evening?'

'Sounds great to me,' said Ruby.

While Tiffany went through to the kitchen to pour the wine, Ruby thought again about the idea that had occurred to her on the way home, but it wasn't until they were both feeling more chilled that she broached the subject.

'I've been thinking,' she began. Rewarded with Tiffany's curious glance, she continued. 'Well, strangely enough, that last client has given me an idea.'

'Really?'

'Yeah. I pulled my knife on the bastard and I couldn't believe his reaction. He seemed to think it was some sort of game. So it set me thinking.'

Ruby paused, giving Tiffany chance to take in her words before she hit her full on with her idea. By this time Tiffany was staring at her with a confused expression on her face, and when Ruby knew she had her full attention, she came out with it.

'I'm thinking of becoming a dominatrix.'

'You're joking!'

'No, seriously.'

'But why, for fuck's sake? I thought you'd just been really freaked out by that guy.'

'Yeah, because he hit me. But what if it was the other way round? I'd be the one doing the hitting.'

'OK,' Tiffany said, drawing out the word while she tried to come to terms with what Ruby was saying.

'Think about it. It makes sense. I could earn a fortune as a dominatrix and I actually think it's something I'd enjoy.'

Tiffany laughed. 'Well, to be honest, you'd probably be good at it.'

Ruby returned her laughter. 'Cheeky cow!'

When they'd finished laughing Tiffany said, 'No, seriously, it does make sense. I mean, you've never fuckin' liked men. This might give you chance to take all your hatred out on them. And you won't necessarily have to have sex with them either.'

They both laughed again and when their laughter finally subsided, Ruby said, 'I've been thinking about it all the way home. I honestly think it would suit me. And have you any idea what a fuckin' fortune those girls earn?'

Tiffany was warming to the idea. 'Go for it then, as long as you're the one dishing it out.'

'I'd have to kit the place out,' said Ruby.

'Where?'

'Well, we've got two bedrooms and we only ever use one for ourselves. Why don't we turn the spare room into Ruby's Dungeon?' She emphasised the last two words and then giggled. 'You can also use it for your clients, which means we can't be booked at the same time but that won't matter as I'll be taking a hell of a lot more money as a dominatrix.'

'I don't wanna be a dominatrix,' said Tiffany.

'No, that's OK. We'll put the gear behind a screen so your clients won't have to see it. The room's big enough for that although we won't be able to buy any big equipment. But we'll keep our bedroom strictly for ourselves.'

Tiffany smiled. 'Sounds like a good idea.'

'Great! So, when are we going shopping for the gear?'

11

November 2006

Ruby and Tiffany were standing inside the doors of one of central Manchester's sex shops. Having done some research beforehand, Ruby had a good idea what she was looking for, and a dominatrix friend had been only too eager to talk her through things.

Tiffany giggled as they stood inside the shop entrance. 'What do we do now?' she asked.

'We have a good look round, that's what,' said Ruby, striding across the shop floor till she came to the first display stand, which was full of vibrators in various colours and sizes.

'We won't need them,' she said.

'What about a strap-on?' asked Tiffany.

'Yes, good idea.' Ruby looked around till her eyes settled on another display stand. 'Over there.'

They walked over and Ruby began picking up the goods and examining them while Tiffany giggled.

'This one will do,' said Ruby, passing a strap-on to Tiffany who giggled again as she held it up high. Ruby looked at her scornfully. 'You keep hold of the goods while I have a rummage around.

She continued walking through the store with Tiffany trailing behind, passing a set of shelves full of DVDs and another display stand containing sexy lingerie.

'I've got plenty of that,' she casually remarked. 'It's the rubber gear I'm after.'

Tiffany nodded her head towards a rail of black clothing. 'Over there.'

Ruby headed in the direction Tiffany had indicated, her girlfriend still following behind. Then she picked up a rubber catsuit and examined it. 'This looks great. I wonder if they've got one in my size.'

They searched the rail till they found Ruby's size. 'Come on,' said Ruby. 'I want to try it on.'

It fit perfectly and Ruby smiled at Tiffany as she showed her the outfit. 'Good start,' she said.

Tiffany pretended to whistle and, as Ruby turned towards the cubicle, she patted her on the backside. When they emerged from the changing rooms Tiffany was carrying the catsuit Ruby had handed to her. Ruby spotted the section with the S&M equipment and made her way towards it. Then she began picking up objects and examining them.

'Excellent. They've got a brilliant selection.'

Tiffany watched in amusement as Ruby handled a leather paddle then a wooden one and slapped them against her hand to test them. Then she did the same with a number of leather whips. She noticed that Tiffany was also examining some of the equipment, holding them high and gazing at them with a puzzled expression, confused about their purpose.

Tiffany was on the verge of laughter again as Ruby said, 'Um, I think I'll go for one of each.'

Then Tiffany reached up to a shelf and pulled out a latex gimp mask, before pulling it over her head. She giggled. 'What do you think, Rubes?'

'Stop fuckin' about! This is serious,' snapped Ruby.

Tiffany looked at her with her most endearing expression, but Ruby was having none of it. 'What's wrong, Ruby?' she asked. 'Why are you so serious?'

'This isn't a game, Tiffany. It's business. So we have to take it seriously, same as we would for any other fuckin' business.'

'Oh, OK,' said Tiffany, looking put out.

But Ruby was riled and for the next half hour she was glad to see that Tiffany was keeping a straight face while she followed her round the shop. Grabbing a shopping trolley, Tiffany then helped her to select the items she would need for her new venture, and they filled the trolley up.

'What about this?' Tiffany asked, walking over to a cage.

'We've no room for it,' said Ruby. 'We'll have to settle for smaller items that we can put away when they're not in use so your clients don't see them. I think we'll have enough to be going on with though.'

She looked down at the items in the trolley as Tiffany followed her gaze: whips, chains, a harness, wooden and leather paddles, handcuffs, gimp masks, blindfolds and nipple clamps, amongst other things.

'Yes, I think you'll definitely have enough,' said Tiffany, and Ruby finally rewarded her with a smile as they made their way to the pay desk.

*

Crystal was sitting in Ruby's living room sipping coffee, although Ruby guessed she would probably have preferred something stronger. She was jittery and it was obvious to Ruby that she was still taking drugs. Across from them sat Tiffany.

Even though Ruby still saw Crystal often, she hadn't had chance for a good chat with her in the last couple of weeks. She'd been too busy getting things ready for her new dominatrix role. 'So, how are you feeling?' she asked.

'Better. Not as weepy, y'know.'

'Good,' said Ruby. 'I knew you'd get there. And how's business? Anyone giving you any hassle?'

'No, it's fine. That pimp called Trevor tried to muscle in but I told him where to go.'

'Good for you. If he gives you any aggro, you let me know. I'll soon fuckin' sort him out.'

'Nah, it's OK. I ain't scared of that little worm,' said Crystal.

Ruby wondered whether Crystal meant what she said or whether she was just displaying bravado for her benefit. Her friend often confused her; sometimes Crystal could seem so meek and yet, at others, she showed a lot of bottle. Maybe, like a lot of the girls, she had an inner strength that she sometimes relied on to get her through. Or maybe it was the drugs that had changed her.

'Glad to hear it,' said Ruby. 'Don't let that little shit or any of the others push you around. Remember what I said, you gotta learn to stand up for yourself, girl.'

'Sure,' said Crystal. Then she seemed pensive before saying, 'There's something you should know actually, Ruby. I've been meaning to tell you for some time but I didn't want to worry you.'

'Go on.'

'Well, you know I still visit Gilly, don't you?'

Ruby sighed dramatically. 'Yeah.'

'Well, he still talks about getting his revenge for grassing him up.'

Ruby felt a rush of fear, but she quickly disguised it from Crystal and from Tiffany, who was looking concerned. 'He hasn't got much chance of that from the nick, has he?' She laughed falsely.

'No,' said Crystal. 'But he says he's gonna do it as soon as he's released.'

'Shit!' said Tiffany.'

Ruby looked at her partner. 'Don't let it bother you. He'll have got over it by then.'

But, despite her brave words, she was worried that Gilly would never get over it. Still, it would be years before he'd be released so she'd put it out of her mind for now and deal with it when the time was right.

Crystal smiled weakly, and Ruby changed the subject. 'Anyway, there's a reason I've asked you here today. There's something I want to show you, and you're gonna love it!' She and Tiffany exchanged smiles, both aware of the surprise that was awaiting Crystal.

They walked her through to the spare bedroom and Crystal stood next to the door, staring around the room inquisitively. Then Tiffany crossed the room and pulled back the screen. A look of amusement flashed across Ruby's face as she watched Crystal's reaction.

'Are they what I think they are?' asked Crystal, looking at the instruments on the far side of the room, which Ruby and Tiffany had carefully laid out.

Ruby nodded. 'Oh my word!' said Crystal. She walked a little closer so she could examine the items. 'Jesus, Ruby. What the fuck?'

Ruby grinned. 'It's Mistress Ruby now.'

'Haha. So have you become a dominatrix?'

'Not yet but you can see I'm all set up for it. I've had the walls soundproofed as well, which cost a bloody fortune.' Then she smiled mischievously. 'I don't want the neighbours hearing the clients squeal.'

Crystal visibly cringed, then asked Tiffany, 'Are you gonna do it as well?'

'No fuckin' chance!' said Tiffany, stepping away from the instruments as though they were contaminated.

'Aren't you nervous?' Crystal asked Ruby as she picked up a leather whip and ran her fingers along it.

Although Ruby had been apprehensive about her new venture, she played it down. 'No more than when I first started on the game. So, if I could do that then, I'm fuckin' sure I can do this. Besides, it only works one way. There's no way I'm letting any of the bastards lay a finger on me! And if I make sure I'm always the one in control then how can it go wrong?'

'Haha, good for you,' said Crystal. 'I think you'll do well at it.'

Ruby picked up another of the leather whips. 'I think so too. All I need now is my first client and I'll be all set to go.' Then she lifted the whip and brought it down so hard it made a cracking sound as it whizzed through the air. She smiled at the other two girls before saying, 'Bring. It. On.'

12

December 1991

Trina was disappointed that her mother wasn't going to talk to the Gallaghers' parents about picking on her brothers, but she couldn't blame her in a way. The whole family had a terrible name around the area. Mr Gallagher was known for getting drunk and picking fights in the local pubs and Mrs Gallagher was always falling out with her neighbours because of her troublesome sons who made their lives a misery, tearing around the streets on their bikes and making a racket until late at night.

Trina would have kept to her own resolution not to get involved with the Gallaghers if she hadn't bumped into Shaun with one of his friends a few days later. She caught sight of them in the distance and decided to walk past and ignore them. But as she drew nearer, the boys began to taunt, making fun of the fact that Jarell had run home in tears. Trina's feeling of injustice resurfaced and anger began to bubble within her.

She tried to keep her temper at bay until she had passed them, and she was doing well until the racist taunts started.

Trina could take no more. She turned around and went for Shaun. She was so quick that he didn't even have chance to back away before she grabbed hold of him and planted a punch on his nose.

Shaun screamed and pulled away from her, then raised his hand to his nose. 'You bitch!' he yelled. 'You've bust my nose. Wait till I tell our Kyle about this. You'll be for it!'

He backed away, clutching his nose and yelling dramatically. Trina was shocked by Shaun's extreme reaction, given what had actually happened. It was only a small punch that didn't even leave a mark and Trina shrugged it off. He was a coward and a typical bully. It was OK for him to pick on others but he didn't like it when someone did it to him.

When Trina returned home, she couldn't resist telling her brothers but unfortunately her mother overheard Ellis repeating what she had said.

'You foolish child!' she scolded. 'Do you realise what you've done?'

Trina looked at her mother, bemused. 'But it was only a soft punch,' she said. 'I didn't even hurt him.'

'It doesn't matter how hard you hit him; he obviously didn't think it was soft if he went home yelling. Why didn't you leave things alone like I told you to? Do you think a family like that will let this go? You've just made a whole heap of trouble for yourself, my girl.'

Trina didn't say anything. She just stared at her mother in shock as she felt a tremor of fear pulse through her.

After her mother's warning that the Gallaghers would

seek revenge for thumping Shaun, Trina avoided the family for a few days, especially Kyle Gallagher who was two years older than her, and vicious. If she saw them in the distance she turned and walked the other way until she was well out of view. Trina told her brothers to avoid the family too.

It was while she was taking a short cut through a back alleyway that she saw Kyle and two of his friends. They were surrounding someone and Trina could tell they were being mean to whoever it was. Then the other person came into view and Trina realised it was Jessica. The breath caught in her throat and for a moment she stood motionless, taking in the scene.

'You're that fuckin' Trina's friend, aren't you?' said Kyle.

'No, I'm not,' said Jessica, and Trina could hear the fear in her voice.

'Well, how come we see you hanging about with her?' asked Kyle.

'I don't. I don't even like her. She just keeps pestering, trying to make friends with us because she hasn't got any other friends. None of us like her.'

'You're a liar,' said Kyle, grabbing hold of Jessica's arm and leaning forward menacingly till his face was close to hers.

Kyle and his friends had their backs to Trina so they didn't spot her. But Jessica did. Trina felt her eyes upon her and prepared to run before the boys realised who Jessica was looking at. She quickly took to her heels and as she turned and ran, she heard Jessica scream in pain.

Trina rounded the corner so she was out of sight. Then she heard Jessica shout her name. 'Trina, help me!' but

Trina kept running, getting as far away as she could from the boys.

When she had made some distance, she became aware of them pursuing her. She heard heavy footfall then Kyle shouting, 'Come here, you bitch! I want you.'

Trina didn't even turn round to check how close they were. She didn't stop till she got home and fled through the door.

'What on earth's the matter with you?' asked her mother.

Trina plonked herself down on the tattered old sofa, panting heavily, and her mother waited while Trina's breathing steadied.

'Kyle and his friends were after me,' she gasped. 'They hit Jessica because they thought she was my friend.'

'What did I tell you, child?' scolded her mother. 'This won't end here, you mark my words.'

Trina's heartbeat had already accelerated after her run but now she felt a rush of blood pulse through her body as fear consumed her. 'Can't you have a word with his mam?' she asked, desperately.

'Oh no, my girl. I told you before, you can't reason with those sorts of people.'

'What can we do then, Mam?' asked Trina, a note of hysteria in her voice.

Her mother seemed to pause for ages before she replied. Then she sighed heavily before speaking. 'There's not a lot we can do, Trina. Just keep away from them and let's hope it blows over.'

13

February 1992

For weeks Trina followed her mother's advice and kept her distance from the Gallaghers and their friends. Trina had started hanging out in the local park rather than in the streets near to her home, hoping she would be safer there. Laura and Holly sometimes came with her but Jessica wouldn't have anything to do with her since the day Kyle and his friends attacked her.

The first time Trina bumped into Jessica after the attack, Trina could see the panic in Jessica's eyes.

'My mam says I can't hang around with you anymore,' she said. 'I was beaten up because of you.'

Her tone was more resigned than hostile. She seemed timid as though she had finally been defeated, and Trina felt a pang of guilt knowing she had deserted her when Kyle and his friends had attacked. Despite how cruel Jessica had been to her in the past, even she didn't deserve that.

Trina didn't know what to say. An apology didn't feel appropriate; neither did an aggressive retort. So, instead, she shrugged and walked away.

After that day, she rarely saw Jessica outside. When she did see her, she was usually accompanied by adults. It made Trina realise just how much the attack by Kyle and his friends must have shaken Jessica. Trina was worried about further reprisals from the boys and took care to keep away from them.

It was several weeks later when they finally caught up with her. Trina had carried on hanging out in the park but she had become complacent as time passed by. So, when Kyle and his friends appeared in the park, they took her completely by surprise.

Trina was with Laura, sitting on a grass verge at the edge of some bushes, facing each other as they chatted about friends, school and their families. Trina remembered glancing admiringly at Laura's straight blonde hair. She would have loved to have had hair like that.

But Laura didn't seem so fixated on her. Instead she was looking over Trina's shoulder at something behind her. Then Trina noticed the shocked expression that appeared on Laura's face. She turned around to see what had surprised her friend.

By the time Trina spotted Kyle Gallagher with two of his mates, Laura was already up on her feet. It was common knowledge amongst all the local kids that he was out to get Trina. She turned back round and also sprang to her feet, the shock of seeing Kyle making her temporarily indecisive about whether to stay or run. The sight of Laura sprinting through the park spurred Trina into action and she set off after her friend.

But Trina wasn't fast enough. Within no time the boys

had surrounded her and there was no way past them. Trina looked desperately at Laura's retreating back.

'Fetch help!' she shouted.

Then she looked at the boys: Kyle, with a cruel sneer on his face, and his two friends. The three of them were equally intimidating; all bigger than Trina, all nasty looking and all ready for revenge.

It was the first time Trina had been frightened of other kids. She was so used to being the intimidating one. But these three weren't part of her usual social circle. They were older, bolder and much more ruthless.

Even fear of her father didn't compare to this. With her father she could usually anticipate the outcome of his wrath; a sharp slap on the thighs or a good shouting at. She'd grown so used to it while he was at home that the rapidly pounding heartbeat had dissipated with each occurrence.

But this was different. She didn't know what to expect, only that it would be bad. And as she stared at the callous faces of the boys, she felt not only her own rapid heartbeat, but a strange sensation in her mouth. The taste of fear. It felt as though her throat had constricted while her tongue swelled and her breath shortened, and she gulped in air, desperately trying to feed her lungs.

The boys dragged her into the bushes so they were off the main pathway and out of view. Then she felt the first blow, which was quickly followed by others. A volley of punches, slaps and kicks around her head and body. Each blow felt sharper than the last and she cried tears of pain and humiliation as they rained punches down on her and tore at her clothes.

Trina quickly realised with startling clarity that this was more than just a playground tussle. It was a terrifying and devastating assault by three cruel boys who knew no bounds. Despite her fear, Trina didn't give in without a fight. Even as the attack was taking place she spat at them, clawing at their faces and calling them foul names, which just made them hurt her even more.

Prior to the incident, Trina had felt that she was as tough as any boy, but now she couldn't escape the physical differences. And she detested that failing. When she realised that fighting back wasn't helping her, Trina begged them to stop. But her anguished pleas were met by sniggers and excited squeals; her distress reflected in their whoops of joy.

Then Kyle pulled out a knife and thrust it at her. Trina knew it had pierced her skin. She didn't feel pain at first; just a dull sensation as the knife sliced across her face. She instinctively put her hands up to her cheeks then pulled one away to examine it. It was covered in blood. Trina let out an agonised yelp, which sounded like an animal in pain.

The boys ran, leaving behind a traumatised ten-year-old child, sobbing into blood-soaked hands. She had been marked by the attack both physically and emotionally.

Daisy was enjoying some valuable time with her sons, helping her youngest, Tyler, with his colouring book while her older two sons drew pictures. When she heard a loud knock at the door, she tutted, not welcoming the intrusion, which meant she had to leave her sons while she answered it. Before she even got to the door, somebody knocked again, this time even louder.

'Alright, alright, I'm coming,' she shouted as she bustled down the hall.

She was surprised to see Laura on the doorstep, out of breath and tearful.

'Some boys have got Trina in the park,' she panted. 'Kyle Gallagher and some others.'

As soon as she heard Kyle's name and linked it to Laura's troubled state, Daisy became alarmed.

'Wait there!' she said.

Then she dashed back into the living room, told Ellis and Jarell she had to go out and left them to look after Tyler while she hurried from the house.

'Come on,' she said to Laura, rushing up the street, 'show me where they are.'

They soon arrived at the park and Laura took Daisy to the spot where they had been when the boys arrived. But there was no sign of Trina.

'It was definitely around here,' said Laura, growing more tearful as she searched around in vain for her friend.

Daisy glanced around the park, frantically hoping to catch sight of her daughter but she couldn't see her anywhere.

'Are you sure this is where you were when the boys caught up with her?' asked Daisy.

'I think so,' said Laura, looking anxiously up and down the pathway as though hoping it would tell her something. 'It was about this far from the gate.'

Daisy realised that, to Laura, there was nothing along the pathway to differentiate one spot from another. It all looked the same; a wide pathway with a field on one side and a grass verge on the other, bordered by bushes. At a loss for what else to do, she began to shout Trina's name. Laura followed suit and, as they shouted, they wandered up and down the pathway taking care not to go too far from the area Laura had indicated.

At one point Daisy thought she heard a voice. 'Shush,' she said to Laura, then she called Trina's name again and listened for a response.

Daisy could just about discern a voice calling, 'here' but it was frail and she wasn't sure whether it belonged to her daughter. She followed the direction of the voice and called Trina's name again.

'Here. In the bushes,' came the faint reply.

This time there was no mistaking her daughter's voice and, with a feeling of trepidation, she headed into the bushes with Laura following her. Daisy could feel the tension within her escalating, her mind full of worries about what she might find. Then she spotted her.

Trina was kneeling down on the muddy ground, her jeans covered in soil and twigs. Her top was torn from the shoulder down, exposing her inadequate child's vest which clung to the outline of a tiny, pert breast. There was a further rip lower down but Daisy was drawn to the area above her daughter's shoulders. Trina was holding blood-soaked hands over her face and Daisy could see the blood seeping through her fingers.

'Oh my God!' yelled Daisy, shocked. 'What have they done to my poor girl?'

Daisy saw how her daughter's tear-filled eyes narrowed at her reaction, and she quickly tried to compose herself, knowing that she needed to be strong for Trina.

She pulled Trina's hands away so she could examine her face, noticing that her hands were covered in mud as well as blood. She flinched at the sight of a large open wound that cut across one side of Trina's face, and was worried that her daughter might already have contaminated it with her muddy hands. It was still pumping blood and Daisy quickly lifted the hem of her skirt and held it to the wound, pressing it at either side to stem the flow. Trina screeched in pain.

'It's alright. Shush, my child,' said Daisy, soothingly. 'I need to stop the blood. Then everything will be just fine.'

She could see Trina tense as she tried to be brave and hold back the tears, and a deep hurt blazed within her. Trina, her precious, only daughter. What had she done to deserve this? Her only crime was in trying to protect her younger brothers as any good sister would do. And as Daisy thought about the lasting damage that this attack would have on her daughter, she struggled to contain her own tears.

But she tried to put her heartrending thoughts to one side. She needed to focus on one thing at a time. Daisy felt sure that a wound that size would need stitches but she wanted to stem the blood loss first. After that, she would need to get Trina to hospital. And once the professionals had patched her daughter up, then she would think about how to deal with the fallout.

14

Daisy looked across at her daughter who was playing with her younger brother, Tyler, and trying her best to act as if everything was alright. But Daisy knew it wasn't. As she took in her daughter's damaged face for the umpteenth time since they had returned from the hospital, she felt a profound sadness. She knew that her daughter would be scarred for life, and that the mental scars would run much deeper than the physical one.

The doctor had said that the wound was three centimetres in length and deep. Therefore, there had been no alternative but to stitch it once they had cleaned it. Daisy had admired her daughter's bravery; the way she had clenched her teeth and balled her hands into fists to fight back her tears as the nurse stitched her up.

At the moment the wound looked bad, but the medical staff had assured both Daisy and Trina that it would eventually fade. Unfortunately, this had given Trina false hope that it might fade to nothing. Daisy hadn't had the heart to tell her that although it wouldn't look as bad as it did now, it would always be there. An upsetting reminder of a wicked act.

Daisy hadn't gone to the police; she didn't dare. The fear of reprisals was too strong to take that chance. But she knew she had to do something. What sort of mother would she have been if she let this go without taking any action at all? She looked at the clock. Mr Gallagher would still be at work. It was therefore the best time to pay a visit to Mrs Gallagher while her own children were occupied; Trina and Tyler in the house and Ellis and Jarell playing outside. Mrs Gallagher was the least fearsome of the two Gallagher parents but, nevertheless, the thought of visiting her struck fear into Daisy.

'Trina, I'm just going out for a few minutes. Will you keep an eye on Tyler for me please?'

'Yeah, sure. Where are you going?'

'Nowhere important. Don't worry, I won't be long.'

She'd chosen not to tell Trina yet, just in case her visit wasn't fruitful. Nevertheless, Daisy was determined that, now she'd made the decision, she was going to see it through, no matter how daunting it was. She slipped out of the house with her heart hammering inside her chest and soon arrived at the Gallaghers' home.

Daisy felt anxious as she knocked on the Gallaghers' front door, anticipating an aggressive reaction from Mrs Gallagher. She became aware once more of her rapidly beating heart and as she lifted the knocker her hands trembled so much she lost her grip on it. The knocker slipped from her hand, landing softly against the door plate and letting out a low, tinny sound. Undeterred, Daisy took a deep breath, squared her shoulders and lifted the knocker again, this time tapping it firmly against the door plate several times.

As Mrs Gallagher opened her front door she looked Daisy up and down with a scowl on her face and Daisy almost lost her nerve. Mrs Gallagher wasn't imposing in the physical sense, as she was slight in frame and a bit shorter than Daisy, but she had the harsh, pinched features of someone used to doing battle. Her whole demeanour was aggressive, from the narrowed eyes and clenched jaw to the balled fists and irate tone of voice.

'What do *you* want?' she demanded.

'Hello, Mrs Gallagher,' said Daisy, trying to disguise the tremor in her voice. 'I've come about your son, Kyle.'

Mrs Gallagher tutted. 'I might have known,' she said. 'He's always getting the blame for summat.' She sighed dramatically as though bored of complaints about her son. 'What is it now?'

'He's attacked my daughter, Trina.'

'Well, she must have done something to deserve it.'

'There was a bit of trouble with your other son, Shaun, so I think Kyle was retaliating but...'

Mrs Gallagher jumped in before Daisy had chance to finish speaking. 'That's it then. She must have done summat to Shaun for my Kyle to attack her. Anyway, what do you mean by attack? They're only bleedin' kids when all said and done.'

'It was him and his friends.'

'And have you been to see their parents? I bet you bleedin' haven't, have you? No, it's always my Kyle that gets the blame. Talk about give a dog a bad name...'

This time Daisy cut in. She was getting tired of

Mrs Gallagher's diatribe and her irritation emboldened her. 'I don't know who his friends are. Perhaps he could tell you. But he was the one with the knife.'

Daisy could see the stunned look on Mrs Gallagher's face. 'Knife! What the fuck you talking about, knife?'

'Kyle cut Trina quite badly. She had to have stitches for a deep cut on her cheek.'

'You're joking!' said Mrs Gallagher, staring at Daisy, her mouth and eyes wide with shock.

'I wish I was,' said Daisy, her tone measured as she tried to stay calm. 'The doctors say she'll be scarred for life.'

Mrs Gallagher reached a hand forward and placed it on Daisy's forearm. The gesture of concern surprised Daisy. 'You sure it was my Kyle?' she asked.

'Definitely,' said Daisy. 'Trina knows him, and her friend saw them attack Trina too.'

'For shit's sake!' said Mrs Gallagher. 'I don't fuckin' believe it. What next?'

It was obvious to Daisy that the other woman was shocked and appalled at what her son had done. It seemed like she had a whole heap of troubles on her mind. Daisy felt bad at bringing even more trouble to her door and for a moment she was tempted to utter an apology. But then she checked herself. After all, Trina was the victim, not Kyle, so she stayed silent and waited for Mrs Gallagher to speak again.

'Right,' she said. 'Leave it with me. I'll sort Kyle out. And I'll find out which of his bleedin' mates were with him as well.'

'Thank you,' said Daisy and she was about to walk away until she realised that Mrs Gallagher hadn't given her any real assurances. 'Trina's very nervous about going outside,' she said. 'She's worried that the boys might attack her again.'

'They won't,' Mrs Gallagher bit back. 'Don't you fuckin' worry! I'll take care of that.'

Daisy realised that this was the best she could expect from a woman like Mrs Gallagher. There was no point waiting for an apology so she thanked her again and returned home, relieved that the encounter was over and at least she had achieved something. In fact, the meeting had gone much better than she could have expected. As she reflected on things on her way home she realised that it was probably because the boys had crossed a line that even someone with Mrs Gallagher's fearsome reputation wouldn't tread.

Daisy didn't tell Trina about the outcome of her visit to Mrs Gallagher straightaway. She wanted Trina to stay indoors a bit longer to give her time to come to terms with what had happened before she faced the cruel world outside. It was two days later when she decided to broach the subject.

'Trina, you don't need to worry about going out anymore,' she began. 'Kyle Gallagher and his friends will leave you alone now.'

'Why? Have the police been to see them?'

'Not exactly, no,' said Daisy, sighing as she wondered how best to word this. 'Let's just say I have Mrs Gallagher's word that they'll leave you alone.'

'Oh,' said Trina, seemingly disappointed, and Daisy felt as though she had to add some more comforting words.

'They won't come near you now, but if any of them says

anything I want you to tell me straightaway. I'm sure they won't though.'

Trina just nodded and carried on with what she was doing.

Later that day Trina decided to venture outdoors. The first people she bumped into were Jessica and Laura. It was obvious from Jessica's reaction that Laura had told her about what had happened and, instead of avoiding her as she usually did, Jessica stopped to talk.

'It's quite big, isn't it?' she said.

Trina was surprised that Jessica hadn't mentioned her own experience at the hands of Kyle and his friends, and Trina's unwillingness to get involved. She had expected animosity with Jessica criticising her lack of involvement, perhaps even telling her she deserved what she got. But instead there was a note of empathy in Jessica's voice and Trina realised that the enormity of what had happened to her surpassed all that had happened previously.

Trina fingered the scar. 'Yes,' she said, with a hint of bravado. 'Kyle Gallagher did it with a knife.'

'I know,' said Jessica. 'I bet it hurt, didn't it?'

'A bit,' said Trina, enjoying the attention.

Then Jessica lowered her voice to a whisper. 'That Kyle Gallagher's horrible. Him and his friends really scared me. My dad wanted to go to the police but my mam said it was best not to because they hadn't done any real damage. Did your mam go to the police?'

'No, but my mam says him and his friends won't bother me again.'

'Why not?' asked Jessica.

'My mam went to see Mrs Gallagher and she told her they'd leave me alone now.'

'Is that all?' asked Jessica. 'Why didn't she go to the police? What they did was really bad, wasn't it, Laura?'

Laura nodded her agreement.

'My dad would have gone to the police if they'd have done that to me,' Jessica continued. 'He said they can't expect to get away with going around using knives. They want locking up. I bet your mam was frightened of going to the police because of what Mr Gallagher would do.'

Trina didn't know how to respond so she shrugged then said, 'I'm going to the shop. See you later.'

As Trina walked away Jessica's comments played on her mind. Why hadn't her mother gone to the police? It wasn't right. Why did her mother trust the word of Mrs Gallagher who was known for being argumentative and aggressive? But, deep down, Trina knew the answer to her own questions. The Gallagher family were fearsome and that was why Kyle Gallagher got away with such bad things.

The worry that Kyle might even go back on his mother's promise, and attack her again, sent a shiver of fear through her. But she became annoyed at her own fear. Trina didn't like that feeling of powerlessness or the knowledge that she and her family were so vulnerable. She already had a mistrust and dislike of all males, but her powerlessness at the hands of the opposite sex fed those insecurities and a burgeoning ill-feeling.

15

April 1992

Trina looked across the room at her two cousins, Josh and Calvin. While Ellis was trying to impress them by telling them about the mischief he had been up to, they largely ignored him. They soon became bored, and turned their attention to Trina instead.

'What was the name of the lad that did that to you, Trina?' asked Josh.

'Kyle Gallagher.'

'You heard of him?' he asked his brother.

'Nah, does he live round here?' Calvin asked Trina.

'Yeah, just up the road.'

'How old is he?' Josh asked.

'Twelve.'

'Aah, small fry,' said Calvin. 'I wouldn't have let him get away with that. I would have kicked that knife right out of his hand then smacked him in the mouth.'

'I would have kicked the shit out of him,' said Josh.

'She can't fight them, she's only a girl,' Calvin chipped in.

'I didn't have a chance,' said Trina, growing agitated.

'Anyway, there wasn't just him. He had two friends with him too.'

'Were they small fry too?'

Trina shrugged.

'Go on,' Calvin persisted. 'How old are they?'

'About the same as him.'

Calvin hissed. 'Ha, like I said, they're small fry.'

Trina soon grew tired of her cousins' interrogation. It wasn't as if they were offering to help. Her mother wouldn't have allowed any reprisals anyway for fear of stirring things up even more with the Gallaghers.

She walked out of the living room and headed towards the kitchen. She was about to push the door open when she heard the voice of her Aunty Tamara. Even louder than usual, she sounded irate, and Trina paused to hear what she was saying.

'I couldn't believe my eyes, Daisy. It's terrible! They want shooting.'

'I know,' said Daisy, resignedly. 'They hurt my Trina real bad, even tore the clothes off her. I don't think she'll ever be the same again. The poor child has no idea how badly this will affect her for the rest of her life, and I haven't the heart to tell her.'

Trina heard a tremor in her mother's voice as she spoke the last few words, and she felt the breath catch in her throat. It got to her that her mother should get so upset when discussing what had happened. But then she dismissed it; her mother had always been a bit of a softie anyway.

Not wanting to witness an emotional scene or, worse still, an awkward silence followed by a swift change of topic, she returned to the lounge. As it was raining, her mother had forbidden them to go outside. She therefore had no choice but to carry on listening to her cousins as they boasted about their designer gear and the cool friends they hung about with. Her mind wasn't on them, but on her scar. Where she had initially felt brave, she no longer did. Instead she now saw her scar as a failing.

The first time Mrs Gallagher saw Trina's scar was several weeks after the attack. Trina had had her stiches taken out a while ago and, although the scar didn't look as bad as it had done, it was still bright red and the flesh was raised. Her mother had told her that in time it would become smoother and the redness would fade, and she had seen no reason not to believe her.

As soon as Mrs Gallagher spotted Trina's scar, she failed to hide her look of alarm and repulsion. Her eyes were fixed on Trina's face for what seemed like an eternity, her brows drawn tightly together, before she became aware of Trina's concern and swiftly looked away. Shock waves tore through Trina's consciousness. Did it really look that bad?

In the weeks following the attack, Trina had had many pitying looks from adults, some of them whispering knowingly amongst themselves. She'd tried not to think about it too much. They were bound to gossip; after all, Kyle had used a knife on her, which was enough to disturb even the most hardened gossips.

Up to now Trina had done her best to avoid looking at the scar in the mirror, hoping it would disappear in time or at least lessen substantially as her mother had assured her. Now, though, she was beginning to view the scar in a different light. She'd become fed up of the stares and whispers and was already longing for the time when the scar wouldn't be as noticeable. But Mrs Gallagher's reaction made her anxious.

Back indoors she couldn't stop thinking about her scar and went to the bathroom to examine it. Locking the door behind her, she stepped gingerly up to the mirror and studied it. It was an angry red and cut diagonally across the fullest part of her cheek. She ran her finger along the length of it, feeling the raised flesh at either side of the cut. Then she looked at it again, in detail.

As she studied it in the mirror, she realised that it would always be there; perhaps smoother and less discoloured, but still there. And it would always label her as the girl who had been attacked for trying to stand up to the boys. Suddenly her breath caught on a sob and tears gushed from her eyes. She sank down onto the cold bathroom floor, weeping bitterly for the girl she once was. In that moment she realised that she would never again be that girl. Her life had been changed irrevocably by one callous act.

Eventually Trina exhausted herself, and she could cry no more. But she didn't want any more tears. What good would they do? She promised herself that it was the last time she would cry about the scar; now she just had to accept it. But her overwhelming feeling of bitterness and resentment against those responsible would never go away; just like the scar.

Trina detested Kyle Gallagher and his friends for what they had done to her, but her anger wasn't just directed at them. She resented her parents too; her father for not being there to protect her, and her mother for failing to do so.

16

November 2006

Ruby checked her appearance in the full-length mirror. She had been putting in extra hours at the gym knowing that the rubber catsuit she had chosen for her role as dominatrix was very unforgiving. As she caught sight of her reflection, she felt a sense of satisfaction. The outfit worked perfectly, hugging her toned body, and the black rubber with accompanying cat eye mask also emphasised her role.

As she patted down her hair and adjusted the mask, she felt a flutter in her chest. Her first client was due in five minutes and, although she knew him, she couldn't help but feel a bit anxious. What if she couldn't pull it off and the clients were dissatisfied?

Ruby quickly swallowed down her nerves, telling herself that if it didn't work out then she'd just have to go back to what she was doing before. She still had her old clients anyway and knew that it would take some time till she built up her reputation as a dominatrix and the new clients joined her.

Ruby heard the sound of the doorbell then the patter of Tiffany's footsteps as she went to answer it.

'Yes, come in. She's ready for you,' she heard Tiffany say.

Ruby took a deep breath and braced herself as she saw the doorknob turn and Tiffany led her client into the room then smiled and left them alone.

'Hi Ruby,' said Victor, an older man who had been visiting Ruby for the past few months.

Victor was a very ordinary looking man. Small and balding, he had a habit of talking too much and loudly, and Ruby guessed that he must have been lonely. He'd previously told her about his visits to other dominatrices and had hinted at receiving the same services from her.

At the time she had instinctively turned it down and, at first, she'd been surprised when he continued to visit her. But then she surmised that, like a lot of clients, he had his favourite girls that he continued to visit regularly. But it didn't stop him hinting again almost every time he visited her with an obsequiousness that she found pitiful. Maybe it was her natural dominance that he found appealing.

When Ruby had told Victor about her new line of work he was delighted. His excitement was palpable and Ruby had laughed about it afterwards with Tiffany, telling her that she had almost expected him to start frothing at the mouth. He'd become so exhilarated as she talked him through her various services, and he'd given his enthusiastic input as to what he would like to happen.

Now, as he walked through the door of Ruby's Dungeon, he had the same excited expression on his face. His look of eagerness made Ruby feel empowered and her nervousness rapidly disappeared.

'It's Mistress Ruby!' she said, in response to his greeting. Her tone was stern as she cracked the whip she was holding, and she was rewarded with his expression of nervous glee. 'Get over there and take your clothes off. Then wait until I summon you.'

Victor dashed eagerly to the other side of the room where Ruby had removed the screen and laid out her instruments of torture ready for his arrival. As she watched him scurrying across the room, she smiled to herself. Maybe this line of work would turn out well after all.

'Well, how did it go?' asked Tiffany, getting up from the sofa.

Ruby grinned. 'It was a breeze.'

'Really? What did you have to do?'

'Whip him, beat him and talk to him like he was a piece of shit.' They both laughed then Ruby added, 'He fuckin' loved it, couldn't get enough of it! And, he's got a few Internet friends who are into the same sort of thing so he's going to put the word out.'

She waved the wad of notes that she had been holding. 'Look at this, three times what I would normally have earnt in that time. If I get enough clients, I should soon get back what I shelled out to set up the room.'

'Brilliant!' said Tiffany. 'You still wouldn't get *me* doing it though.'

'Don't worry, you won't have to. Oh, and he suggested I get my own website to promote my services.'

'Are you going to?'

'Might do. It's worth thinking about.'

'Wow! Sounds like it's gonna do well,' said Tiffany.

'Dead right,' said Ruby, walking up to Tiffany and putting her arms around her. 'We're gonna be rich, girl. And when we are, I'll be able to buy you anything you want.'

Tiffany kissed Ruby on the cheek then looked at her admiringly and smiled. 'I knew you could do it.'

Ruby could see the look of joy on her girlfriend's face, and she felt a warm glow inside. To think, she'd been nervous about her first session. Why? It couldn't have gone better. And now that she'd got that out of the way she was looking forward to a very lucrative future for herself and Tiffany.

17

May 2007

Ruby's client was right on time and as she went to answer the front door, she adopted her Mistress Ruby persona. He didn't hesitate in crossing over the threshold while Ruby shut the door.

She had been working as a dominatrix for a few months now and it was going well, the number of clients gradually increasing. Once she had got the first few clients out of the way she became much more confident in her new role. She was getting to know each of them and their particular fetishes and, she liked to think, they went away happy. The repeat business was evidence of that. The only problem she had up to now was that some clients asked for things she couldn't offer because the equipment required was too big to fit inside her spare bedroom.

As the client stepped inside, Ruby noticed her neighbour opposite. She had only lived there a few weeks and hadn't been particularly friendly since she moved in, often just returning a swift hello but refusing to engage in conversation.

The way the neighbour looked at her drew Ruby's

attention to what she was wearing. Normally Tiffany would answer the door to avoid Ruby being spotted in her dominatrix gear but today she had had to go out. Looking across at the neighbour, Ruby felt she had no alternative other than to brazen it out.

'Hi, alright?' she said, but the neighbour didn't reply; instead she quickly slammed the door shut.

It was obvious the woman wasn't impressed by Ruby's attire. But there was no time to think about that now; she had a client to tend to so she went into the spare room where she found the man already sitting on the bed, and ready to get down to business. She got to work straightaway, placing a dog-collar around his neck, and then telling him he had to address her as Mistress Ruby at all times and do exactly as he was ordered.

Ruby stood at well over six feet in her spiky-heeled, thigh-high boots. Dressed in a black rubber catsuit that clung to her feminine but toned physique and melded seamlessly into the dark leather boots, she was Amazonian in stature.

She looked down at the diminutive man sitting cowered before her and yanked the chain of his dog-collar, a faint smirk of amusement lighting up her strained features as she watched his keen reaction.

'I want you over that stool, NOW!' she commanded.

'Yes,' said the man, nodding obsequiously.

'Yes, what?' she asked.

'Yes, Mistress Ruby,' the man replied, anxious to please.

She pulled sharply on the chain and led him over to a stool placed beneath a rack full of her instruments of torture.

'Bend over!' she ordered, selecting a wooden paddle from

the row of implements. It was less likely to mark than a leather one although far more painful.

He had no sooner bent over the stool than she let the chain fall loose in her hand while she paddled him viciously on his behind, gaining immense gratification as the man yelled in pain. She gauged his reaction just to the point where he could take no more then she put down the paddle and yanked the chain again.

As soon as he was on his feet, Ruby kicked the stool out of the way. The man jumped as the stool crashed and bounced along the black vinyl floor of Mistress Ruby's dungeon, and she felt a frisson of excitement. Now for the next stage.

Ruby grabbed a whip from the rack. Like her boots, it was black leather. It had a sturdy wooden handle and fanned out into multiple tails, each capable of delivering a harsh stroke to exposed flesh. Perfect. Because Ruby knew there were some days when only the whip would do.

'Turn your back to me and stand still!' she ordered, and her client quickly complied.

She stepped back and brought the whip down onto the man's bare back. He yelled. Ruby gave him only a second to recover before bringing the whip down again, drawing satisfaction at the sight of red weals beginning to form on his back and the lashing sound as the whip slashed through the air.

After five lashes of the whip, she gave the man a break. She always did this; it gave her clients a chance to decide whether they wanted to continue or whether they had had enough for the day. She could see his body tense and then relax as he drew in a deep breath.

'Do you want more?' she asked.

'Yes.'

She tutted. 'Yes, Mistress Ruby. What have I told you?'

'Sorry. Yes, Mistress Ruby.'

'It's not good enough. That's twice you've disobeyed me by not using my name. It's time you were really punished.'

Without waiting for the man to react, she brought the whip down on his back five times in quick succession. Then she stopped again, allowing him to recover.

'Are you going to obey me in future?' she asked.

But the man didn't reply. Instead, to her astonishment, he quickly spun round. Then he grabbed the tails of the whip and dragged it out of her hand.

'My turn,' he said, leering at her. He nodded at the zipper on the front of her catsuit. 'Open it. I want to see you in the flesh,' he demanded.

'Get back!' she yelled. 'Mistress Ruby hasn't given you permission. Only Mistress Ruby can give orders.'

She desperately hoped that he was still prepared to act out his role. But the look on his face told her otherwise. He was fevered with excitement, his eyes wide and teeth bared, and it was obvious from looking at him that he couldn't wait to get started on her.

Ruby quickly reached out to the rack and grabbed the dark handle of the knife she had secreted behind the other implements. She flicked a switch and the blade shot out just as the whip came crashing down on her face. Ignoring the smarting pain, she grabbed the tails with her other hand and pulled, closing the gap between her and the man. Then she shoved the knife up to his throat, nicking the flesh till a stream of blood ran down to his chest.

The man stared back at her in alarm. 'No! Please no,' he uttered, his expression no longer animated but frozen like a startled rabbit.

Ruby responded by pulling the knife away and slashing it down his arm, leaving a gaping wound. The man screamed in agony and quickly covered the gash with his other hand. But before he had chance to do anything else, Ruby held the knife to his throat again, so close that he was forced to raise his chin and look straight into her angry eyes.

'Sky!' he yelled. 'Sky!'

'It's a bit too fuckin' late for the safe word!' she hissed. 'This has got fuck all to do with what you paid for. I told you from the start that I give the orders. You NEVER touch Mistress Ruby. Do you understand?'

'Yes,' the man mumbled, hardly able to move his mouth as the knife was so tight against his throat.

'Let this be a warning,' she continued. 'Never, ever step out of line again! I want you off my fuckin' premises. And don't bother coming back. And if I EVER hear of you stepping out of line with a woman again then I'll hunt you down like the fuckin' animal you are, and I'll finish the job off.'

The man didn't say anything; he just stared at her, his pleading eyes wide open with fear, till Ruby pulled the knife away.

'Now go and get dressed then fuck off!' she said, and she watched, relieved as the man picked up his clothes and began to dress.

In working as a dominatrix Ruby had found her ideal role

in life as she had a profound distrust of men. Previously, in her work as a prostitute, Ruby had put up with the depraved and perverted clients by telling herself that it was just a means to an end. They might have thought they were using her but she knew she was the one in control. Men were just there to provide her with money.

But being a dominatrix suited her far better. She didn't have to sleep with the clients, who were mainly satisfied just to be punished or belittled. There were occasional times when a customer stepped out of line, like today, but those times were rare. Most customers knew what was expected of them. Not only that, but they knew of Ruby's fearsome reputation.

Ruby waited while the man got dressed then led him out of the flat. Once he had left her premises, she returned to the dungeon and got the room ready for her next client. Then she tidied herself up and checked her appearance in the mirror. By this time her cheek was smarting and as she caught her reflection, she noticed marks where the whip had lashed her. She put her hand up to her face and as she brought it away, she saw the glistening vermillion streaks of blood on her fingertips.

The breath caught in her throat as she examined her face in detail in the mirror. But it was only a tiny gash and she let out a sigh, relieved that it was unlikely to scar. Nevertheless, the sight of blood on her face unsettled her and reminded her why she had such an intense aversion to the opposite sex.

18

May 2007

A few days later the landlord paid them a visit. Ruby had just seen her last client of the day and was in the bedroom changing out of her rubber catsuit when she heard Tiffany answer the front door followed by the sound of the landlord's voice. Then their voices carried past the bedroom door and Ruby knew Tiffany had let him in.

She quickly finished getting dressed in her jeans and t-shirt then dashed through to the lounge to join them.

'What's the matter?' she asked, switching down the music till the sound of the Sugababes hummed softly in the background.

'As I've just been telling your friend, here,' he began, 'we've had a complaint from one of your neighbours who is concerned about the number of strange men you keep bringing into the flat.'

Ruby immediately got on the offensive. 'Her across the way d'you mean?' Then, without waiting for the landlord to reply, she continued. 'Jesus Christ! What is her problem?

Yes, we do have men coming to the flat, but they're friends and relatives, and they're not strange to us.'

'Really? Well, she mentioned the clothing you were wearing when you let a man inside the flat. She seemed to think there was something a bit suspicious about it. Rubber, she said.'

Ruby forced a fake laugh, but inside she was praying that the landlord didn't ask to take a look around the flat. The S&M gear would be a real giveaway. 'It was a catsuit, actually. We were going to a fancy-dress party and my friend had come to pick us up.'

The landlord didn't look convinced but Ruby could tell that he couldn't think of anything else to say other than accusing her outright of being on the game. It was obvious from the embarrassed way he was squirming that he wasn't about to do that. Then she noticed Tiffany looking desperately at the clock, her features strained. Ruby remembered that Tiffany had a client due. Shit! She had to get rid of the landlord before he arrived. So she continued on the attack, acting wounded by the perceived insult.

'So, you can tell Mrs Busy Body that she's barking up the wrong tree! And now, if you don't mind, Mr Walker, we're busy.'

The landlord looked round as though searching for words he couldn't find. Then, when he still couldn't think of anything more to say, he made towards the door, led by Ruby. But he left her with a few parting words.

'Well, I'm sorry if I might have got it wrong, but if I have any further complaints then I will have to take things further.'

Ruby could tell by his tone of voice that he wasn't

convinced by her story about the fancy-dress party. Nevertheless, she was relieved to see him walk down the hall and head for the stairs. She was thankful for that. It had been a close shave.

When she got back inside the flat Tiffany was fretting. 'Shit, Ruby, what are we gonna do? Now that old cow over the way knows what we're up to she'll be watching us every minute. It's only a matter of time before she complains to him again.'

'Bitch!' Ruby cursed. 'Why can't people learn to mind their own fuckin' business? It's not as if we're doing her any harm.'

'I know, but you know what people are like. What are we gonna do?' Tiffany repeated. 'If she complains again, we could be out on our arses with nowhere to live and back to working the streets. And how the fuck will we get another place? No one wants to rent their property to a couple of prostitutes.'

'Don't worry,' said Ruby. 'I think I've got a plan that should get us out of the shit. It's something I've been thinking about for a while and, after what's happened, I think it's the right time.'

19

September 1993

It was Trina's first day at secondary school and over a year and a half since her attack at the hands of Kyle Gallagher and his friends. By now her scar had faded into a pale thin brown line. It was no longer repulsive to look at but, nevertheless, it set her apart from the other students, as did her good looks, tall, athletic physique and forceful personality.

During their first games lesson, Nicole Pugh made herself known to Trina. By now, the other students were finding out about Trina's tough girl reputation. While she was getting changed for games, Trina could see Nicole standing with a group of friends and sizing her up. Trina was still in her underwear, making her feel vulnerable, when Nicole approached with two of her friends following behind.

'How did you get that scar?' she asked.

'Fighting,' Trina replied, flippantly. Then she added, 'with boys,' and stood staring at Nicole, waiting for her response.

For seconds they stood facing each other, their eyes locked in a death stare. It was Nicole who broke away first and walked back to where she had been standing. Her two friends shot Trina a contemptuous glare before they took off after her. Trina knew she had a problem. She had already heard of Nicole's reputation. Many of the other girls were frightened of her and kept their distance when she was around. Others sucked up to her, wary of getting on her bad side.

They were put on opposite teams for a practice game of netball and Nicole flashed her a sly grin as they took their places. Trina wasn't surprised when Nicole managed to wrangle it so that they were paired against each other; Trina in goal attack and Nicole as a defender.

While they waited for play to start, Nicole glared at Trina but, to Trina's delight, she had to look up as Trina was much taller than her. Trina smirked at her and Nicole returned a look of hatred. For the first half of the game, Nicole marked her closely but Trina still managed to score two goals, her tall frame giving her an advantage.

It was during the start of the second half that Trina and Nicole jumped for the ball at the same time. They collided and Nicole knocked Trina off balance. The ball flew from Trina's hands. Nicole quickly reached for it but the teacher called a foul before she had chance and gave possession back to Trina's team who yelled with joy when Trina scored a goal off the back of it.

Nicole glared at Trina and hissed under her breath. 'I didn't foul; you did, and you're gonna pay for that, bitch!'

'Come on, girls, carry on with the game please,' shouted the teacher.

They resumed play and for the rest of the second half Trina managed to avoid any more encounters with Nicole, but she knew it wasn't over. Nicole waited until the teachers had left them in the changing rooms before she made her move, stepping right up to Trina.

'You pushed into me, you bitch!' she said.

'No I didn't. It was you that pushed into me. That's why the teacher called a foul. Bitch!' Trina replied.

'Who are you fuckin' calling a bitch?' shouted Nicole, giving Trina a sharp slap on her face.

But Trina was ready and she launched herself at Nicole, overpowering her with a series of swift punches. Nicole staggered backwards, looking around for her friends who stayed out of the way, nervous of getting involved. Trina grinned on seeing Nicole's look of despair then carried on raining punches down on her.

It was the games teacher who came to Nicole's rescue, rushing over in alarm as soon as she walked through the door and saw what was taking place. She pushed between the girls, holding them apart while she hollered at them to break it up.

'Right, I want your names,' she said. When she had taken a note of them, she said, 'What a despicable way to carry on in your first week of secondary school! You can report to the head's office after school and tell him I sent you. And I suggest you get yourself cleaned up,' she said to Nicole whose nose was pumping blood.

Trina spotted a slight tremble of Nicole's lip and she could feel an inner glow of satisfaction. She had put Nicole Pugh in her place and everybody would now know that she wasn't to be messed with. She didn't care what punishment she got. It was more important that she had beaten her rival.

For the rest of that day Trina basked in the glory of having beaten Nicole Pugh in a fight. Unknown to her, many of the school tough nuts had been waiting to see which girl came out on top in their year, and they were excited to see a winner. Others clamoured to win Trina's favour, chatting to her as they made their way to classes.

When Trina arrived at the head teacher's office after school, Nicole was already standing outside waiting. Trina had seen Nicole as she walked up the corridor and had expected a hostile reception. But Nicole surprised her by flashing a grin as soon as she arrived.

'He knows I'm here,' she said. 'You're best knocking on the door and letting him know you're here as well. He said he'll deal with us once you arrive.'

Trina shrugged and knocked on the door. A female member of staff answered it and looked at her contemptuously. Then she told her to wait till the head was ready for them before shutting the door again.

Nicole giggled. 'She looked at me like that too.'

Trina couldn't help but smile back. 'You scared?' she asked.

'Nah, they can't do much, can they? They're not allowed to give us the strap anymore. Are you?'

'Nah,' said Trina. 'Teachers don't scare me.'

'You're a good fighter,' said Nicole.

'Thanks,' Trina replied.

'You're good at netball too.'

'I used to play it at primary school. I was the best runner in our year too.'

'Wow! Cool,' said Nicole. She then shifted awkwardly from foot to foot before asking. 'Who do you hang around with?'

'No one really. Just different girls in our class.'

'Do you wanna hang around with me and my mates?'

Trina grinned. 'Yeah,' she said, overjoyed.

It was the seal of approval she had been looking for. She was now a member of the coolest group of girls in her year, which would make her popular. Trina wasn't interested in being a good pupil. She had never been academically gifted anyway. For her, school was more about having a good time, and that meant hanging about with the right crowd.

Within the first week of secondary school Trina had already found her place. Nicole was just the sort of wanton girl that Trina's mother would have warned her against but that didn't bother Trina. She was determined to fit in and have fun no matter what the cost.

20

August 1994

'Trina, would you bring the washing in from outside please?' asked Daisy.

'Why?'

Daisy looked at her daughter, astonished, and Trina knew she was finding it difficult to cope with the way she had changed since starting secondary school almost a year ago. 'Don't ask why, child. Just do as you're told!' she said.

'But why should I? Why can't they do it?' asked Trina, nodding in the direction of her brothers, Ellis and Jarell, who were toy fighting on the living room floor.

'Because I asked you,' said Daisy. 'And will you stop that fighting!' she said to her sons before turning her attention back to Trina, adding, 'Anyway they're too young.'

'No they're not! Ellis is nine now. I helped you when I was nine,' said Trina.

'Do I have to ask you again? Why does everything have to be an argument with you? You never used to be like this,' said Daisy. 'You're a girl. You should be helping around the house.'

Trina had been on the brink of helping, her shame at letting her mother down battling with her bid to be her own person. Ever since she had become friends with Nicole, she had been testing the boundaries. Nicole was always telling her what a mug she was for helping her mother when her brothers got away with it, as well as offering advice and criticism on other aspects of her life.

Why couldn't she stop out late at night? Why didn't she get more pocket money from her mother? Why didn't she ask her mother to buy her some new, more fashionable clothes?

It had made Trina think about things. Previously she'd been willing to help her mother around the house and to fit in with whatever else her mother wanted her to do. It was automatic, something she'd always done. But the more she found out about her friend's lives, the more she was starting to rebel. It wasn't that she didn't love her mother; she had a deep love for her, but when it came to respecting her it was another matter.

As soon as she said the words, 'you're a girl' it was like igniting a flame of fury within Trina and she immediately made her mind up. There was no way she was going to help her mother with the housework on the basis that she was a girl. Unlike her mother, she didn't think that women had to fit into a specified role. She resented men and the hold they had had over the family throughout her life, and she wanted to break away from the path her mother had set.

'That's rubbish!' she yelled. 'We're not living in the dark ages now, y'know. Ellis and Jarell should help too.'

'How dare you defy me, child!' her mother yelled back.

'And don't speak to me in that tone of voice. Are you going to help out or do I have to punish you?'

'What are you gonna do?' asked Trina, mockingly.

'Right, that's it. Go to your room and don't come back out till I tell you. You can go without your tea too.'

'For God's sake! I'm not a little kid, y'know, I'm twelve,' said Trina, stomping up the stairs.

'Well start acting like it then,' her mother shouted after her.

Trina stormed into her bedroom and slammed the door behind her. It took her a while to calm down and, while she did, she kept thinking about the injustice of it all. Her friend, Nicole, was right; her brothers should help out more. Why did she always have to do everything her mam said just because she was the oldest and a girl? It was like being an unpaid skivvy and, when all was said and done, they were her mother's kids, not hers, so why should she have to help look after them?

She also began to ponder on all the other injustices in her life and became trapped in a cycle of negativity. Why did her friends always have more fashionable clothes than her? Why did she always have to tell them her mam couldn't afford for her to go to the cinema with them? And why did she always have to be in as early as her brothers?

Since she had started secondary school Trina was becoming more and more rebellious, not only in the home but at school too. She wasn't interested in study, only in enjoying herself and being popular. And if being popular meant getting into trouble then that was what she would do.

Once she had exhausted all negative thoughts and calmed

down, Trina became bored. She had been looking forward to meeting Nicole and some of the other girls later. Nicole was great fun to be with and Trina enjoyed getting up to mischief with her and having a laugh. But if her mother insisted on making her stay in her room then she'd miss out on meeting her friends.

Trina wandered over to her bedroom window and looked out at the tiny patch of garden, which her mother kept neat. She saw the washing still lined up meticulously on the line and for a moment she regretted not helping. It wouldn't have taken her two minutes. But no, why should she? Most of the clothes didn't belong to her anyway.

Her eyes drifted back towards the house, which had a back extension to the downstairs with a flat roof. It had been added before they moved in to give the house more kitchen and dining space. As she looked through the window, Trina saw her mother go out into the garden and start bringing the washing in. While she worked, she hummed a tune but it wasn't a cheerful tune; it sounded melancholy. Trina felt a momentary stab of guilt but quickly pushed it aside.

An idea was beginning to form in her head, but she couldn't act on it until her mother was back indoors. She lay back down on her bed and waited till she could no longer hear her mother humming. Then she went to the window again to check her mother was out of sight. She'd gone back indoors. Good!

Trina eased the window open and looked down. There was only a short distance to the extension roof. It would be easy to drop down onto it. The extension was a lot higher up from ground level though so that might prove difficult to climb down. She carried on looking for a while, trying to decide whether it was worth the effort.

Why not? she thought. At least it would mean she would get to meet her friends so, to her mind, it was worth taking the risk. She eased herself out of the bedroom window and straddled the ledge. Then she swung both legs over it. She gripped the ledge with her arms and hands, and slowly lowered herself so her feet touched down lightly onto the roof.

Next she tiptoed across till she was at the outer edge of the extension. She lay down softly, peering over the edge to see through the kitchen window. There she spotted her mother who was chunnering away to herself, as usual, something about the magpies creating a racket again. Trina stifled a chuckle, knowing that her mother would be blaming the magpies for the noise she had made while walking across the roof. At least that meant she had done a good job of keeping her steps light.

Trina looked around her, assessing her options. Then she spotted the guttering and noticed that it led to a drainpipe at the far corner. The window finished about two thirds of the way across the extension wall, so the far corner would be the best place at which to descend to ground level without being spotted. She tiptoed across the roof again, this time making her way to the drainpipe, away from the window.

Easing herself over the edge proved a bit trickier this time. But Trina was a tall, athletic girl and she knew she could do it. At only twelve, she was also light enough for the drainpipe to support her weight. She swung her legs down, her feet gripping tightly onto one of the drainpipe brackets. She heard a bang as her feet hit the drainpipe and cringed, hoping she hadn't raised her mother's suspicions.

Trina waited a few seconds but couldn't hear anything so she climbed down the wall, holding onto the drainpipe with her hands and feet till she had safely reached the bottom. Then, without waiting to see if her mother had heard her, she ran. She continued running till she was safely out of her street and on the way to Nicole's home.

A feeling of euphoria swept through her, and she grinned to herself. She'd done it! She'd got out of the house and her mam hadn't been able to stop her. There was every chance her mother would find out later when she came upstairs to check on her. But Trina wasn't bothered.

She felt a sense of freedom. It wasn't just about defying her mother. That was the easy part. No, it was also about becoming her own person.

21

August 1996

It was a lovely summer evening in the school holidays and Trina was hanging out in the local park with Nicole. They had been firm friends ever since they had started secondary school almost three years ago, and now they were both fourteen. Trina had grown into a very attractive girl, still tall and slim but with ample curves.

Her striking eyes were a deep, dark brown with a brilliant sheen which lit up her face. She also had full lips, a perfectly formed nose and high cheekbones and, although the scar was still visible, it was no longer repulsive, forming a smooth fine line across her left cheek.

Nicole was on a similar wavelength to Trina; they were both tough, athletic girls who liked to push the boundaries. Lately they had started drinking after dark. They and a group of friends hid out in a clearing behind some bushes and guzzled from cans of cider, chatting and giggling till they felt merry.

'So, go on, tell me, how was last night?' Trina asked.

A mischievous smile lit up Nicole's face. 'It was great. We

started snogging first but then he wanted to go further so we did.'

'What, you mean, all the way?'

'Yeah, why not? It's not like it's the first time, is it?'

'Did you use anything?' asked Trina.

'No, he pulled out just in time.'

'Jesus, Nicole; you wanna be careful! You don't want to end up pregnant.'

'Don't worry, I won't. He's bringing some condoms with him next time.'

'What was it like?' asked Trina.

'Fuckin' brilliant! I loved it.'

Just then they were joined by two other friends, Emma and Clare, who were carrying a plastic bag containing several bottles of alcopop, a drink that Trina had never seen before, and puffing on cigarettes. They stopped and pulled two bottles from the bag then started drinking from them.

'Why are you drinking fruit juice?' asked Trina.

'It's not,' said Emma. 'It's booze but it's got fruit in it. Do you want to try some?'

Trina took a swig from one of the bottles. 'Eh, that's nice,' she said. 'Can I have a bottle? I'll let you have some of our cider.'

They did a trade-off, then Trina soon returned to the conversation she had been having with Nicole before the two friends arrived.

'Hey, have you two done it?' asked Trina.

'Done what?' they both responded.

'Had sex?'

'Yeah,' said Emma but Clare stayed quiet.

'Fuckin' brilliant innit?' said Nicole.

'Ew no, I didn't like it,' said Emma. 'It fuckin' hurt and then he came all over my legs and made a right mess.'

The other three giggled then Nicole said, 'That's because he's crap at it. You need to do it with someone who's good. Alex is brilliant.' Then she turned to Trina and asked, 'Why haven't you and Zac done it yet?'

Zac Poole was a friend of Alex. He was a year older than Trina and one of the cool kids of his year. With boyish good looks, and a reputation for fighting, Trina had been overjoyed when he'd bumped into her in the park and asked to take her out. Not only did all the girls fancy him, but it also felt good to be the girlfriend of someone with his reputation.

'I dunno. We've done other stuff but we've not gone all the way yet.'

'You wanna watch he doesn't go off with someone else. He could have any girl he wants. Alex told me there's a girl he fancies in his year and if he doesn't get sex with you, he's gonna ask her out.'

Trina didn't comment but thoughts were cascading around in her head. Although it felt good to be linked to Zac, Trina still had a profound mistrust of the opposite sex, which stemmed back to her childhood. Memories of her errant father, the seedy rent collector, her cocky cousins and the vicious boys who had attacked her were always at the back of her mind. But she didn't feel comfortable confiding in her friends about all of that.

After they had been drinking for a while, and Trina was feeling more drunk than usual, they saw Zac and Alex appear through a gap in the bushes. The boys knew where

Trina and Nicole hung out by now, and they had come to see them.

Nicole walked straight over to Alex, draped her arms around his neck and kissed him passionately, and it wasn't long before they left the space in the clearing to find a more private spot. Zac approached Trina, and the other girls stood to one side, giving them some space.

'You wanna come for a walk?' he asked, and Trina nodded then followed him out of the clearing.

As they walked along the pathway he handed her a cigarette then took one for himself and lit them both. They smoked while they walked along arm in arm. Trina missed her footing a few times and giggled when Zac helped her to regain her balance. She felt euphoric, partly from the effects of the booze and partly because she was getting attention from Zac Poole.

'Where are we going?' she asked.

Zac nodded towards the park building in the distance, and smiled. 'In there. We can have a sit down.'

'Oh, OK,' said Trina.

They eventually reached the building. It was open at the front with a bench running along the back of it. They sat side by side, concealed in the shadows. Zac hadn't made much of an effort at conversation on the way there but now he reached across and put his arm around her shoulder.

'Come on, let's have a snog,' he said, pulling her towards him till their lips met.

Trina complied with his wishes and as they kissed, she felt his hand on her breast. It gave her a shiver and she longed for him to go further. His hand soon moved to her neckline then slid under her top and inside her bra. When Trina felt his hand brush against her nipple a shiver of pleasure ran through her and she pushed her body against him, yearning for more.

He pulled away from the kiss but kept his hand inside her clothing, teasing each of her nipples in turn. 'You like that, don't you?' he said, and Trina nodded, her inhibitions lost to the alcohol.

His other hand was soon inside her jeans, venturing downwards till he found her vagina and slipped a finger inside. Trina let out a squeal. The pleasure felt so intense and she continued to push against him till she was writhing in ecstasy on the bench.

'Come on, let's do it,' he said.

In Trina's alcohol fuddled mind, she wanted sex. It felt so good with him that she wanted to carry on and she also knew it was what he wanted. It would keep him with her and boost her standing amongst her friends. But when he entered her, it was a let-down.

Trina yelped as she felt a sharp pain between her legs. Zac took it as a yelp of joy and carried on plunging inside her. She gritted her teeth until he had finished. Having come this far, she could hardly back out now. It was soon over and Trina pulled her clothes back up. She was quickly sobering up; all desire had now left her and all she wanted to do was return to her friends.

Zac looked across at her, noticing the displeasure on her face. 'You were a virgin, weren't you?' he asked.

'Yes,' said Trina.

'Good,' said Zac. 'I'm glad I was your first. I don't like slappers.'

He was smiling and Trina realised that he had gained

far more pleasure from the act than she had. For a few moments they made pointless conversation till Zac walked her back to the clearing. A knowing look passed between Trina and the other girls. But, once Zac was gone, Trina didn't feel like discussing the experience with them. Instead she made her way home alone, still feeling tipsy but with the feelings of euphoria now gone. It was getting late by the time she got back.

'What on earth are you doing home at this time, child?' her mother complained as Trina walked through the door. 'And you've been drinking,' she added, pushing her face up to Trina's and smelling her breath. 'Don't bother denying it; I can smell it on you.'

'I only had a bit,' said Trina, with attitude. 'Anyway, you drink so how can you have a go at me for doing it?' She was already ignoring her mother's tirade as she made her way up the stairs.

'You listen to me when I'm talking to you, young lady!' Daisy shouted after her.

Trina kept walking, knowing there was nothing her mother would do to stop her. What could she do? If she grounded her, Trina would only sneak out. And if she stopped giving her money to spend, Trina would find another way to get it. Her mother didn't even know half the tricks Trina got up to, such as walking to school so she could pocket her bus fare. She had no hold over someone as mentally strong as Trina.

The following day in school Nicole couldn't wait to hear about Trina's exploits.

'Did you do it?' she asked.

'Yes, we went all the way,' said Trina, smiling proudly.

'Did you like it?'

'Yeah, it was good,' said Trina.

She didn't want to admit to her friend that she hadn't actually enjoyed it. In fact, it had been painful. But she wasn't going to let Nicole or anybody else find out how she really felt. Instead it would remain her secret. Trina wanted Nicole to think she enjoyed sex as much as she did. She needed to fit in and to do so she had to be seen to be doing all the things her crowd did, and that included having sex with boys.

At break time Trina and Nicole bumped into Zac and Alex. Normally Zac didn't say much to Trina in school, but this time he made a show of putting his arm around her and proudly showing her off as his girl. Then he sneaked a kiss out of view of the teachers. When Trina broke away from the kiss, she noticed the admiring glances from other girls and a self-satisfied smile graced her lips. She had now earnt not only the respect of her friends but Zac's acknowledgement too.

Trina might not have enjoyed the sex act but it didn't bother her that much. Having gained Zac's acknowledgement she wanted to keep hold of him, knowing that the longer she was with him the more it would boost her reputation. Being with Zac gave her status. It was her ticket to the cool club. In fact, it was even more than that. Trina had discovered that her sexuality was the ultimate weapon with which to wield power over men. And it was a potent aphrodisiac.

22

June 2007

Now that the landlord was onto them, Ruby and Tiffany were afraid of being evicted. But Ruby had thought of a solution and she could tell Tiffany was intrigued as she stared back at her with a puzzled expression on her face. Then she said, 'Go on then, what is it?'

'Well,' began Ruby, 'I think we should get another place, a bigger place; one with loads of rooms that we can rent out to other girls so we can take a mark-up from what they earn.'

'What, like a brothel, you mean?'

'Yes, that's exactly what I mean.'

'And how the fuck will we manage that? We can't exactly go to the bank for a loan and show them our business plan, can we?'

'We won't have to. Victor will put up the money.'

'Victor? You mean that creepy little man that comes to you for a good beating?'

'Erm, the client who comes to me for my dominatrix services, don't you mean?' said Ruby, with a tone of mock authority.

Tiffany laughed. 'Listen to you!'

'Well, if I'm gonna do this, Tiffany, then I'm gonna do it right. Anyway, yes, that's Victor. He mentioned it a while ago, but I just said I'd think about it. I must admit, the fact that he's so creepy did put me off a bit. But, he's so into the whole scene and just wants to be a bigger part of it.

'Anyway, last time I saw him he said he'd put the money up but I would be the one running it as he needs to protect his reputation. And he said he'd share the profits with me on a fifty-fifty basis. Apparently, he's loaded and has lots of businesses. And, he's even found a place that he thinks will be perfect. I've been mulling it over for the last few days.'

'Really? It sounds interesting. But, won't it mean we'll be under his control?'

'No, you're wrong, Tiffany. He's the one who's under my control. He'll do anything I say, and he'll have a fuckin' smile on his face while he's doing it too. Besides, what's the alternative? Stay here and wait to be thrown out?'

Then Ruby's tone softened and she stared into Tiffany's eyes. 'I want the best for us, Tiff. I feel like all this is my fault for letting clients come back here in the first place, and I want to make it up to you.'

'Aw, thanks, Rubes,' said Tiffany. 'But don't forget, we're in this together. And I suppose you have got a point.'

'Definitely, Tiff. Just imagine, it'll mean we can book in clients at the same time instead of having to take turns.' Ruby was becoming animated by now, her words tumbling out of her in a rush to share her thoughts with Tiffany. 'And I'll be able to have a proper dungeon. Not just a space in a bedroom. A proper dungeon! I'll be able to get all the big equipment. The clients are always asking for it: stocks, cage, sex sling, the fuckin' lot!'

'Erm, maybe it is worth thinking about. I could help you man the desk too and it'll be great fixing the place up together. We could go and have a look at some other places where our friends work and see how they've kitted them out.'

'Course we can. Tell you what, why don't we go and see the place he's found and take it from there? If we don't like the look of it then we don't need to take it any further.'

'Sounds good to me,' said Tiffany. 'But I'm not agreeing to anything till I've seen the place and had chance to have a good think about it.'

'I wouldn't expect you to,' said Ruby stroking her girlfriend's shoulder affectionately. She was so glad she had Tiffany's support, and welcomed her enthusiasm. Life didn't seem so bad when you had someone loving and caring to share it with. 'Trust me, Tiff,' she said. 'It'll all work out fine.'

The following day Ruby went to visit her mother. When she walked in the living room Tyler was sitting playing on his games console as usual.

'I'll go and make us all a cuppa,' said her mother. 'Tyler, why don't you come off that thing for once and talk to your sister?'

Tyler flicked his head around briefly. 'Hang on a minute. Let me just finish this game,' he said.

Ruby smiled and ruffled his hair then sat down on the sofa until he'd finished. She heard her mother shout through from the kitchen, 'Aren't you gonna tell your sister your good news?'

Tyler then seemed to stop playing mid-game. When he got up, the look on his face suggested he felt a little ashamed for ignoring Ruby, and he took the seat next to her on the sofa.

'Soz,' he said.

'No worries,' said Ruby, smiling. 'I've grown used to your obsession with that thing by now.'

Tyler's face became more animated as he said. 'You'll never guess what?' Then, after a dramatic pause, he added, 'I've got a place at Manchester Uni.'

'You're joking!' said Ruby.

'No, straight up. Two of my mates are going there too. I can't wait.'

'Aw, that's brilliant!' said Ruby, throwing her arms round him. 'I'm so pleased for you. You've done really well, little bruv.'

'Less of the little,' laughed Tyler, standing up as if to demonstrate his height then stepping towards his mother who had just come in through the door, and taking one of the drinks from her.

'Hasn't he done well?' asked Daisy.

'He has,' said Ruby, and as she looked at her mother, she noticed a look of pure pride on her face.

'Aye, I'd be the first to say it, but me kids have all done well for themselves. You and your other two brothers have all got your own homes and good jobs and now our Tyler's going to university.'

The way her mother slowly emphasised the word university gave Ruby a warm glow, and she went over to her and put her arms around her.

'You've done well, Mam. I'm really pleased for both of you,' said Ruby.

Seeing her mother like that made her realise just how well her mother had coped considering the circumstances she'd had to endure. She was happy for her but, at the same time, she regretted the harsh opinion she had formed of her when she had been a rebellious teenager. Her mother wasn't feeble at all. She was a strong woman who had kept a good home and held down two jobs to provide for her children. And she'd done it all by herself.

Ruby also felt a little guilty because her mother didn't know the truth about what she really did. And Ruby was even more determined that she would never find out. After the life she'd had, her mother deserved her bit of happiness and Ruby decided there was no way she was going to spoil it for her.

23

June 2007

It was another three days before they got chance to view the property Victor had found, which was a large flat above a discount shop, two miles from the city centre in Rusholme. Ruby had rung the estate agents to arrange a viewing and had taken the first available appointment when she, Tiffany and the estate agent were all free.

It was early evening when Ruby headed towards Rusholme in her gleaming BMW feeling a rush of excitement. Ever since she'd told Tiffany about her plans the idea had come to life in her imagination and as she got closer to the viewing appointment, she could feel her heart fluttering as the thoughts whirled around inside her head. Now, as she rushed through the city traffic, she shared some of her ideas with Tiffany.

'I'll take the biggest room. I'll need it to fit all my equipment in. It'll be nice to have a proper dungeon. We can even have a sign put on the door, saying, Ruby's Dungeon. I'm gonna kit the place out really nice as well.'

'Whoa!' said Tiffany. 'You're getting a bit ahead of yourself, aren't you? We haven't even seen the place yet.'

Ruby just smiled enigmatically, but she decided to keep quiet for the rest of the journey, despite her excitement. She'd give Tiffany chance to see the place first before she ran her through the rest of her plans. She was driving along Platt Lane, former home of the Manchester City football ground, when her phone rang.

'Shit,' she said, knowing it would be impossible to answer it while she was driving, especially as it was inside her handbag, tucked away inside the foot well of the back seat.

'Want me to answer it?' asked Tiffany.

'Nah,' she said. 'It'll probably be a client. I'll ring them back later.'

They soon arrived at Wilmslow Road, and parked in a back street behind the stretch of road known as the curry mile because of the abundance of Asian restaurants. It was a vibrant hub of activity featuring not only restaurants but a variety of shops.

Ruby had always liked this stretch; it was so colourful and animated. And as for the aromas that came from the restaurants, Ruby found herself salivating as soon as she parked the car and got out.

In the early evening the neon lights of the restaurants and shops added to the area's visual appeal, highlighting the brightly-coloured saris, sparkling gold jewellery and tantalising sweets and pastries, which had all been expertly arranged in the shop windows. People chatted enthusiastically as they headed for the popular restaurants, admired the shop displays and bought their fresh produce.

Ignoring her sudden desire for food, Ruby said to Tiffany,

'It's somewhere on the main road, the shop's called P & M Discounts.'

She was striding so fast in her eagerness to get there that her girlfriend found it difficult to keep up with her. It didn't take long to find P & M Discounts, and Ruby was pleased that it was the largest shop on the main road. Perhaps the upstairs flat would be large too. She also liked the location. It was the sort of place where people came and went a lot so maybe their activities wouldn't be as noticeable as they would in a more residential area.

As with many flats above shops it was accessed via a door to one side. Ruby pressed the doorbell and waited for a good while. When nobody came to answer the bell after a few seconds she rang it again.

'Perhaps the estate agent hasn't arrived yet,' she said.

'Yeah, maybe. It's a couple of minutes to the appointment so he might be here any minute.'

Ruby shrugged and pulled a face. 'Maybe you're right, Tiff. We'll give him a bit longer.'

Ruby and Tiffany waited outside but when there was still no sign of the agent after ten minutes Ruby's enthusiasm started to wane and she kept looking impatiently at her designer watch.

'Why don't we go into the shop and get a few bits while we're waiting?' suggested Tiffany.

Ruby was worried about missing the agent while they were inside the shop but she was getting fed up of waiting so she agreed to Tiffany's suggestion. As they walked around the shop Ruby kept looking out of the window to see if anyone resembling an estate agent approached the flat, but she didn't notice anyone.

The person on the checkout had seen them outside and he commented as they were paying for their goods. 'There's nobody upstairs yet. It's only just been sold.'

'Sold?' asked Ruby, alarmed. 'It's for sale, don't you mean?'

'No, it's sold. My cousin's just put an offer in and had it accepted.'

'You're fuckin' joking!' said Ruby, forgetting her manners because she was so annoyed with the agent. She turned to Tiffany, 'You sort this lot out while I go outside to phone the estate agent and see what the fuck they're playing at!'

The checkout assistant flashed a nervous look at Tiffany but Ruby ignored it. She was too concerned about having a word with the estate agent.

Once Ruby was outside she pulled her phone from her handbag, noticing as she did so that the agent had tried to call her. But that was only half an hour ago. That would have been the call she received when she was on the way. What the hell was the estate agent doing leaving it so late to let her know that the flat had already been sold?

As soon as the receptionist answered the phone, Ruby gave her name and demanded to speak to the agent who should have been meeting them, a Mr Browning. 'What the hell do you think you're playing at, sending me to view a flat that's already been sold?' she blasted down the phone.

'I'm terribly sorry, Miss Henry. I did ring to let you know but I wasn't able to get hold of you.'

'Yes, half a bloody hour ago! What use is that? We were already on the way here by then.'

'I do apologise. We only agreed the sale earlier today and

I've been tied up all day so it was the first chance I had to call you.'

'A likely story. More like you couldn't be arsed.'

'Miss Henry, I'm sorry but I'm afraid we don't tolerate that kind of language from our customers.'

'Tough. Try this for language, you're a fuckin' arsehole!' Ruby could hear a gasp on the other end of the phone and she guessed the estate agent was about to cut the call so she quickly shouted. 'Stick your fuckin' properties where the sun don't shine you useless little shit!'

As she stood staring at the phone in her hand, livid, Tiffany stepped tentatively towards her.

'Erm, I'm guessing it was bad news.'

For the next few seconds Ruby explained the situation to Tiffany, cursing the estate agent and adding a few choice expletives.

Tiffany tried to cajole her. 'Don't worry, Ruby, we'll find something else.'

'I doubt it. Properties that can be used as a whorehouse are fuckin' hard to come by.' Then she noticed the hurt expression on Tiffany's face and regretted being so sharp with her. 'Come on, let's get back home,' she said, 'then we'll have to have a think about where we go from here.'

Ruby and Tiffany had only just arrived home and were standing outside the door to their flat while Ruby found the key in her handbag. She was just about to put it into the lock when they heard someone thundering up the stairs. It was the landlord, Mr Walker, and Ruby could see even from a few feet away that he wasn't very happy. As she and Tiffany waited to see what he wanted, she noticed the envelope he was carrying.

'There,' he said, handing the envelope to Ruby.

Curious, Ruby stared at it then slid her forefinger under the seal to prise it open.

'I'll save you the trouble,' growled the landlord. 'It's your notice to vacate. I want you out within a month.'

Ruby looked up at him, her expression fierce. 'What?' she demanded.

'You heard. I've had more complaints from the other residents.'

'But it's rubbish!' Ruby complained. 'It's her over the way stirring it up with everyone. She's just making trouble for us cos she's a miserable old cow who doesn't like anyone having friends.'

'Oh no it isn't!' the landlord snarled, rounding on Ruby till his face was only centimetres from hers. 'I've been keeping my eye on you two. I've seen the number of men that come and go, and you can't tell me they're all just friends. I know exactly what you two are bloody well up to, so don't try telling me any different.'

'We're not up to anything!' said Ruby, 'And you can't prove we are either.'

'I don't need to prove anything. I know what's going on here, I'm not bloody stupid and if I want you out then I'll bloody well have you out!'

He turned and stormed off down the stairs with Ruby shouting after him. 'You won't get away with this. We haven't done anything wrong!' But she knew her words were wasted. Then she turned to Tiffany, her shoulders slumped as she asked, 'What the fuck do we do now?'

24

December 1996

For several months Trina continued to enjoy her status as Zac's girlfriend. As the summer faded, the nights became cooler and the prospect of having sex in the park became increasingly unappealing. After Trina had complained yet again about having to spend time in the park where it was cold and dark, Zac arranged for them to go to his house.

It was only the second time she had been there as it was difficult for Zac to find a time when the rest of his family were out. Trina knew he wasn't interested in introducing her to his parents. There was only one thing Zac was interested in with Trina, but that suited her because it meant they stayed together.

They couldn't go to her house either, not for what Zac had in mind. As Trina had three brothers as well as her mother, there was nearly always somebody at home. And the idea of introducing Zac to her mother was out of the question. Daisy was a God-fearing Christian woman who would be horrified at the thought of her daughter having a boyfriend when she was still so young.

This particular night, although the rest of Zac's family were out, his younger brother was in. Even after Trina had been there a while, his younger brother continued to hang around and Trina could tell that Zac was becoming increasingly irritated with him.

'Why don't you just fuck off out, Matt?' Zac said to him.

'Because it's too cold,' said Matt, 'and, anyway, why should I, just so you can shag *her*?'

Matt looked scornfully at Trina before leaving the room. Zac got up and dashed after his brother to have a word with him. As Trina sat on the sofa patiently waiting for Zac to come back, she strained to overhear what was being said, but couldn't hear anything apart from a lot of whispering. Then Zac returned, alone.

'Come on, we're going upstairs to my bedroom,' he said.

'But... don't you share it with Matt?'

Zac grinned. 'Don't worry, he isn't there. He's in the kitchen.'

Trina followed him upstairs and as soon as they were inside his bedroom, they sat down on his bed where Zac immediately began kissing Trina passionately and putting his hands inside her clothes. She couldn't settle, on edge in case Zac's brother should walk in or, worse still, his parents might return. She pulled away, and Zac looked at her quizzically.

'What's wrong?' he asked.

'What if he comes in or if your mam and dad come home early?' she asked.

'He won't. Don't worry, I've fixed him,' said Zac, smiling enigmatically. 'And my mam and dad never come home before the pubs shut. So, are we going to do this, or what? Anyone would think you didn't fancy me anymore.'

Trina hesitated for a moment, glancing around her and trying to think of another excuse. She really didn't feel comfortable having sex with Zac's brother downstairs. It had been different in the park; they always made sure they were well out of view of other people and it was usually dark, so someone passing by wouldn't be able to see them properly anyway. Besides, most of the people in the park at that time were doing the same so it somehow made it acceptable.

As she glanced around, Zac followed her eyes then got up and walked over to a chest of drawers. He picked up a box and handed it to her. 'Here, I forgot to give you this for your birthday.'

Her birthday had been a week prior and she'd dropped various hints about it, eventually giving up and presuming he hadn't bothered. But now she felt pleased as she looked at the box in her hands. It was slightly battered but that didn't matter. She could see from the name on the box that it was perfume and she pulled it open and grasped at the fancy bottle inside, spraying it on herself and smiling as she held her wrist up for Zac to sniff.

'Thanks, it's lovely,' she said.

'That's alright,' said Zac, sitting back down next to her on the bed.

He didn't waste time in getting back down to business. Trina was about to protest again but then she thought about the lovely present he'd bought her and felt bad about pushing him away. He must have thought a lot of her to buy such an expensive-looking bottle of perfume. And, it wasn't as if she hadn't had sex before, so, although Trina still didn't feel comfortable, she went along with his wishes. It didn't last long, Zac plunging straight into her while they were still half-dressed. He had almost finished when there was a knock on the bedroom door.

'Shit!' said Trina, pushing him away and scrambling for her underwear and jeans.

'What?' yelled Zac.

'Time's up,' came Matt's voice from the other side of the door. 'You said fifteen minutes.'

'For fuck's sake! Wait a minute,' said Zac, pulling his trousers up then pulling the bedroom door open. 'Why couldn't you fuckin' wait till I got downstairs?'

'Because I want my money now,' said Matt, holding out his hand.

Trina stared at Zac and Matt, feeling shocked and demeaned when she realised that Zac had bribed his brother to stay out of the room. Not only that, but Matt had been timing them, which was why Zac wanted to get it over and done with as soon as possible. Suddenly the whole situation felt degrading.

'You bastard!' she yelled, getting up from the bed. She stopped at the bedroom door and glared at Zac. She was consumed by anger and wanted to tell him exactly what she thought. But when she caught sight of his brother grinning at her, words failed her. Instead she spat at Zac, not stopping to witness his anger when it hit him in the face. Then she stormed out of the house.

Despite Trina's wounded pride at what Zac had done, she

didn't want to see the end of the relationship. She enjoyed being seen as part of his crowd and he was good fun to be with most of the time. But there was no way she was going to make up with him without getting an apology first.

What irked her even more was that she'd been in such a rush to get out of his house that she'd left her precious bottle of perfume behind. She'd been so chuffed to receive such a fancy bottle of perfume and couldn't wait to impress her friends. But if she and Zac didn't make up, she could say goodbye to the present as well as him.

For days she sought him out at school, hoping he'd come over and apologise. Then she'd play hard to get for a while before accepting his apology and agreeing to see him again. But she didn't see him for three days. On the fourth day, she was walking along the corridor when Nicole spotted him.

'Don't look now but Zac's on his way towards us,' said Nicole.

Trina couldn't help but take a look. She saw him in the distance and decided she would make eye contact briefly as he drew nearer then play it cool. He was a few metres away when their eyes met and she quickly looked away. For a few seconds she could feel herself stiffen on seeing some of his friends in her peripheral vision as they passed by, Alex stopping to pat Nicole on the shoulder and whisper something.

Trina knew Zac was with him and she could feel her skin prickle as she became aware of his close proximity, expecting him to speak to her at any moment. But he didn't. And Nicole turned to her, affronted on her friend's behalf.

'The cheeky bastard!' she said. 'Did you see that? He just walked straight past.'

'It's alright. I'm not speaking to him anyway,' said Trina, trying to put on a brave face.

Word soon got around that Zac had snubbed her, then other rumours started. Zac was supposedly interested in a really pretty girl in his year and was going to ask her out. Her name was Rebecca Statton and Trina knew of her. While she was very attractive, Trina doubted she would go out with Zac. Rebecca was too studious and well-behaved to waste time with a bad boy, but there was a chance that Zac would put pressure on her until he'd won her round.

Trina's next move was to play off some of her admirers against each other in the hope of getting Zac jealous and perhaps making him see what he was missing. She had already met one of them after school and embarked on a pointless date where they spent time walking round the shops and chatting before he bought her chips and she went back home.

Her second date was with a boy called Ryan in her year who took her to the cinema to see *Golden Eye*. Ryan was a tall, blond boy, good looking but the quiet type and not cool like Zac. Still, it would be good to be seen with him and maybe it would bring Zac to his senses.

When they arrived in the cinema foyer, she was thrilled to spot two of Zac's friends in the crowd with two girls. Trina was pleased that they had seen her too and hoped news of her date would soon get back to Zac.

While watching the film, Trina noticed Zac's friends a few rows in front. One of them kept glancing curiously behind so she started kissing Ryan to give him something to look at. It was when she casually gazed ahead, to see if Zac's friend was still looking, that she spotted Zac. He had arrived late and was joining his friends while chatting and laughing with Rebecca Statton whose hand he was clutching.

Trina was livid, not only because Zac had moved on, but also because he appeared so happy. And he'd taken Rebecca to the cinema, which was something he'd never done with her. Deciding she couldn't sit through the film while watching Zac with Rebecca she got up to leave.

'Hang on! Where are you going?' asked Ryan.

'Home!'

'But you haven't seen the film yet,' he said.

'I've seen enough,' she said. 'Don't worry, you don't have to come with me. You can stop and watch.'

Then she went, leaving Ryan to watch the film alone.

A maelstrom of thoughts ran through her mind. She was annoyed, upset and humiliated. He hadn't even had the decency to finish with her before he started parading his new girlfriend around. Damn Rebecca Statton! Trina was so consumed with anger at Zac's treatment of her that it didn't occur to her that she had also been seen with other boys. In her mind the other boys were nonentities anyway but Rebecca Statton was something else altogether. All the boys fancied her!

Trina felt like crying, but it was more a feeling that she *should* be crying although she knew she wouldn't. It was only when she got over her initial shock at Zac's behaviour that she realised she wasn't really upset about losing him. Trina wasn't actually in love with Zac; she was in love with the idea of being a part of Zac's life and her upset was more concerned with losing face now she had been officially dumped.

She was dreading facing everyone at school when they found out she was no longer with him, but Trina knew she'd get through it. She'd play it down and pretend she wasn't really that bothered anyway. It wasn't that far from the truth because Trina had used Zac for her own ends, same as she'd done with the other boys. She was beginning to realise more and more that boys just didn't appeal to her in that way.

25

September 1997

Trina was now fifteen and had just begun her last year of secondary school. Zac Poole had left school the previous summer and she hadn't heard from him since. Trina didn't know what she wanted to do once she had sat her GCSEs. Ideas about working in a hairdressing salon or a fashion shop had floated around in her head but she hadn't yet decided. What she was certain of was that she didn't want to go on to sixth form. She was bright and astute but hated studying and knew it wasn't for her.

For the last year she'd drifted in and out of short-term relationships with boys. Although none of them appealed to her on a long-term basis the relationships were mutually beneficial. She gave the boys sex and they treated her to cinema and bowling trips whilst also enabling her to fit in with the crowd. Currently she wasn't seeing anybody and, if she was honest with herself, she was happier that way. All boys got on her nerves after a while.

It was the weekend and Trina was sitting in her mother's living room watching TV when a car pulled up outside.

Large, silver-coloured and gleaming, it was much flashier than the cars that usually parked on her street and Trina went to the window, curious about who was driving.

She gazed in awe at the beautiful vehicle, but when the driver stepped out, she felt a mixture of disappointment and intrigue. It was her cousin Josh, and his brother, Calvin, was getting out of the passenger side. She was disappointed that they were visiting because, at eighteen and nineteen they hadn't outgrown their spitefulness and were still mean to her, but she was also intrigued as to why they were driving such a flash car.

Without waiting for them to ring the doorbell, Trina rushed into the hallway and answered the door.

'Oh, it's you,' said Calvin. 'Is Aunty Daisy not in?'

'She's in the kitchen,' Trina bit back. Then she shouted. 'Mam, Josh and Calvin are here to see you.'

They strutted through to the lounge, each of them dripping in gold. They were wearing chunky gold chains around their necks and sovereign rings on their fingers. In addition to the jewellery was the usual mix of expensive designer sportswear.

When Daisy came through to the lounge she eyed them cautiously and nodded at them. 'Would you like a drink?' she asked formally.

Josh grinned. 'Yeah that would be nice. Coffee, three sugars.'

'Same for me,' said Calvin.

'Can't Trina make the brews?' said Josh. 'I've come to show you my new car.'

Just then Trina's three younger brothers ran into the

house. 'Is that your car, Josh?' Tyler gushed. 'Can I have a ride in it?'

'Me too,' said Ellis and Jarell but Trina stayed silent, refusing to join in with their adulation.

Josh smiled widely as Daisy walked over to the window to examine the car. 'Sure,' he said, cocking his head back smugly. 'Once we've had a drink.'

'Good grief!' said Daisy. 'How on earth did you come by the money for that?'

'Hard work,' said Josh.

'Yeah, hard work and good contacts,' said Calvin, grinning.

Daisy tutted and backed out of the room. 'I'll make you both a drink then I suppose you can let us all have a run out in it, the boys first then me and Trina.'

While Daisy made the drinks, Trina's younger brothers fussed over Josh and Calvin, asking them about their clothing, jewellery and car. Trina hated the way her cousins patronised her younger brothers and showed off what they had. But, although she was loath to admit it, she wanted a run out in the car just as much as her brothers did.

When she grew tired of listening to their condescending and scornful comments, Trina went to help her mother fetch the drinks through to the living room. She was glad when it was finally time for her and her mother to have a run out in Josh's car. Calvin came with them while the younger boys waited in the house and, as she stepped out of the front door, Trina swelled with pride at the admiring glances from neighbours.

Trina jumped straight into the front seat, enjoying the

feel of the plush leather upholstery and admiring the fancy dashboard with its CD player. Josh started up the engine and the sound of *Gangsta's Paradise* by Coolio blasted out of the in-car speakers.

Daisy jumped, to the amusement of Trina and her cousins, and then said, 'For heaven's sake, Joshua, turn it down. It's enough to deafen us.'

Josh reached over to the volume control and flashed Trina a sarcastic grin before turning the music lower. Trina settled back into her seat, staring out of the window as they blasted up the street, and relishing even more envious glances from their neighbours. As they sped through the streets, Trina kept one eye on the dashboard and the other on the road ahead. She was intrigued by all the fancy dials that swivelled around.

It wasn't long till they reached the motorway. Trina wound down her window, taking delight in the sense of speed and the feel of the wind hitting her cheeks and gusting through her hair. It was the biggest thrill she'd felt for a long time but it was soon over.

When they got back indoors, she couldn't resist the urge to quiz Josh about the car despite her determination not to feed her cousins' overblown egos.

'How much did it cost?' she asked.

'Shedloads,' said Josh, cockily.

'Did you have to save for ages?' she enquired, naively.

Both of her cousins laughed but they waited till their aunty was out of the room before they continued their discussion.

'We don't save,' said Calvin. 'But we have to do some bad stuff to get what we want,' he bragged while Josh shot him a warning look.

'What sort of stuff?' Trina persisted.

'Stuff you shouldn't fuckin' know about,' snapped Josh.

'Yeah, you don't need to know,' said Calvin, following his brother's lead. 'You wouldn't be tough enough to do what we do. Girls can't cut it.'

'Bet I would!' said Trina, affronted at the insult.

Josh snapped at his brother again. 'That's all she needs to fuckin' know!'

She didn't have a clue what they were talking about but she was nevertheless annoyed that they should think her incapable because she was a girl. It was that same old familiar insult and it got to her every time.

'Anyway, bro, we gotta go now,' said Josh, signifying the end of the discussion.

They went through to the kitchen to say goodbye to their aunty. Daisy saw them to the front door then went through to the lounge to watch as they set off in the car. Trina's brothers pursued the car excitedly with their friends as it roared down the street.

Daisy tutted again. 'Poor Tamara. I don't know how she puts up with it. Heaven knows what they'll be getting into next,' she muttered cryptically.

When her mother went back into the kitchen, Trina was left alone with just her thoughts for company. Although her cousins' insults had riled her, she couldn't help but be impressed by the car and their expensive clothes and jewellery.

She thought about how they might have come by the car and other expensive items. By piecing together her mother's cryptic comments as well as the few things her cousins had told her, she guessed that they had somehow acquired them by illegal means. At this point, though, she had no idea about the extent of their illicit dealings.

As far as Trina was concerned they were just her two goofy cousins, Josh and Calvin, and she didn't see any reason why she shouldn't have what they had. If they could get hold of those things then why couldn't she? In fact, she'd make sure she got what they had. She wasn't sure how she would manage it but somehow or other she would one day say goodbye to her life of poverty and have all the things she desired and deserved.

26

April 1998

Springtime soon arrived and the date for leaving school loomed closer. But Trina still hadn't made a decision regarding her future despite her mother's concerns. By now Daisy was running two jobs to provide for her family and pay the bills; cleaning in the daytime and bar work in the evenings. Trina had noticed the way her knuckles were often raw and how tired she became due to the late-night hours in the pub.

But instead of feeling pity for her mother, Trina felt contempt. How could Daisy possibly hope to give her advice about her future when she so obviously hadn't made a success of her own life? Trina didn't dwell on her mother's misfortunes, choosing instead to spend as much time as possible out of the home. As the nights became longer and warmer, she was enjoying hanging out at the park more frequently with Nicole and her other friends. She hadn't paid much thought to her GCSEs; the idea of studying didn't appeal to her.

She and Nicole hadn't been in the park long one night,

and had just started drinking some alcopops. They were hidden in a small glade behind some bushes, which had a narrow opening, giving them a view of anyone passing by on the pathway through the park. Trina had her back to the bushes when she heard someone walking past. She looked at her friend, Nicole, standing opposite her, and noticed how her eyes narrowed curiously as she peered through the gap.

'What's wrong?' whispered Trina. 'Who is it?'

'Not sure. Wait there,' said Nicole, passing Trina her drink and making her way through the bushes and onto the pathway.

After a moment's hesitation, Trina put down the two bottles of alcopop and followed Nicole through the clearing in the bushes. If her friend had run into a problem then she wanted to find out what it was.

Once on the path she found Nicole hugging another blonde girl. Trina wasn't sure who the girl was; her body was obscured by Nicole and her head was facing downwards, resting on Nicole's shoulder.

'Jesus, Shelley! I can't believe it's you,' said Nicole, releasing the taller girl from her embrace and holding her at arms' length so she could look at her. 'You look great! How the fuck did you find me?'

'It wasn't hard,' said Shelley. 'All the kids hang about in this park. I just asked some girls over there if they'd seen you and they sent me here.'

The word *kids* didn't sound as though it was intended as an insult, more a statement of fact. Trina recognised the name, Shelley; it was Nicole's older sister. As soon as Nicole moved away Trina could see Shelley full on. She looked older than them and beautiful with blonde hair and lovely blue eyes. The attraction was instant.

Although Trina had been attracted to girls before, she'd never felt a pull like this. She'd previously dismissed it, knowing deep down that she fancied girls but telling herself it was maybe just a phase. But now she knew for sure.

As Nicole fussed over her sister, Shelley smiled back at her, enjoying the attention and the feeling of sisterly warmth that passed between them. Then Shelley's eyes locked with Trina's and Trina felt a moment's discomfort; her intensity of feeling unsettling her. Nicole spotted her sister's wandering gaze and spun around.

'Trina, I can't believe it!' she said. 'This is our Shelley. I've not seen her for months.'

She was delighted at seeing her older sister and Trina beamed a big smile at both of them. 'Hi!' she said, feeling herself blush under Shelley's scrutiny.

Trina recalled Nicole mentioning that her older sister had left home under a cloud. Her memory was hazy with the details but now she wished she'd paid more attention to what Nicole had told her. Now, as she looked at Nicole's striking sister, Trina was eager to find out as much as possible about her.

For a few seconds they surveyed each other. Shelley was similar in looks to Nicole but prettier. She was wearing a short A-line skirt and a cropped top with a slouchy jacket layered effortlessly over the top, adding just the right volume to her slim frame. Her makeup was perhaps a little overdone but, in a way, it added to her charm.

The bright red lipstick, frosted eyeshadow, blue eyeliner and lashings of mascara were very much in fashion.

Nevertheless, the way they had been liberally applied would have looked tarty on someone older, but with Shelley's elfin features, her makeup seemed to transport her from innocence to streetwise sophistication.

'Trina's my best mate,' said Nicole. 'I've told you about her before. We have some right laughs together.'

'It seems an age since I was palling around with my mates at school,' said Shelley wistfully.

'I bet you're glad you're not there now,' said Nicole. 'It's shit.'

'Course I am. I'm doing alright for myself now,' said Shelley.

'Where you living?' asked Nicole.

'I've got a two-bedroomed flat in Whalley Range. You'll have to come and see me but don't let my mam know.'

'Oh no, I won't,' said Nicole. 'She'd kill me.' Then she seemed to sense a change in her sister and quickly added, 'I'm sure she'll be alright in the end though. You know what parents are like.'

'It's alright,' said Shelley. 'I don't need them. I'm doing alright now,' she repeated.

As the conversation continued, Trina became mesmerised by her. She seemed so grown-up and switched on compared to them. Trina felt childish and unknowing compared to Shelley, who had an edge to her. It was in everything about her; from her stylish clothing and striking features to her mannerisms. She noticed her body language; the flirty way she tossed her long blonde hair and the way her smile seemed to mask a hidden depth. She would become momentarily lost in thought but then quickly recover, hinting at a life of tough decisions.

And when she spoke, she just seemed to know everything they were feeling as though she had experienced it all already but in a more enjoyable and shocking way. She was also knowledgeable about the wider world; a world outside of school and family life.

The more Trina watched and listened to Shelley, the more smitten she became. It was a revelation and she knew straightaway that she'd found what she'd been looking for. She had fallen instantly and unremittingly in love.

27

April 1998

The following day at school Trina couldn't wait to find out more from Nicole about her older sister, Shelley.

'Your sister's really nice,' she gushed. 'Why did she leave home?'

'My mam and dad kicked her out.'

'Why?'

'She got into loads of rows with them about drinking and staying out late. Then my mam found out she was shagging around, and she went fuckin' ballistic. They had a massive row and Shelley walked out. My mam told her not to bother coming back so Shelley told her to fuck off.'

'Jesus! You don't think they'll throw you out for coming in late, do you?'

'Nah. They're always giving me grief, but I think they're secretly scared of me walking out too. I can tell they miss our Shelley.'

'Is it the first time you've seen her since she left?'

'No, I've bumped into her a couple of times. Once she

sent me a message to meet her in town so I did, but that was months ago.'

'How does she manage?' asked Trina.

Nicole looked around her to make sure nobody was listening then she whispered, 'She's on the game.'

'What?' asked Trina. Then a flash of Nicole's eyes told her she had heard correctly and she added, 'You're joking!'

'No,' said Nicole, grinning.

'Jesus! I wonder what it's like,' said Trina.

'Fuckin' awful from what she's told me. I mean, she gets loads of dosh. Some of 'em buy her clothes and perfume. One even bought her a gold chain but she has to put up with a lot of pervy clients too.'

'How d'you mean?' asked Trina.

'Dirty old bastards that want her to do all sorts. You wouldn't catch me doing what she does.'

'How did she get into it?' asked Trina, fascinated.

'I don't know; you'd have to ask her,' Nicole replied sharply as though she was growing bored of Trina's questions.

'I can't believe it. You wouldn't think she was the type, would you?'

'What do you mean?' asked Nicole with a note of irritation in her tone.

'Well, she's really pretty. I thought they were all supposed to be old slappers.'

'Fuckin' hell, Trina. Why you so interested in our Shelley? Anyone would think you fancied her or summat.'

Nicole's words hit Trina like a slap in the face, and she recoiled. Was it really that obvious? She hoped not. But Nicole seemed to interpret her reaction as offence and she played down the comment.

'Sorry, I was only joking,' she said, grinning at Trina.

'I was only interested,' said Trina. 'I've never come across anyone who does that before.'

'You mean a tart,' said Nicole, cynically.

Trina shrugged. 'That sounds bad. She's probably only doing it because she needs the money.'

'Whatever,' said Nicole and Trina got the feeling that her friend wanted to end the conversation.

She was a bit annoyed by Nicole's attitude and normally she would have faced her with it. But her embarrassment stopped her from doing so. The comment about her fancying Shelley was made flippantly but Trina didn't want Nicole to know that she had actually hit on the truth.

Trina was curious about Shelley. She was at an age where she wanted to find out about life in all its sordid detail and the fact that she had a crush on Shelley intrigued her even more. To her mind, Shelley was bold and fearless as well as stunning. Instead of doing what her parents demanded of her, she was making her own way in life, and the fact that she earned a lot of money doing it made Trina eager and determined to find out more.

It was over a week before they saw Shelley in the park again. Trina and Nicole were both delighted to see her. Determined to conceal her discomfort at the attraction she felt, Trina joined in with Nicole and Shelley's conversation. When Nicole's latest boyfriend came to find her, it was obvious to Trina and Shelley that she wanted some time alone with him.

'It's alright,' said Shelley. 'I don't mind if you want to be with him. I've got to go anyway.'

Seizing her opportunity to find out more about Shelley, Trina said, 'Which way are you walking? I'll come with you.'

They left the park, Trina walking keenly alongside Shelley. 'Have you got to go to work?' she asked when they were on their way out of the gate.

'Yeah. Well, I don't have to really but I'd miss the money if I didn't,' she said. Then she added casually. 'I suppose our Nicole told you what I do.'

'Yeah,' said Trina. 'But I'm not arsed.' She then thought about her clumsy wording and said. 'I mean, it doesn't bother me. I wouldn't hold it against you, not like some people.'

Shelley laughed. 'Glad to hear it,' she said, and Trina couldn't help but feel that she was somehow being patronised.

She felt awkward carrying on the conversation, worried she might have offended Shelley but then curiosity prompted her to delve further.

'What's it like?' she asked, hoping Shelley didn't mind her probing.

'It's OK,' said Shelley, candidly. 'People make out that it's bad but it isn't really. Most of the clients are alright. I earn loads of money and some of them even buy me presents. One guy bought me a gold chain and he keeps asking me to go on a cruise with him.'

'Would you?' said Trina, fascinated.

'No, not with him,' laughed Shelley. 'He's an ugly

old bastard. Besides, I could be earning shedloads from my other clients instead of going on some boring boat trip with him.'

'Does it not bother you, going with blokes that are ugly?'

'Nah, at the end of the day it's not about fancying the clients. It's about what you can get out of it. I have had a couple of fit ones though.'

'Really?' asked Trina.

'Yeah, but you don't get many of them. Most of 'em are old and fat. Like I said, it's more about what you can get out of it, and I need the money to pay my rent and bills.'

'Does it cost a lot to live on your own?'

'Yeah. Well, I've got a two-bedroomed flat so until I can get someone to flat share, I have to find all the money myself.'

Trina stared in awe at Shelley, mesmerised, not only by her but by her lifestyle. She was so matter-of-fact about what she did, and made it sound like a viable option. Trina had previously thought that a prostitute's life was the lowest of the low but listening to Shelley made her realise that it wasn't so bad after all. Having listened to what Shelley had to say, Trina now saw it as a good opportunity to make easy money, and she was impressed.

28

April–May 1998

'Are you fuckin' serious?' yelled Nicole when Trina told her about her idea.

'Deadly,' said Trina, nonchalant. 'Why not? I sleep with boys anyway so why not get paid for it? It's not like I've got anything else lined up for when I leave school, is it?'

'You don't know what you're talking about,' said Nicole. 'Some of those men are bad bastards. They can hurt you. Our Shelley had a black eye once when she came to meet me.'

'Pffft. What's a black eye?' said Trina. 'It's nothing.'

'But some of them rape her as well.'

Trina laughed. 'How can they have raped her? That's what they fuckin' pay for, innit?'

A look of confusion flashed across Nicole's face and Trina could see that she wasn't able to back up her argument.

'They're ugly as well,' she quickly added when she couldn't think of anything else to say.

'Yeah, I know. Well, most of them are. You do get some fit ones though.'

Trina didn't reveal all her thoughts; that it made no

difference whether they were good looking or not because she felt no desire for men anyway.

'You seem to fuckin' know plenty,' Nicole continued. 'I suppose our Shelley has put you up to this, has she? Wait till I fuckin' see her!'

'No, she hasn't. It was my own idea but I asked her about it. She earns loads of money and gets presents bought for her.'

'But it's not fuckin' worth it!' said Nicole. 'Imagine the name you'll get for yourself. You should hear what the rest of my family say about our Shelley.'

'Do you think I give a fuck about that?' asked Trina. 'They won't know anyway. You don't think I'm telling my mam, do you? She'd have a fit.'

For a few moments neither of them spoke. Trina's mind drifted to thoughts of all the men in her life and her negative view of them – her absent father and lecherous landlord, and her patronising cousins who always seemed to have plenty of money. Well, she'd show them! Why should she care about any of them? She'd soon be able to afford nice things too. Trina had found the perfect way to use men for her own gain and no matter what anybody said she was determined to go ahead.

Eventually Nicole spoke. 'Where will you do it?'

'What do you mean?'

'Well, where will you take the men? Where will you live?'

'Your Shelley needs a flatmate to help her pay the rent. I'm gonna ask her if I can move in next time we see her.'

Nicole scowled. 'I might have fuckin' known! My mam and dad are right about her, she's nothing but trouble; and you don't know what you're letting yourself in for.'

'For fuck's sake, Nicole, chill! It'll be fine. In fact, I'll let you know what you're missing. When you see all my cash, maybe you'll want a piece of the action too.'

'No fuckin' chance! You can stick your money where the sun don't shine.'

Nicole's hostile words put an end to the conversation and they continued to walk along the school corridors in silence until they reached the science labs for their next lesson. But while they remained silent, Trina's mind was running wild with thoughts of the glamorous lifestyle she was about to embark upon.

Living away from home would be great. She'd be treated like an adult at last instead of having to take orders from her mother. Trina dreamt about the wads of cash she could earn and the nice things she could buy for herself; clothes, perfume and makeup. She could wave goodbye to her pain-in-the-arse brothers, come and go as she pleased and eat and drink whatever she liked.

But the thing about her new life that appealed to her most of all was the opportunity to share it with the desirable Shelley. And despite all Nicole's dire warnings, Trina couldn't wait.

'What do you mean, you're moving out?' asked Daisy, in shock.

'What I said. I'm moving out. Tomorrow,' said Trina.

'By the heavens above you'll do no such thing!'

'Too late, I'm already doing it.'

Daisy glared at her daughter. 'Now you listen to me, child! You're barely sixteen. How do you think you'll survive out there? It's a harsh world. Look at me, having to hold down two jobs just to make ends meet. And who's going to keep an eye on the boys while I'm working at the pub?'

'Not my problem,' muttered Trina.

'I beg your pardon?'

Trina rounded on her mother. 'What I said. Why should I have to watch out for them all the time?'

'Because the money from the cleaning job isn't enough. Do you really think I'd be working in a pub if I could help it?'

'That's up to you. It's got nowt to do with me. I won't be here so they'll have to look after themselves. I'm sick of getting roped in to help with everything. How come I'm the only one who does any housework, anyway?'

'Don't you dare speak to me like that! You're not the only one who does any housework.' Daisy snapped. 'It might have escaped your attention, Trina, but I work damn hard to keep a nice home for you and your brothers.'

'Yeah, and so do I. And what do they do? Nothing!'

'Now you listen to me. I won't have you leaving this house, not over my dead body! You're underage anyway. And what will you do? Where will you live? I don't suppose you've thought of any of that, have you?'

Trina smiled smugly. 'Yes, I have. I'm moving in my friend's flat with her.'

Daisy tutted, her expression one of indignation. 'And who is this friend? What's her name?'

'She's just a friend, no one you know.'

Daisy eyed her daughter warily. 'I hope you're not moving in with some boy!'

'No, course I'm not. It's a girl.'

'And who's paying the bills on this flat?'

'Both of us.'

'With what? You can't live on thin air, Trina.'

'I know that!' Trina snapped. 'She's got me a job at her place.' She noticed the inquisitive expression on her mother's face and swiftly added, 'It's a restaurant in town. I'm gonna be a waitress.'

This seemed to silence Daisy for a while and she strode across the room then plonked herself down in her armchair. After a few seconds deep in thought, she continued.

'Why can't you stay at home and do this waitressing job?'

'Because I don't want to. I'm sick of it here. All I ever seem to do is look out for them lot,' she said nodding towards her brothers' bedroom, 'and help out in the house. I want more, Mam.'

'Heaven's above, Trina!' said Daisy, becoming distraught now. 'Do you not think I've got enough to deal with, without having to worry about you too?'

'You don't need to worry. I'll be fine.' Trina crossed the room to where her mother was sitting then placed a conciliatory hand on her shoulder. 'I'll still come to see you.'

'Well, perhaps I should be coming to see you too. Where is this flat?'

'I'll ring you with the address once I'm settled in,' said Trina. Then she shut down the conversation by leaving the room.

The following morning Daisy had calmed down a bit. She tried again to dissuade Trina from leaving but this time her tone was softer. Eventually she seemed to resign herself to the fact that her daughter was definitely going. As Trina struggled down the stairs carrying her school bag and an assortment of carrier bags filled with clothes and other items, her mother eyed her through tear-filled eyes. She tutted as Trina dropped one of the bags, spilling its contents, then plonked the others at the foot of the stairs while she picked everything back up.

'Is that any way to live?' Daisy asked. 'You've got a perfectly good home here and yet you're living out of carrier bags.'

'It's only till I get there. I'll have my own room with a wardrobe and chest of drawers,' Trina said proudly.

'This sounds like one hell of a generous friend. Are you sure there isn't some catch?'

'No!' Trina replied, but she could feel herself flushing slightly. She quickly began arranging her bags in the hallway to divert her mother's attention then said, 'Can I ring a taxi?'

'I suppose you'll have to with all those bags to carry,' said Daisy.

Daisy didn't offer to let Trina use her battered old suitcase and Trina didn't bother asking. It was partly because she didn't want to push her luck even further, but also because she wanted to prove her independence. Neither did Daisy offer to help with her bags, but Trina knew she wouldn't. Why would she help her leave when she didn't want her to go?

The taxi soon arrived and, despite her resolve, Trina could feel herself becoming emotional. She bit back the tears as she hugged her mother and promised to get in touch as soon as possible. Then she was inside the cab. As she looked out of the window at her old family home, a feeling of excitement shot through her. She'd done it! She'd left home and set out on her own, venturing confidently and unaware into her new life.

29

July 2007

It was Ruby and Tiffany's night off and they had decided to stay home and chill. Normally, as they ate their Chinese takeaway and sipped wine they would have been feeling relaxed. But not tonight.

It was almost three weeks since the landlord had served notice on them and they were no nearer to finding anywhere to live. With the threat of eviction looming they had started to pack up their stuff but their attempts were half-hearted. It was hard to decide what to take when you didn't know where you would end up or whether you would even have a home.

Ruby had lost count of the number of places they had viewed since the landlord had served notice on them. But none of the properties were suitable. They were either too small, too run down or in residential areas where they would attract too much attention. She had been right; finding a property suitable for a whorehouse wasn't easy.

The situation was also putting a strain on their relationship. Ruby hadn't realised just how much Tiffany relied on her to sort things out. In the past she had always been able to come up with a solution to most problems, but now even Ruby with her strength of character couldn't conjure up a suitable property.

Tiffany put down her knife and fork and slid her empty plate across the dining table then took a slug of the wine. 'What are we gonna do, Rubes?'

Ruby shrugged. 'I dunno. Well, I know what you'll do but the bastard doesn't want me, does he?'

Ruby was referring to one of Tiffany's clients who had offered to put her up if she didn't find anywhere to live, which had caused a massive argument between her and Ruby. She knew she had overreacted to the situation, but it was due to the strain they were under.

Tiffany reached out and placed her hand on top of Ruby's. 'Aw, Rubes, please don't start that again. I'm sorry I mentioned it now. I told you I don't want to go anywhere without you but, you never know, I might be able to persuade him to take you in too. But if that doesn't happen, maybe we could squat somewhere. I know someone who...'

'And what would we do with all our nice stuff?' snapped Ruby. 'We can't take it to a fuckin' squat with us, can we?'

'OK, it's only a suggestion. It's not my fault we're in the shit, Rubes. I'm only trying to help. Besides, if push comes to shove you can always go back to your mam's.'

'Yeah, without you. And what d'you reckon my mother would think if I brought you round to meet her? She could hardly introduce you to her church friends as my lesbian girlfriend, could she?'

Despite her angst about their situation, Ruby managed a

slight grin as she thought about the shocked reaction of the congregation at the church her mother attended.

Tiffany laughed. 'You never know, she might surprise you and greet me with open arms. Maybe she's always secretly dreamt of having a lesbian for a daughter-in-law.'

Ruby couldn't resist joining in with Tiffany's laughter. When she'd stopped laughing, she said, 'Seriously though, the whole situation with my mam is awkward. She still hasn't got a clue what I do for a living. For the last few years she thinks I've been working in a nightclub. I couldn't tell her I worked in a restaurant anymore; she kept bloody wanting to visit me there. At least I know she's not into nightclubs.'

'I don't know how you've kept it up all these years,' said Tiffany, 'especially when you're round there visiting her every week. Anyway, we'll have to come up with something about where to live,' she added, looking once again to Ruby for the answers. 'What about Victor? Can he not find us a place?'

'I told you, he left me to look for a property because he was too busy with his other businesses. And, to be honest, Tiffany, I don't want him to think I can't hack it. After all, he'd be putting me in charge so I need to prove myself. He asked how things were going last time I saw him and when I said I still hadn't found anywhere he looked well disappointed.'

'OK, what about other cities then? Liverpool or Leeds maybe?'

Ruby replied despondently, her voice low and drawn. 'We'd be starting from scratch. I mean, which of our clients would want to go all that way? Besides, I think Victor will want it based in Manchester. After all, that's where he lives and it's where most of his contacts are. And there's no guarantee that we'd find a property any easier in another city.'

'Erm,' said Tiffany, but she failed to come up with any other suggestions.

'Come on; let's watch a bit of TV. Maybe we'll think of something tomorrow,' said Ruby, switching on the television and glancing at Emmerdale on the screen. She wanted an end to the conversation, which was only making her feel tenser as she realised how dire their situation was becoming.

Later, they were just clearing up the dirty pots when they heard a knock on the door and Tiffany went to answer it.

'If it's that bastard landlord or her from across the hall, I'm gonna make them wish they hadn't bothered,' Ruby grumbled as she listened to Tiffany padding down the hall then returned to the living room and topped up their glasses.

But she could tell by the way Tiffany greeted their visitor and the distant sound of a familiar man's voice that this wasn't a grudge call. Within seconds Tiffany was standing in front of her with Victor in the background.

'Hi, Victor,' said Ruby, with an inquisitive tone to her voice as she stood up to greet him.

Victor was all smiles as he returned the greeting and she guessed that he had made a surprise visit expecting her services. 'I'm sorry, Victor but...' She paused, indicating the glasses of wine in front of her, 'we're having a night off.'

'No, it's OK,' said Victor.

As the words spilt out of him while his head bobbed excitedly up and down Ruby wondered, not for the first time, how he managed to cut it as a successful businessman.

But appearances could be deceiving she supposed and, from what he had told her, he was certainly sharp when it came to business.

'I'm actually here to share some exciting news with you,' he continued, 'well, that is, presuming you haven't already found a new place.'

Ruby sat up, her attention now fully on Victor. 'No, actually we were just talking about that. We've looked at loads of places but none of them were any good for what we want.'

'That's alright, because I think I've found somewhere that will be just the job. It's above a nightclub in Manchester. North. Do you know it?'

Ruby was smiling now, remembering with fondness the nights she'd spent in North as a teenager when she'd first started on the game and was still discovering the world around her. She had enjoyed watching some of the characters that frequented the nightclub and had been fascinated by the behaviour of its many eccentric patrons.

Appropriately based in the bohemian Northern Quarter, North was edgier than the more popular Manchester clubs and had a diverse clientele ranging from wide boys and gangsters to legitimate businessmen and the occasional minor celebrity. The lure of North stemmed from its appeal to a wide range of people of different ages and its laidback vibe. The music was also varied, from chart toppers to dance club classics; in fact, anything that people would want to dance to. And, as somewhere at which to base an upstairs brothel, it was ideal.

'Course I know it,' said Ruby. 'I've had some wicked nights out there.'

'I bet you have,' said Tiffany. Then she laughed. 'Me too.'

The girls couldn't hide their excitement. 'It's a decent sized club, Victor. What's it like upstairs?' asked Ruby.

'Oh, the upstairs is a good size too.' Then he seemed to leer across at her as he said, 'It'll be perfect, I think, but it'll need some work. Don't worry about that though; I'll meet any costs as long as you send me itemised bills.'

Ignoring the creepy feeling that Victor sometimes aroused in her, Ruby focused instead on the prospect of having a building they could use. 'It sounds like you've done well, Victor. How the bloody hell did you wangle it?'

Victor tapped the side of his nose with his finger. 'A friend of mine owns the nightclub. He's selling off the upstairs part of the building to raise funds for another business venture.'

'Won't he mind about it being a brothel?' asked Ruby.

Victor grinned in his usual leering manner. 'No, in fact, he'll positively welcome it. He'll probably even send a few customers in our direction.'

'When can we go and see it?' asked Tiffany.

'I'll find out when I can get hold of the keys then let you know when to arrange an appointment.'

'Brilliant,' said Ruby. 'This sounds like a celebration.' Then she picked up the bottle of wine. 'Fancy a glass?'

'No, no, not for me,' said Victor, his words spilling hastily from him again. Then he made a show of looking at his watch, his head twitching as he did so. 'There's somewhere I need to be but I just thought I'd drop by first to give you the good news.'

'Brilliant!' Ruby looked across at Tiffany and smiled. 'We really appreciate it. Thanks very much.'

Then Victor bid them goodbye, promising to get in touch

soon, and was gone. Ruby could tell from his eagerness to get away that he was probably on the way to meet another of his girls. She left Tiffany to see him to the door. Then, as soon as Tiffany walked back into the lounge, Ruby jumped up off the sofa, ran over to her girlfriend and threw her arms around her.

'Hurrah! Good old Victor,' she yelled.

For precious moments the girls jumped around the room cheering and yelling at the top of their voices.

Then Tiffany stopped all of a sudden. 'Shush. What about the neighbours?' she whispered.

'Fuck the neighbours,' said Ruby, pointing the V sign in the direction of her neighbour across the hallway and pulling faces as she continued jumping up and down and laughing. 'We're out of here anyway in just over a week so what have we got to lose?'

Tiffany laughed too but when she calmed down, she said, 'We should really see it first before we get too excited.'

Ruby smiled enigmatically. 'I don't think it'll be a problem, Tiff. That Victor's no fool no matter what he might look like. And if he says it's a goer, then it's a fuckin' goer. She held the bottle of wine up once more, and shook it around to illustrate the small amount remaining in the bottom of the bottle. 'Come on, girl; let's grab another bottle from the kitchen. This is a celebration!'

30

After weeks of refurbishment, the club was almost ready. Ruby couldn't believe her luck as she glanced around the waiting area of the massage parlour (or 'the club' as she preferred to call it). It met her vision precisely, striking the right balance of plush and inviting as well as sultry and seductive, and she couldn't have been more pleased.

The sumptuous carpet was deep pink and the room was lined with burgundy Chesterfields. In the corner was a coffee machine where clients could grab a complimentary coffee and then sit down on the comfy sofas while the girls made them welcome. The walls were painted cream and the ceiling was dotted with rose-coloured, dimmed spotlights, giving the room a warm glow. The tasteful prints adorning the walls and the potted plants standing in large pots added to the room's homely feel.

As soon as she and Tiffany had viewed the rooms above North nightclub, Ruby had known they were what she was looking for. True to his word, Victor had found them the perfect place; it was a little run down and in need of a makeover, but in terms of the number and size of the rooms, it was ideal. There was even an area that could easily be separated from the club for Ruby and Tiffany to use as their own private apartment. As well as a refurb, the place had wanted a great deal of imagination but, as Ruby walked around the building, ideas started to form in her mind.

Ruby knew there was still a bit of work to be done in her own apartment and one or two of the other rooms, but that wouldn't take long, and they would soon be up and running.

At Victor's advice, Ruby had officially named the place Ruby's Massage Parlour due to UK laws against running a brothel. But there was an unwritten understanding between the management, the girls and the customers that the services on offer included far more than massage.

'Ruby's Dungeon' was inconspicuously situated in an attic room at the top of the building accessed via a door marked, 'Private'. Another private door led to Ruby and Tiffany's living quarters, which were also at the top of the building, but separate from the dungeon. Only Ruby and Tiffany had keys to the private rooms.

Now, Ruby was sitting in the waiting area with Tiffany, getting a feel for the place while they waited for their visitor, Rose, to arrive. It wasn't long before Ruby heard the sound of heels tapping on the stairs and she guessed Rose was here. The sight of a voluptuous blonde confidently announcing her arrival told her she had guessed right.

'Come and take a seat,' said Ruby, trying to act cool but secretly delighted at Rose's appearance.

Rose was aged around thirty and very well-maintained. She was average height with blonde, straight hair and her attractive features were defined by heavy but skilfully applied makeup. Ruby imagined that, apart from the liberal application of makeup, Rose had probably had some cosmetic help with her looks, which were a little too perfect but nevertheless attractive.

Likewise, Rose's figure was like something out of a playboy's dream; huge breasts, tiny waist, flat stomach and rounded, well-toned hips. The whole package was displayed in a low-cut, figure-hugging dress that sat just above the knee.

The only thing that marred Rose was her voice, which was loud and high-pitched. *I guess there are some things that even plastic surgery can't put right*, thought Ruby sardonically but, nevertheless, she was thrilled by everything else about Rose. Even before the interview began Ruby knew she wanted Rose working for her. The punters would love her!

'We're holding interviews here for now,' Ruby said, trying to maintain a professional approach despite her excitement at the thought of having Rose on the books. 'Some of the rooms are still being refurbished. Would you like a coffee then I'll tell you a bit about how we operate?'

Rose declined a drink so Ruby began explaining things straightaway. 'We operate as a massage parlour, but you're free to offer extra services to the clients. We'll take a daily fee from you for use of the room, and we'll manage the bookings. If you receive any private bookings then you'll have to let us know so that we can put them in the diary to avoid double-booking.'

Rose stared wide-eyed at Ruby, her eyelashes fluttering intermittently, as Ruby went through all of the procedure before asking her about herself. It turned out that Rose had been in the industry for a number of years and had recently worked at another brothel in the city until it was shut down. That meant that she already had her own clients who would continue to visit her at Ruby's brothel.

The interview couldn't have gone better and, after she had asked Rose whether she was happy with the rates and the set-up, Ruby offered her the job straightaway. She and Tiffany then watched as Rose wiggled her way out of the room and down the stairs out of the building.

'Wow!' said Tiffany, once Rose was gone. 'I wish all the girls looked like that.'

'OK, calm the fuck down,' said Ruby, whose attempt at light-heartedness missed the mark.

Tiffany giggled, 'I'm thinking about business,' she said. 'Why, what are you thinking?'

Ruby smiled back. 'That she's a fuckin' good catch for a new brothel. But don't worry about the other girls. We've got a good selection. Don't forget, not all the clients have got the same tastes. Some like more of a natural look.'

'True,' said Tiffany who giggled again. 'She is fuckin' gorgeous though, isn't she?'

Ruby thumped Tiffany playfully on the arm. She couldn't help but feel a little jealous when she saw her girlfriend admiring other women. But she knew she needn't have worried; Rose was obviously not gay as she'd mentioned a male partner and, besides, she knew Tiffany only had eyes for her.

As she sat there with Tiffany, admiring the cosy ambience of her waiting area and thinking about the imminent opening of her very own brothel, Ruby felt like her life couldn't possibly get any better. She had everything she could ever have wished for; a partner who loved her unconditionally and her own business, which not only gave her independence but was also going to make her very rich. She couldn't wait to open her doors to the public and get things started.

Aaron Gill was lying back on his prison bunk smoking a joint and chatting to his cellmate who was in the bunk below. He'd been inside for over two and a half years now and was much calmer following regular sessions with a prison counsellor. His appearance was still slim thanks to the coke that he managed to get hold of inside. But he wasn't quite as skinny as before due to the unhealthy prison food and the large amount of time spent inactive.

He had adapted to life on the inside, disguising his middle-class accent for the street talk he had used in his role as Gilly, pimp and drug user. He was wise enough to realise that he'd fit in much better that way. Gilly had also kept his nose clean while he'd been on the inside, knowing that it would lead to an earlier release.

When he'd viciously beaten up Crystal and left her for dead, he'd really lost the plot. But that level of violence and anger, which had led to his incarceration, was no longer evident. Gilly also knew that it didn't pay to dwell on the reasons why he was here in the first place – the fact that he'd lost the woman he adored, Maddy, thanks to that silly cow, Crystal, and her obsession with him. And the fact that her bitch of a mate, Ruby, had grassed him up.

Maddy had been perfect, and so different from the girls

he normally dealt with. He had never revealed his real identity to her, knowing she'd run a mile if she found out she was seeing a pimp and drug user. But then Crystal had given the game away, convinced in her own stupid mind that he was two-timing her.

He'd already dealt with Crystal, but Ruby was another matter and the bitter feelings about what Ruby had done gnawed at his insides. Gilly recognised that it wouldn't take much for those feelings to result in a violent rage. Every time he thought about it the adrenalin pumped furiously through his body, the veins on his neck protruding and his hands clenching in tight fists. But he held himself in check each time he spotted the signs, carrying out his mind exercises just like his counsellor had taught him.

'Tell you what,' Gilly said to his cellmate, 'I can't fuckin' believe I've only been in this dump for two and a half years. It's gonna be years yet before I can fuck off out of here.'

'No worries, mate, it'll come round quicker than you think. You still gonna sort out the bitch that put you in here?' his cellmate asked, picking up on Gilly's thoughts.

Gilly grinned to himself. 'Sure, but I'd be mad to fuckin' lose it again and end up back in here... Oh no, I'm gonna play it a bit more cagey this time. But, don't you worry, one way or another, I'll get the bitch.'

31

September 2007

'Ruby, Victor's here,' said Tiffany as she led him to the desk where Ruby was taking the bookings. The club had now been running for a few days and Victor had called in to see how things were going.

Ruby looked up from her computer, pleased when she saw Victor's reaction as he strolled through the waiting area, eyeing up the girls as well as the décor, with a beaming smile on his face.

'Well, well,' he said, smiling. 'You *have* done a good job.'

'You ain't seen nothing yet,' said Ruby. 'Wait till you see the rest of the rooms.'

'Sounds good,' he said, looking over to where the girls were seated.

Ruby picked up on his thoughts. 'Come on, I'll introduce you to the girls first. I've asked them all to come in especially so they can meet you.'

They walked over to two of the Chesterfields where the girls were seated, chatting animatedly. As they approached

Ruby could sense Victor's mounting excitement. His pace had quickened and his head was twitching.

'Girls, this is Victor, the owner,' said Ruby. 'He's here to meet you all.'

A couple of the girls looked shocked. Ruby understood their reaction; Victor wasn't exactly what you would have expected from a brothel owner, his nervous twitching belying his status as a shrewd businessman. But then the glamorous Rose stood up and held out her hand, and Victor leered in appreciation.

Ruby introduced her. 'This is Rose. She's come from Denny's place so she already has her own clients.'

'Good, good,' said Victor as his eyes roamed over her perfect body. Then he switched his focus to the next girl along, and held out his hand.

'This is, Ria,' said Ruby, introducing a small, pretty, Asian girl with captivating, large brown eyes.

'Aah,' said Victor, shaking her hand vigorously while his head nodded in time. 'Our Asian Princess.'

Ruby laughed. 'Sounds like a good title… She's come from Denny's too so she's also brought some clients over with her.'

Victor's head twitched again. 'Excellent! It looks like they had some very pretty girls at Denny's.'

Ruby then introduced Victor to the other of the three girls from Denny's, an overweight girl called Pammy who wasn't quite as pretty as Rose and Ria. His reaction wasn't as enthusiastic, but Ruby knew that Pammy was also a good find. She catered to those clients who preferred a larger woman and, although she wasn't the best looking girl on her books, she oozed sensuality. And the other good point as far as Ruby was concerned was that she'd brought almost as many clients with her as each of the other two girls.

She continued introducing the girls, pleased with her selection. As well as the younger girls, there was an older lady who Ruby thought would make an ideal MILF and a posh girl who had dropped out of university. Ruby could tell by Victor's reaction that he was impressed.

'It's lovely to meet you all,' he said, his eyes roaming excitedly from girl to girl. 'I hope you'll be very happy with us.'

Ruby could tell what he was thinking; he was looking at the girls with his own desires in mind. Despite her experience as a prostitute, this was one thing she didn't like about Victor. While she was trying to take as professional an approach as possible, here was Victor leering at the girls, his smutty mind working overtime. She quickly led him away.

'Come on, I'll show you the rest of the place.'

As they walked from room to room, they chatted. Victor surprised her when he said, 'I'm not sure Pammy is right for us.'

'Why?' demanded Ruby.

'Well, she is a bit overweight, isn't she? And she's not as attractive as the other girls.'

Ruby was quick to defend her choice. 'But the customers love her, and she's brought quite a few with her from Denny's.'

'Really?'

'Yes, almost as many as Rose and Ria, actually.'

Victor looked pensive for a moment. 'OK. Keep her for now. We'll see how she goes.'

'I thought I was running the place,' said Ruby.

'Of course,' said Victor, all officious. 'But as you're new to the business world I will be offering my guidance on occasion. Anyway,' he continued, shutting down any potential comeback from Ruby, 'how are things going otherwise?'

Ruby, although a bit irritated by his attitude, was eager to prove herself. After all, she felt lucky to have been given this opportunity. 'Good, good,' she said. 'Obviously all of the three girls from Denny's have brought some customers with them, like I said. It's a bit slow with the other girls until word gets around but we've already had some customers come up from the nightclub.'

'Excellent. I'm sure it won't be long till it really takes off,' said Victor.

'Yeah, it's good that we're getting custom from North, but if any of them are too pissed or they step out of line, I'll send them packing.'

Victor placed his hand on top of Ruby's. 'Good. I knew I could rely on you to run a tight ship.'

Ruby quickly pulled her hand away and carried on talking as she led him into the first of the girls' rooms. Like the waiting area, the rooms were a mix of cosy and seductive with subtle lighting and comfortable furnishings.

'All of the rooms have the same layout with the exception of one which I'll show you last.' She then pointed to a cabinet across from the bed. 'The girls provide their own baby wipes and condoms and anything else they want to bring. We ask them to keep them in the cabinet so in the event of a raid we can deny all knowledge.'

She then walked out of the room and into a shower

room. 'This is one of the shower rooms I told you about. We have one to every two bedrooms so the clients and the girls can take a shower and we'll make sure we always have a supply of clean towels.'

'Excellent,' said Victor, smiling. 'It seems you've thought of everything.'

Ruby couldn't resist smiling back, proud of what she'd achieved so far. Once she'd shown him round all the rooms she led him to a door marked Private. 'There's only one room left to show you apart from my living quarters, which I assume you don't want to see.' As Victor nodded his assent, she added, 'You can probably guess what the last room is.'

Victor's face broke out into a huge grin and Ruby could see spittle forming in the corners of his mouth. As she put the key in the lock and turned it, Victor's head jerked involuntarily in his eagerness to see the inside of Ruby's Dungeon.

'Obviously, I couldn't give the room its proper name like I wanted to,' she said when they had arrived at the top of the stairs. 'It would have been a bit of a giveaway if any coppers came snooping.'

But Victor wasn't listening. He was too busy walking round the room and examining the apparatus, his eyes gleaming. This room had a different feel than the others; it was darker, the walls painted a vivid red and the floor laid with black vinyl. There was a bed in the corner with a metal frame so that chains and other restraints could be attached, and it was covered with scarlet satin bedding. The equipment was placed around the room like a grotesque gymnasium and, as Victor inspected the stocks, cage and some of the whips, he could hardly contain his excitement.

He turned round and looked at Ruby with a lewd grin. 'You've done well. I can't wait to try it out.' Then he asked, 'Where will you offer your other services, y'know, those that don't involve S&M?'

'I won't,' snapped Ruby, suddenly irritated. 'And it isn't S&M. I'm a dominatrix. I inflict pain, I don't take it. And I won't be offering any other services. If the clients want that they've got plenty of other girls to choose from.'

Victor looked slightly taken aback and for a moment Ruby regretted being so sharp with him. It was a common mistake that a lot of clients, made but it still annoyed her when they expected S&M services.

Ruby had already decided that the only role she would perform in addition to jointly running the club with Tiffany was that of a dominatrix. She'd also had a rethink regarding Tiffany. They had enough girls offering their services so she wouldn't have to get involved in anything other than running the club. Ruby had had enough of having to sleep with men for money or imagining what they were doing to her girlfriend. In fact, the only reason she was still offering dominatrix services was because it paid so well. And, aside from that, she enjoyed it.

As Victor continued to explore the room she waited by the door. Eventually, satisfied that he had seen all there was to see he joined her, ready to leave the room. She turned and pulled the door open and, as she did so, she felt Victor's hand pat her buttock as he said, 'Well done, Ruby. I'm proud of you and I'm sure we'll do well out of this joint venture.'

'Not if you don't take your hand off my backside,' she said between gritted teeth.

'Oh, sorry,' said Victor, quickly pulling away from her,

his face red and his head twitching. 'I must have got carried away with all the excitement.'

Ruby was furious. Despite the number of years she had spent on the game, she hated men taking liberties with her and thought she had finally said goodbye to that part of her life.

'Like I said, Victor, I don't offer any other services. I'm a dominatrix, that's all.'

'Yes, yes, of course,' said Victor. 'My apologies.'

Ruby was still angry but, despite her resentment at the feel of Victor's roaming hands, she let it go. She felt she had no choice. Victor held the purse strings and without him she wouldn't even have her massage parlour. But if any other client should ever dare to overstep the mark with her, they would get exactly what they deserved.

32

May 1998

Trina hadn't known what to expect of Shelley's flat, but nevertheless it was a surprise. In her mind she'd built Shelley up; everything about her seemed edgy and glamorous so Trina supposed that subconsciously she'd expected the flat to fit in with this ideal.

It was in a large Victorian house in Whalley Range, approached through the main front door and then up some stairs to the first floor where there were two other flats. The front door of Shelley's flat led onto a hallway, which was in need of a coat of paint and there was a faint musty smell in the air. Shelley led her through to the lounge, which was the first door on the left. It held an interesting mix of high-end furniture, high tech electrical goods and more outdated furnishings.

Several shabby cushions looked out of place on the trendy leather sofa, and the two armchairs pre-dated the sofa by about twenty years. The TV was huge and there was a sophisticated stereo system mounted on a battered, old-fashioned table. Here the décor was also in need of an update, but the musty smell had been masked by a powerful air freshener.

'Do you wanna cuppa or do you wanna take your bags to your room first?' asked Shelley who was dressed today in tight-fitting jeans and a cropped top, her makeup heavy but still enhancing her pretty features.

'Can I take my bags to my room?' asked Trina, curious to see what it was like.

'Course,' said Shelley.

Trina followed her down the hallway and through another door to the right. When she entered the room, Trina couldn't hide the look of disappointment on her face, which she guessed Shelley must have noticed as she said. 'I know it needs decorating and that. I've not got round to it yet.'

'Oh, it's OK,' said Trina, eyeing the torn wallpaper, curtains with a fading flower design, mismatched bedding and old-fashioned dark wood wardrobe. 'I can soon decorate it.'

Shelley smiled. 'Come on, I'll show you the rest of the flat.'

The rest of the flat was in a similar state except Shelley's bedroom, which was bigger than Trina's and had a modern wardrobe and chest of drawers.

'I've bought some stuff for the flat,' said Shelley, 'but I've got a bit to do yet.'

'It's fine,' said Trina. 'We'll be able to make it really nice.' Then she asked, 'Where do you take them?'

'Who?'

'The customers. Where do you take them?'

'The clients?' said Shelley. 'You don't think they come back here, d'you?' She laughed. 'Not a fuckin' chance! I don't want any of 'em knowing where I live.' Then, seeming to sense Trina's discomfort, she said, 'Come on, let's go and have that cuppa and I'll tell you the drill.'

When they were sitting back down in the lounge, Shelley began talking.

'It's one of my rules,' she said. 'I never bring clients back here and I don't want you to either. You don't always know what or who you're dealing with so it's best they don't know where you live.'

Trina couldn't hide a look of alarm so Shelley quickly added, 'Oh, don't worry. Most of them are alright but you get the odd weirdo. The other reason I don't bring clients back is because I don't want the other residents complaining. It could land me in a lot of shit if they report us to the police, not to mention the landlord.'

'OK,' said Trina. 'Where do you take them then?'

'It depends what they want. Some take you back to a hotel room, a few take you back to theirs but most of 'em just take you somewhere deserted so no one can see you in the car.'

'What, you mean, you have to do things in the car?' asked Trina.

Shelley laughed, 'Don't worry,' she said. 'It's no biggie. There's plenty of places you can go round here where no one can see what's going on. You'll soon get used to it.'

'OK,' said Trina again, trying to hide her trepidation.

'Oh, and don't tell them your real name,' said Shelley. 'For the same reason that you don't let them know where you live. If you get a dodgy client, the less they know about you the better.'

Trina stared at Shelley, stupefied, as she listened to her

list of instructions: *Always use a condom, agree a price up front, avoid anyone who stinks of booze or smells dirty.* The list went on until Trina found herself becoming quite anxious.

'It's fine,' said Shelley. 'As long as you have your wits about you, it'll be OK. Like I say, you'll soon get used to it.'

This time Trina just nodded, keeping her anxious thoughts to herself.

Shelley then went on to describe the various services Trina could offer and how much she should charge for them.

'You don't have to offer all of them,' she added. 'It's up to you, but you get more clients if you offer more.'

'It's OK,' said Trina. 'I don't mind.'

'You still up for it then?' asked Shelley.

'Yeah, course,' said Trina, putting on a brave face.

The following night Trina tried to hide her nerves as she prepared for her first night on the game. She was standing in front of the bathroom mirror putting on her makeup while, in the background, the Spice Girls sang about what they really really want. Again, Shelley had offered her advice, suggesting what she should wear and what makeup to apply.

'You should deffo wear a short skirt,' she said. 'And make sure it's clingy as well. The clients love long legs and a tight arse.'

Despite her nerves Trina preened at the perceived compliment, especially coming from her object of desire. Shelley smiled in response. 'In this game you've gotta make the most of what you've got,' she said.

It was almost time to go and Trina could feel her heartbeat speeding up as she sprayed herself liberally with the bottle of Obsession that Shelley had lent her. Shelley seemed to pick up on her unease as she said, 'Before we go, there's a little something I always take. It helps you get through it.'

She pulled a bag of white powder from the sideboard in the living room and dipped a finger in it then held it to her nose.

'What is it?' asked Trina.

'Coke. Try some,' Shelley said, offering Trina the bag.

'Oh, I'm not sure,' said Trina.

'It'll make you feel better.' Shelley smiled that wonderful smile of hers and added, 'I promise.'

Trina didn't know whether it was the need for something to calm her down or Shelley's gentle persuasion, but she soon capitulated and had a snort of the coke. For a moment she didn't feel anything. But then the rush hit her and she felt much more confident; euphoric even.

Shelley smiled again. 'Right, I think you're ready. Time to go.'

They walked the short distance to where the red light district was situated. To Trina it didn't seem what she would have expected from a red light district. Unlike the area she came from, all the streets were tree-lined and some of the houses were huge.

It had once been an affluent area but many of the large houses were now being rented out to the criminal element. Where the trees had once added to the area's appeal, to Trina they gave the neighbourhood an eerie atmosphere, acting as cover for anyone who was up to no good, their vast branches overhanging the pavements and reaching out like the tentacles of an octopus. In the darkness of night-time she kept expecting someone to pounce out at her from behind one of the huge tree trunks.

After a few minutes Shelley said, 'Right, we're here. You stand here and I'll move further along.' Trina looked at her in alarm; by now she was finding it difficult to mask her growing unease, despite taking the cocaine.

It wasn't long until a car pulled up and the driver wound the window down. Shelley approached the vehicle and although Trina couldn't hear everything that was said she saw Shelley nod in her direction then she stood aside while the driver looked across and shook his head as if in distaste.

Shelley stepped back towards Trina. 'Right, this one's mine. Don't forget everything I told you,' she said, stepping back up to the car and jumping inside.

Then the car sped off and Trina was alone. She was immediately beset by panic and an urge to flee, especially as the rejection by Shelley's first client had sapped her confidence. Trina tried to calm down, telling herself that it was no big deal as she'd had sex plenty of times before and felt nothing. But then she thought about what she was about to do and what she had become.

Something about the word 'prostitute' struck terror into her and Trina thought about the implications. She was no longer dealing with naïve schoolboys, but was selling her body to men. Strange men. Old men. Fat men. Dirty men. She tried to shake off her negative thoughts and focus instead on the money and the list of instructions Shelley had given her.

Then Trina noticed a car pull up and as the driver wound down the window she realised he had stopped for her. For a few moments she hesitated while the driver watched her. He didn't look too bad; oldish but not bad looking, and clean. And the car was nice too.

When she didn't make a move, the driver revved his engine, the sound marking his impatience and prompting Trina to make a decision. She took a deep breath, crossed the pavement and prepared to do business with her first client.

33

May 1998

Trina stooped till she could see through the car's window, and the man's eyes met hers. 'How much for full sex?' he asked.

Trina gave him the price suggested by Shelley and his face remained impassive as he said, 'OK, get in.'

She did as she was told and the man took off. Trina had no idea where they were going till the car pulled up in a car park behind a block of flats. The man hadn't spoken throughout the few minutes' journey and Trina had also kept silent. She didn't know what to say to him and felt foolish starting a meaningless conversation so she kept her gaze on the road ahead. Nevertheless she could sense the man eyeing up her legs.

When the car stopped the man said, 'Are you new to this patch?'

Trina glanced across at him. 'Yes,' she said, but she didn't reveal that it was her first time.

'Press the button on that side for the seat to go back,' he said, and Trina followed his instructions, noticing her skirt ride up even further as she shot back. Again, she felt panic stirring within her but before she had chance to react the man was on top of her unfastening his flies. She quickly passed him a condom.

It was soon over and Trina felt relief as the man climbed off her, pulled up his trousers and passed her the money. While he was occupied, she slipped her briefs back on and it wasn't long before he threw the used condom out of the car window then started the engine.

'Do you want dropping back where you were?' he asked.

'Yeah,' said Trina, keeping her eyes on the road again till she got back to her spot then opened the car door and jumped out.

Once Trina was back on the pavement, she noticed how much her legs were trembling. She felt tears in her eyes but she fought them back, unable to understand why she was so upset. This was what she had wanted after all. And it wasn't that bad. No different from the boys at school really except the man was older and he'd paid her.

Now she'd had her first client, packing it in wasn't an option as far as Trina was concerned. What else would she do to earn so much money? And she needed to earn money to carry on living with Shelley. Where else would she go? She dreaded the thought of going back home to a life like her mother's, full of drudgery and menial, low-paid jobs.

Then she thought again of the money. She'd done it! She'd just got paid twenty-five pounds for five minutes work. Trina's hand closed around the bunch of notes in her pocket. It was a long time since she'd had twenty-five pounds all to herself, and the thought of earning even more urged her on. Ignoring her trembling legs and persistent nervousness she looked out at the road, noticing the cars passing by, and waited for her next client.

The night was a revelation. Each time a car pulled up Trina would feel a fresh surge of trepidation but she pushed herself on, thinking of the money and her new-found freedom. The clients varied in looks. Their attitudes varied as well. Most of them were alright with her but she had one that talked down to her and was a bit rough.

She soon got used to the drill; she'd ask the client what service he wanted then agree a price with him before she got in the car. During that time she would size up the client and make sure she was comfortable about going off with him.

Trina hoped to catch sight of Shelley again, knowing she'd draw comfort from seeing a friendly, familiar face but she only saw her once and they didn't have chance to talk much before a car pulled up and Shelley got inside. But as the night drew on Trina became less nervous and finally, in the early hours of the morning, she decided she'd had enough for the night and made her way back to Shelley's.

When Trina arrived at the flat it was empty; Shelley wasn't home yet. The first thing Trina did was to take out the money and count it. She'd been keeping a mental note of how much she'd earnt until she'd lost count. Now, as she counted the notes in her hands, she felt a rush of excitement. £155 for one night's work!

Trina was delighted and all the angst of the night quickly evaporated as she dreamt of how she would spend the cash. She was already getting used to this way of life and the sense of satisfaction at the end of the night when she'd earnt her wad.

It wasn't long before Shelley arrived home. 'Well, how was it?' she asked. 'Did anyone give you any grief?'

'Not too bad,' said Trina. 'There was one guy who was a bit of a dick, but he didn't bother me too much.' Then she waved her cash, 'Look, I got £155.'

'Well done,' said Shelley. 'There'll be plenty more where that came from. That's if you want to carry on.'

'Yeah, course I do.'

Shelley smiled. 'Well, in that case, I think we should have a celebration.'

Shelley opened the plastic bag she had been carrying and pulled out a bottle of champagne.

'Wow! Have you just been and bought that?' asked Trina.

'No, my last client gave it to me. He's got a bit of a thing for me so he likes to bring presents.'

Trina laughed. 'Aah, bless him,' she said and for a few seconds they both giggled till Shelley pulled two glasses from the cupboard and filled them up.

'To us,' she said, chinking her glass against Trina's.

Trina liked the sound of those words and she felt content. This was where her future lay; with the delectable Shelley, making shedloads of money and buying all the things she'd ever wanted to buy.

They stayed up for a couple of hours, chatting, sharing amusing stories about their clients and taking coke. Despite Trina's earlier trepidation she didn't think she'd ever felt so happy. She didn't particularly like selling herself to strange men, but she knew she could cope with it in view of the rewards. Not only did she have freedom and money but she also got to live with Shelley who she was becoming increasingly drawn towards.

34

June 1998

Daisy stood with her arms folded, looking down at her daughter who was occupying the sofa in her living room. 'What I don't understand,' she said, 'is why you can't tell me where you live. It's been weeks now since you left home and I've still not been to see where you're staying.'

'Aw, Mam, not that again!' said Trina.

'Don't you *Aw Mam* me,' snapped Daisy, to which Trina shrugged in response. Then Daisy added, 'What's the problem with where you're living anyway?'

'I told you, there's no problem. I just don't want you interfering.'

'But I worry about you, child,' said Daisy, her tone now conciliatory. 'You're so young to be living on your own. I don't know why you couldn't stay here till you're older...'

'I don't live on my own,' Trina cut in. 'I share a flat with Shelley and she's eighteen.'

'Don't split hairs with me, Trina. You know what I mean. Anyway, eighteen is still very young.'

Trina shrugged again but Daisy wasn't finished. 'Well, if

you won't let me come and visit you at home, you could at least tell me the name of the restaurant where you work,' she said.

'No chance!' said Trina. 'You'd only embarrass me. You'd probably bring that lot with you as well.' She looked upwards, indicating her brothers who were upstairs.

'You mean your brothers?' asked Daisy. 'They're your own flesh and blood, Trina.'

'Yeah, don't I know it,' muttered Trina.

'I beg your pardon, child.'

'Nothing,' said Trina, 'but you know what they're like. They'd probably be running wild around the restaurant and showing me up.'

Daisy sighed before relenting. 'I don't know, you won't tell me where you live or where you work. How can you expect me not to worry? But, at least you're here now so I suppose I should be grateful for small mercies.'

Trina felt a pang of guilt. It was only the second time she'd visited home in the six weeks since she'd left but it was difficult to fit it into her busy life. Most of her evenings were spent working till the early hours or out enjoying herself, and the days were spent sleeping off the late nights. And when she wasn't working, or out having fun, there was always something that needed attending to. Shopping. Washing. Cleaning.

A quick glance around her mother's living room told her that her mother hadn't been keeping on top of her own cleaning since she had left home. Trina again felt guilty even though she told herself that it wasn't her responsibility. But, no matter how much she tried to brush it off, she knew it was a sign that her mother was finding it difficult without her. Daisy was a house-proud woman and she wouldn't let dust and grime gather in her home unless she couldn't help it.

Trina thought of how it had been with her mother struggling to hold down two jobs and relying on her to keep her brothers in order and help out in the home. She knew that as well as having all the household chores, Daisy would also be finding it difficult financially. She always had.

Feeling remorseful, Trina reached inside her handbag and pulled out fifty pounds. 'Here,' she said, holding out the notes, 'have this.'

Daisy looked at her with an expression of surprise. 'Lord above! Where on earth did you get that from?'

'From working. Where do you think? I want you to have it.'

Daisy continued to eye her sceptically. 'But you're only a waitress. You can't possibly afford to give that much away.'

'It's fine,' Trina scoffed. 'I get loads of tips. It's a posh restaurant. We get some rich people in there.'

Daisy didn't hesitate for much longer. 'Well, as long as you're alright with it,' she said, reaching out for the money then placing it in a jar inside the cupboard. 'Thank you, Trina. That's very good of you,' she added. Then she went over to Trina and wrapped her arms around her, holding her tight for precious moments.

Trina's face lit up with a satisfied smile and she decided that she would make the effort to visit her mother more often in future.

When Trina arrived back home, Shelley was in the bathroom.

Trina couldn't resist going into her own bedroom and stepping over to the dressing table she had recently bought for herself. There she opened up a small jewellery box and pulled out her gold and ruby necklace. For the umpteenth time since she had treated herself to it, she put it on and admired herself in her dressing table mirror. The ruby was pear-shaped and held in a gold clasp and it glistened under the bedroom light.

Trina knew she'd rarely have chance to wear the necklace. It was too risky wearing it for work; there were too many muggers hanging about late at night. Neither would she be likely to go to the sorts of places where she would wear a ruby necklace. But, nevertheless, she'd had to have it. As soon as she'd seen it in the jeweller's window, she knew she would buy it. And why shouldn't she? After all, she deserved some reward for the work she did.

In the last six weeks Trina had become used to the job. She didn't like it; in fact, a lot of the clients made her skin crawl and she hated what she had to do with them. But she loved the rewards. It was so good to be able to treat herself; she'd spent enough years going without. Apart from the ruby necklace, she'd bought herself new clothes and makeup and was steadily improving the state of her bedroom.

Trina also enjoyed flat sharing with Shelley. She was good company and they often had a drink together and a laugh, as well as a snort of cocaine before they went out to work.

When it came to looking after the flat, Trina did most of the tasks, but it was her own choice. Being used to doing housework for her mother, Trina had become house-proud and she accepted that Shelley perhaps just wasn't made that way. But what Shelley lacked in housekeeping skills she more than made up for in other ways. Trina was mesmerised by her and loved being in her company.

While she was in the bedroom Trina decided to check through her money. It was something she often did, enjoying the feel of it in her hands and the knowledge that it was all hers to spend as she pleased. As she counted through it she was surprised, because she'd thought she had £10 more. She checked again to make sure. No, there was definitely £10 less than she had thought.

Then Shelley appeared at the bedroom door and Trina brushed off her concerns about the money. Perhaps she had spent more than she realised. Shelley was fresh out of the shower, wearing only her underwear, with her hair still wet. Droplets of water had trickled onto her black see-through bra, making it even more see-through in places where the moist material clung to her naked flesh. Shelley often walked round the flat wearing only her underwear; it was another of the things Trina liked about living with her.

'What do you fancy for tea?' asked Shelley.

Trina grinned salaciously, but kept her true thoughts to herself. 'We could have some pizzas out of the freezer if you like.'

'Yeah,' said Shelley. 'That'll be good. Then we can have a quick snort before we go to work.'

Trina smiled and made her way to the kitchen to pre-heat the oven while Shelley finished getting ready. The sight of Shelley in her flimsy underwear had side-tracked her, driving all thoughts of the missing money out of her mind for now.

35

June 1998

Trina and Shelley were having a night off. Having treated themselves to a meal in a nice Italian restaurant followed by a few drinks, they were now back at the flat and were both feeling merry.

'Fancy some Charlie?' asked Shelley.

Trina nodded and for a few minutes they indulged in some cocaine. She was on a high as she and Shelley again exchanged stories about clients, and laughed raucously.

'There's one of 'em that's a right weirdo,' said Trina. 'He spends ages just feeling my legs before he gets down to it. I have to keep reminding him that he's only paid for a fuck.'

Shelley laughed. 'Some of 'em are like that. It all depends what turns 'em on. He's obviously a leg man and you *have* got really nice legs.'

'Aw, thanks,' said Trina, smiling. Because of the drugs and drink she was feeling bolder than usual as she added, 'You've got nice everything.'

She gazed intensely at Shelley who was sitting to the side of her on the sofa, with just a small gap between them.

Shelley didn't seem uncomfortable at the intensity of Trina's gaze. Instead she smiled back and said, 'So have you.'

'Yeah, sure,' said Trina. 'That's why you get all the clients.'

'Heh,' said Shelley. 'You get your fair share and don't forget I have my regulars. Once you've been at it a bit longer you'll build up your regulars too. You've probably already got some.'

Trina shrugged. 'A few,' she said, noncommittally.

'Seriously,' said Shelley. 'You're a good-looking girl, Trina. Don't put yourself down.'

'Aw, thanks,' said Trina again.

Shelley's eyes never left her and for a few moments Trina gazed back, neither of them saying anything. Trina was still feeling the effects of the coke. She felt high, full of energy and confident, and Shelley's compliments were adding to her feelings of euphoria. She had an urge to speak and break down the wall that seemed to stand between them.

'You're gorgeous,' she said, shuffling nearer to Shelley, and gazing longingly into her eyes. 'I've thought it ever since the first time I saw you.'

'Thanks,' said Shelley, her state of intoxication smothering any discomfort she would normally have felt at such an ardent declaration. Instead she gently patted Trina on the shoulder to acknowledge the compliment.

This was all the encouragement Trina needed and, as Shelley continued to stare back at her, Trina leant forward until her lips were touching Shelley's. They began to kiss, Trina feeling Shelley's lips move in time with her own, and she placed her hand on the back of Shelley's head, gently running her fingers lovingly through her hair. Then Shelley stopped and abruptly pulled away as though she had just come to her senses.

'What the fuck are you playing at?' she yelled.

She jumped up from the sofa and Trina noticed that her face was a mask of fury. 'But I thought it was what you wanted,' she said, already feeling her face flush with shame.

'Was it fuck! I ain't no lesbo,' Shelley shouted.

This was a side to Shelley that Trina had never seen. In her mind she had built her up into something almost godlike. But now her anger contorted her attractive features until she didn't even look like the same girl. Trina was confused and embarrassed. 'But you kissed me back,' she implored.

'No I fuckin' didn't! I didn't even realise what was happening. I thought we were just mates. And then you go and do summat like that!'

'I'm sorry,' said Trina. 'I honestly thought you felt the same. I'm sorry,' she repeated. 'I promise it won't happen again.'

'It better fuckin' hadn't do,' said Shelley. 'Because if it does, you'll be out on your fuckin' arse and your feet won't touch the ground.'

Trina got up off the sofa and dashed to her room, muttering her apologies repeatedly as tears of humiliation stung her eyes. When she reached her room, she flung herself on her bed and gave way to her sorrow.

Shelley's threats hadn't bothered her. Under any other circumstances she would have retaliated and let Shelley know she wouldn't be pushed around. But this was different. Trina was feeling rejected and bewildered as well as humiliated. In her eagerness to have Shelley for her own she had misread the signals, and she cursed herself for her foolishness.

The following morning, they had a serious talk. Trina felt mortified as Shelley asked, 'How could you have got the impression that there was anything between us other than mates?'

'Dunno. Like I say, it won't happen again.' Trina hung her head in shame.

'Right, well what's happened has happened. Don't worry, you can still stay… as long as you don't fuckin' do anything like that again.'

Trina looked up coyly. 'No, course I won't; not now I know the score.'

'OK. Well I think we need some rules if you're staying here.' Shelley paused, giving Trina time to take in her words before she continued. 'From now on we both need to keep covered up in front of each other. If you need to come into my bedroom for anything while I'm there you need to knock first so I can make sure I'm dressed. I'll do the same for you too. Oh, and the bathroom door needs to be locked whenever one of us is using it.'

Trina agreed to all Shelley's requests, but she just wanted the conversation to be over as soon as possible. It felt as though Shelley was enjoying prolonging her discomfort.

She didn't want to leave the flat. Trina still had mixed feelings about Shelley and was upset that she'd ruined everything between them. But it was apparent from Shelley's anger and her expression of scorn that things would never be the same between them from this day onwards.

36

July 1998

It was a few weeks later. Although it was late afternoon Trina was still in bed as she'd worked till the early hours. She was about to get up when she heard a loud knocking on the front door. She waited for some moments to see if Shelley would answer it. But the knocking continued so Trina slung on her dressing gown, wiped the sleep from her eyes and went to see who it was.

She was surprised to find an angry looking middle-aged man on the other side of the door. He was tall and balding but, despite his age, he had a powerful frame. His stance was rigid and his expression stony.

'Where is she?' he demanded. 'And who the hell are you?'

Trina's first thought was that it might be a client who had somehow found his way to the flat and she immediately became cautious. 'Wait there a minute. I'll go and get her,' she said, as she tried to shut the door.

The man jammed his foot inside the door to stop it closing. 'Oh no you bloody well won't! 'I know your game; you'll leave me standing here.' He began pushing his way past Trina. 'It's my bloody property and I've as much right to be here as anyone. More so, in fact. Who the bloody hell are you anyway?'

His attitude annoyed Trina and she was about to tell him that she also had every right to be there as she was Shelley's flatmate. But something held her back. This angry man was obviously the landlord. What if Shelley hadn't told him about her? He might want more money if he knew a second person lived there or he might even throw her out for living there without his permission.

So Trina chose her words carefully. 'I… I'm Shelley's friend.'

The man eyed her suspiciously, his eyes taking in what she was wearing, as he continued to barge past her and made his way into the hall.

Trina quickly explained the reason for her dressing gown. 'Shelley let me stay over last night.' Then she followed him through to the lounge.

'Hang on here, I'll see if she's in her room,' she said, leaving the landlord pacing around the lounge.

Trina could find no sign of Shelley either in her bedroom or the rest of the flat so she went back to face the landlord. 'She's not in; she must have gone out while I was still in bed.'

'How bloody convenient when she owes me two month's rent.'

'Really?' asked Trina, knowing this would affect her, and failing to hide her disquiet.

'Oh yes, and it's not the first time. It's not as if I haven't tackled her about it either. She told me on the phone that she'd be here with it when I called and instead I find she's gone AWOL and got a bloody stranger staying here. So where the bloody hell is she?'

'I've no idea,' said Trina. 'Like I said, she must have gone out while I was still in bed.'

The landlord plonked himself down on the sofa. 'Right, well I'll just have to wait until she gets back. Any idea when that might be?'

Trina knew that Shelley might not be back till the early hours especially if she had gone somewhere and then straight on to work afterwards. But she wasn't about to discuss Shelley's occupation with the landlord. 'I... I don't know. It could be a while though.'

'That's OK, I can wait.'

For a moment Trina stood awkwardly in the lounge not knowing what to do. She didn't usually get easily intimidated, but this man was scary. He was also the person who owned the home where she was living so she knew she had to exercise caution. Trina wanted to get showered and dressed but she was nervous about leaving the landlord unattended in the flat. For all she knew he might take away some of their things to claw back part of the rent arrears.

Thoughts of other scary men from her childhood flashed through her mind. Mr Dodds, the lecherous landlord who her mother had succumbed to in order to keep a roof over her heads, and the two burly bailiffs. She could still picture the bailiffs, one with red hair and a beard and the other with crooked teeth, their faces stern as they callously took possession of their things while her brothers cried and screamed and her mother looked so helpless. It would always stick in her mind; it was the first time she had heard her mother swear or seen her reduced to tears.

Eventually she went through to the kitchen to make herself something to eat, leaving the man in the lounge and listening for any movement from him. She hoped he would get tired of waiting and go away. But after fifteen minutes he was still there, and Trina was becoming increasingly unnerved, a tight knot forming in her stomach. She stepped tentatively back into the lounge to find the landlord still stony faced and sitting on the sofa.

'How much does she owe?' she asked.

'Eight hundred.'

'Wow!' Trina was shocked, especially as she had been paying Shelley her share of the rent on time every month. She thought about the cash she had hidden in her room. Maybe if she paid him some of the rent he would go away and leave her alone. 'OK, to save you waiting I could give you some of the money and then get her to give you the rest.'

'How much can you pay?' he grumbled.

'A hundred.'

'Pffft! Do you think I was born yesterday? Eight hundred quid she owes me, and you're offering me a poxy hundred?'

'Alright, it isn't my fault!' snapped Trina. 'I'm just trying to help out.'

'Well, it's not enough. I want at least half of it and then the rest from her tomorrow. It's your bloody mate's fault for leaving you here when she knew I was coming round.'

'I don't have that sort of money on me. I can do one-fifty but that's it.'

The landlord looked pensive for some moments. 'OK, give me two hundred and I'll collect the rest tomorrow.'

Trina frowned. 'Give me a minute,' she said before going to her room for the money and handing it over to him.

The landlord didn't thank her. Instead he scowled as she passed the money over then said, 'You can blame your mate for leaving you in the shit. So you'd better tell her to be here tomorrow when I come for the rest or I'll be throwing her out.'

Trina wasn't happy with her flatmate at all. Shelley had known the landlord was calling round yet she had left her to face him. Not only that but Trina had to pay him some of her own money to appease him when she had already given Shelley her share of the rent.

Apart from the issue with the rent, Trina had a more pressing problem. She had noticed over the weeks that money was continuing to go missing from her bedroom. The first time it had happened, she thought she might have made a mistake but now she was sure there was no mistake. Trina had taken to checking her money regularly and was certain that some of it had disappeared. It was usually ten pounds at a time, on two or three occasions a week.

The previous night she'd arrived home from work later than Shelley who was already in bed. Trina had automatically checked her money, a habit she had got into lately. She was disturbed to find that this time there was twenty pounds missing.

Trina was angry. There was only one person who could have taken the money. That person was Shelley, and Trina was determined to confront her about it. She'd have to tread lightly though as she didn't want to risk upsetting her and having to leave after she'd invested so much time and money into turning the flat into a home.

Trina had been determined to make the most of her time living there. As well as making her bedroom look more presentable, she had also painted the hallway and bought some cushions for the living room and a modern television stand. Despite Shelley promising to pay towards the things she had bought, Trina never received any money.

She was beginning to see another side to Shelley, who was slovenly as well as irresponsible with money. Then there were the drugs. Since her awkward pass at Shelley, Trina had cut down drastically on her own drug and alcohol consumption, determined to maintain control so that she would never make the same mistake again. She had noticed over the weeks though that Shelley seemed to be taking more drugs, or maybe it was just more apparent to Trina now she was staying sober herself.

Shelley's drug abuse was affecting her moods as well. Sometimes she would be on a high but at other times she was depressed and irritable, which made her unpleasant to live with. In fact, ever since the night when Trina had made her pass at Shelley, the atmosphere had been strained between them.

Trina didn't get chance to confront Shelley till the following day as she was in bed when Trina got home from work. Shelley walked into the living room late that morning wearing a scruffy dressing gown and looking tense, her hair messy, and remnants of last night's makeup emphasising the stress lines on her face. Trina took in her untidy appearance; the girl she had fallen for was no longer evident and she eyed her with distaste.

'Alright?' asked Trina.

Shelley muttered a moody 'yeah' in response while she dashed around the living room, pulling up cushions and opening drawers as though searching for something.

Trina guessed that Shelley was feeling irritable as she hadn't yet had her first fix of the day. She was tempted to leave things till later but decided against it. She had psyched herself up now and wanted to get the conversation over with.

'I need to have a word with you,' she began.

'Can't it wait?' asked Shelley.

'Not really,' said Trina. 'I've been waiting for you to get up so we can talk.'

'OK, just give me a sec,' said Shelley, her tone sharp. 'I haven't even had a drink yet.'

Shelley went through to the kitchen then came back into the living room carrying a small bag but no drink. Then she sat down on the armchair over from Trina, dipped her finger inside the bag and held it to her nose, taking a snort of cocaine up each nostril. 'Want some?' she asked, offering the bag to Trina.

'No thanks.'

Shelley sniffed. 'Suit yourself.' Then she added, 'Well, go on then. You can tell me while I'm waiting for the kettle to boil.'

'I had the landlord round yesterday.' She noticed Shelley blanch as though she had only just recalled his arrangement to call and collect the rent. 'He says you're two months overdue with the rent. Eight hundred quid you owe.'

Shelley shrugged. 'Maybe. I missed him once or twice but it's no biggie.'

'You could have fooled me. He came round here going ape shit! I had to pay him two hundred pounds before he'd go away. He's coming back today for the rest.'

Shelley smiled falsely. 'Don't worry, I'll sort him out.'

'And what about the two hundred quid you owe me? I

shouldn't have had to give him that when I've already paid you my share.'

'You'll get it, keep your hair on!' Shelley snapped.

'Some of my money's been going missing as well,' Trina said, determined to have it out with her now she'd started.

Shelley pulled her shoulders back and frowned as if in surprise but the movement was exaggerated and false. 'You sure?'

'Definitely. I've been checking it regularly. Another twenty quid went missing the night before last while I was at work.'

Shelley shrugged. 'So, what you trying to say?'

Trina paused and took a sharp breath. 'Well, there's only one person who it can be, Shelley, unless you had somebody else in the flat that night.'

'No I fuckin' didn't!' Shelley snapped. 'I told you I don't have clients back.'

'In that case, it must be you who took it,' said Trina, 'and it's not the first time either.'

Shelley snapped again. 'I haven't touched your fuckin' money! I earn plenty of my own. I don't need yours.'

'Well who took it then?' demanded Trina.

'I don't know, do I?'

For a few moments the conversation halted as both girls glared belligerently at each other. But Trina wasn't prepared to leave it at that and have Shelley worm her way out of it like she did when she didn't settle up with her for things she had bought for the flat.

'It's not on, Shelley. It's got to stop!' she said.

'I've told you I've not had your fuckin' money!' yelled Shelley. 'Don't you dare come here laying down the law and accusing me of stealing.'

'It has to be you. There's no one else it can be. And you never pay me what you fuckin' owe me either. I'm sick of it!'

'Right, well if you're sick of it, you know what you can do! Get your own fuckin' place,' shouted Shelley who then stormed out of the room.

For a second Trina was tempted to follow her and put her straight about things. But then she wavered as she thought about her situation. She was lucky to still be living here after her ill-fated pass at Shelley. If she walked out now then she'd have all the hassle of having to find somewhere else to live. She didn't really know anybody else who would put her up so she'd have to find a place of her own. But, at only sixteen, she didn't really know how to go about it, and then there would be all the expense of having to start from scratch.

In the end she decided to stay put for now but she'd have to find somewhere to hide her money to make sure Shelley couldn't get hold of it anymore. And as for all the other expenditure, she wouldn't buy anything for the house in future unless Shelley gave her the money up front.

Hopefully, that should put an end to the money issues. But deep down she knew that the reason Shelley spent so much money was because she had a drug problem. And that was something that wasn't going to go away. If Shelley continued to leave the rent unpaid then it was only a matter of time before Trina would be forced to move out.

37

November 2007

'How was it?' asked Ruby as Tiffany walked into their bedroom and slipped into bed beside her.

'Good. No major problems and the takings were well up for a Tuesday night.'

'Great,' said Ruby, snuggling up to Tiffany from behind and draping her arm across her waist. 'It just gets better, doesn't it?'

Tiffany muttered 'erm' and within seconds she was fast asleep, having worked the night shift on the reception desk. They had been open for several weeks now and the club was going from strength to strength.

Most nights Ruby and Tiffany worked the reception desk together but they each had two nights off a week. Ruby also spent some time with her private clients who she entertained in her upstairs 'dungeon' while Tiffany ran the reception area alone.

After a few hours' sleep Ruby got up and went to make some breakfast. Her kitchen was stunning with polished granite work surfaces, top-of-the-range appliances and the latest gadgets. Like her previous flat, the rest of the apartment was tastefully decorated and furnished, except that, with her increased income, the furniture was even more high-end. Although Ruby and Tiffany's private rooms were only up a flight of stairs from the rest of the club, they looked a million miles away.

By the time Tiffany was out of bed, Ruby had fixed them each a dish of chopped fruit with bran and poured them both a glass of fresh orange. These days Ruby lived a healthy existence. Her healthy lifestyle was also reflected in her regular visits to the gym, which helped to maintain her strong, toned physique.

'How are things with Victor nowadays?' asked Tiffany when they sat down to eat.

'What do you mean?'

'You know, any more roaming hands?'

'Oh no! There was only that first time when I showed him round but I soon put him straight.' Then Ruby had a thought, 'Why d'you ask? He hasn't made a play for you, has he?'

Tiffany smiled. 'No, I think he's probably frightened of what you'll do if he dares to touch me.'

'Good, so he should be. Anyway, I think he's more than occupied now with trying out all the girls we've got available. He's like a kid in a sweet shop and he loves the fact that he gets it all for nowt.'

Tiffany pulled a face, displaying her repulsion. 'I know,' said Ruby. 'Whatever turns you on, I suppose.'

Ruby paused for a moment while she took a mouthful

of cereal then she became pensive. 'Y'know, Tiffany, we've been banging some money away in the last few weeks, haven't we?'

'Yeah, I know.' Tiffany giggled. 'We can't fuckin' spend it quick enough.'

'Well, I was thinking,' said Ruby. 'Why don't we carry on saving till we have a deposit for a place of our own?'

'Really? Is that what you want?' When Ruby nodded, Tiffany asked, 'D'you think we'll get a mortgage?'

'Course we will. It's not a brothel as far as the bank is concerned; it's a massage parlour. Victor's going to make sure it's all done officially through an accountant so we'll have proper accounts to show the bank.'

'Sounds good. Do you not like it here then?'

'Yeah, it's handy being on the premises but... well... sometimes I think it would be nice to have our own home where we can get away from it all.'

'Where are you thinking of moving to?' asked Tiffany.

'Somewhere nice, maybe Sale or Altrincham.'

Tiffany beamed a smile at her. 'Sound. I can't wait,' she said.

Later that evening Ruby, was manning the reception desk while Tiffany had a night off. They preferred to take time off on the quieter nights and manage the desk together at weekends when things were busier. Although it was a Wednesday, the nightclub was open to the public but, like the brothel, it was a quiet night for North. Ruby was enjoying the vibe from the nightclub, the beat of the dance music creating a party atmosphere. *Don't Cha* by the

Pussycat Dolls was just fading out when a new client came in through the door. Ruby took a good look at him as he walked over to the reception desk.

The man was around forty, tall and quite good looking and had made an attempt at casual dress although his clothing seemed a bit too new and squeaky clean to be something that he wore regularly. He smiled confidently as he sauntered up to the reception desk.

'I'd like to book one of your girls,' he said in an accent that was somewhere in between refined and street.

'Come on, I'll show you who's available,' said Ruby, walking him over to the waiting area where two girls were sitting. After introducing them both, she added, 'You can have a coffee and a chat with the girls before you decide who you would like to spend some time with if you like.'

'No, that's OK. I'll take Ria if that's alright,' said the man.

'Good choice,' said Ruby and as Ria stood up Ruby said to her, 'Ria, why don't you tell him about your special massage?'

'Sure,' said Ria, who then led the man to her room.

The arrival of the man had unsettled Ruby and she had a bad feeling about him. All the time he was in Ria's room she found it difficult to relax. This man could spell major trouble for them and she dreaded to think what the upshot of that might be. She just hoped Ria was onto him.

But then she tried to tell herself Ria would be able to handle the situation fine. Ruby had seen the look of recognition on her face and prayed that it meant she would do the right thing. Nevertheless, the half hour that the man spent in Ria's room passed excruciatingly slowly.

Eventually they came out of Ria's room. Ruby saw the

man first as he passed the reception desk and headed for the stairs, muttering a glum 'hello'. She saw his look of disappointment; maybe it was a good sign. Ria went back to the waiting area but, once the man had left the building, she came over to speak to Ruby.

'Everything alright?' asked Ruby.

'Yeah,' said Ria. 'He only had a massage.'

'Good. Did he ask for anything else?'

'No, but I didn't offer it either.'

'Good. Well done, girl,' said Ruby. 'I'm glad you had him sussed. I don't think we need to worry about him anymore, but there might be others so you be careful.'

'No worries,' said Ria. 'You didn't think I'd forget our secret code, did you?'

Ruby went back to the reception area and smiled to herself. Thank God Ria had been on the ball and remembered what the special massage meant! Still, the situation had unsettled her and she made a mental note to remind the other girls just in case.

Ruby had figured him out as soon as she saw him walk over to the reception desk. He was too different from the other clients. His style of dress didn't seem right, as though he was trying too hard to create a certain image. Then there was his over-confident manner; clients visiting for the first time were normally a bit apprehensive. And the final thing that had given him away was the way he was examining the club in fine detail.

He had copper written all over him. She should know; she'd seen so many of them during the years she'd spent on the street that she could easily sniff one out. Apart from those who were trying to impose the law, she had also met plenty who had indulged in the services she offered.

Although his appearance had unnerved Ruby, she still felt confident that if they had any other visits from the law, she would easily be able to handle them. In fact, she thought smugly, she couldn't foresee any problems that she wouldn't be capable of handling.

38

March 2008

'Well I never thought I'd see the day when a daughter of mine would have a house like this. They must be paying you well managing that nightclub, my girl.'

Ruby smiled back at her mother but she couldn't help but feel a twinge of guilt at the lie she'd told her. She hadn't really seen any alternative though. Over the years, as she'd become progressively more affluent, Ruby had invented a stream of lies for her mother, with her imaginary career progressing from restaurant waitress to nightclub employee and eventually nightclub manager.

But, even on the salary of a nightclub manager, the house would have been out of reach so Ruby had come up with the lie that she was co-purchasing it with her 'friend' Tiffany. She had relied on these fabrications to keep a close relationship with her mother because Ruby knew she couldn't have coped with the knowledge that her daughter was not only a lesbian, but the madam of a brothel.

'Come inside,' said Ruby. 'Have a look at the kitchen.'

It was the second time she and Tiffany had been to see

the house, but this time they had returned with Ruby's mother and her youngest brother, Tyler, knowing they would be thrilled to see the place Ruby was going to buy. And it was such a relief to finally be able to show them where she would be living because, since she'd left home, she had never done so. Instead she had made many excuses to prevent them coming round, from living with a difficult flat-mate to the place being too dirty and run-down, until they had eventually stopped asking.

'Wow! Good stuff this innit?' Tyler commented as he marvelled at the modern kitchen with its high-tech appliances.

'My God!' her mother chipped in. 'I bet this is a step up from that other place where you lived. I don't know how you put up with it for so long when you could afford something like this.'

'I did have to save for a bit,' said Ruby, flashing Tiffany a loving glance. 'Anyway, wait till you see the garden.'

They walked through to the comfortable living room then through the patio doors and into the conservatory.

Her mother stared around the room in awe.

'Haven't you seen a conservatory before?' asked Ruby.

'Only on the telly.' Her mother was soon standing at the window looking out into the garden. 'It's beautiful,' she muttered subconsciously.

Ruby grabbed the bunch of keys and inserted one into the back door. 'Come on, I'll show it to you.'

Although it was a modern house, the garden was quite mature, having being cultivated since the first owners had moved in almost twenty years previously. It had a small but adequate lawn and a series of flagged areas punctuated with beds full of colourful blooms. At the far side of the garden was a recessed area housing an arbour, which was surrounded by shrubs and climbing plants, giving it a tranquil feel.

Ruby's mother walked over to the arbour and plonked herself down on the seat. She didn't say anything, but a pleasant smile graced her lips as she gazed around her. Eventually she stood up and shivered.

'You'll have to come round in the summer, Mam,' said Ruby. 'You can sit out then. We might even have a barbecue.'

'It's lovely,' she said, looking about her, and Ruby could have sworn she saw a tear in her eye.

Next, Ruby and Tiffany took them up to the master bedroom and Ruby proudly showed off the stunning fitted bedroom units, pulling open the door to a corner wardrobe.

'You'll get plenty of clothes in there,' said her mother. Then she looked around the rest of the fitted furniture. 'How many wardrobes do you need?' she asked.

Ruby and Tiffany laughed and then took them through to the en-suite bathroom followed by the other two bedrooms and, lastly, the family bathroom.

Ruby was amused by the next comment. 'But I thought you had a bathroom in there.'

'That's the en-suite, Mam. This is the main bathroom.'

Ruby could feel Tiffany's hand on the small of her back, out of view of her family. She smiled affectionately at her while her mother tutted and shook her head as though this level of extravagance was strange to her.

When they'd finally finished having a good look around, Ruby led them all back downstairs where they hovered in the hallway for a few moments before leaving.

'Well, what do you think?' she asked.

'It's well smart,' said Tyler. 'I wish I had an 'ouse like this.'

Ruby turned to her mother who nodded her head. 'I think you've done very well for yourself, Ruby,' was all she said but for Ruby it was enough. She could see that pride was oozing out of every pore in her body.

She tried to dismiss the fact that the pride she felt was based on lies. As far as Ruby was concerned, it didn't matter how she had achieved her financial status; the end result was just the same. And it was wonderful to see how proud she had made her family.

Aaron Gill looked over to his cell door to see the huge frame of a fellow prisoner, Mal, standing in the doorway. Gilly sat up in his bunk.

'Come in mate, shut the door,' he said, knowing he didn't want anyone to overhear them. 'What have you got for me?'

'Some info, but it'll cost.'

'No probs, it's all here,' said Gilly, referring to the cigarettes they had agreed in payment. 'But I want to hear what you've got first.'

Mal sat down on Gilly's bunk. 'She's still using the name Ruby,' he began.

'Yeah, and...?'

'She's running a brothel now, apparently.'

'Really?' said Gilly, annoyed that Crystal hadn't seen fit to share that information with him. 'How long's it been open?'

'Six months.'

'I wonder how the bitch managed to afford that.'

'She's the co-owner apparently but I don't know who the other owner is.'

'No, worries. That's not important. Where is it?'

'Manchester, above a nightclub called North. Have you heard of it?'

Gilly smiled. As a Manchester lad he knew the name straightaway. 'Oh yeah, I know it.'

'I can send some lads round if you like but it'll cost you more.'

'No, it's OK,' said Gilly. 'I want to sort this one out myself.' He reached under his mattress and took out the cigarettes then passed them to Mal.

'Cheers, mate. Anything else you want, just ask,' he said. Then, as he was about to leave Gilly's cell he stopped and asked, 'Haven't you got a few years to serve yet?'

'Yeah, that's right. I got a ten stretch and I've done three. I've kept my nose clean so I probably won't do all that but it'll still be a few years yet.'

'Ah, you'll have forgotten all about who grassed you up by then.'

'That's where you're wrong,' said Gilly. 'And thinking about how I'm gonna get my revenge on that vindictive bitch is all that's keeping me going. After all, I've got fuck all else to keep me busy in this shithole so I've got all the time I need to decide how I'm gonna fix her.'

39

August 2008

Ruby was with a client when she heard the buzzer sound. It was only the second time it had happened in almost a year of running the club. As part of the refurb, Ruby had had buzzers fitted in all of the rooms, which were connected to both the reception desk and her own area, Ruby's Dungeon She looked down at the black leather whip in her hand and quickly flicked her wrist till it swished through the air.

'Stay there!' she yelled at the man kneeling naked in front of her before she dashed from the room, confident that he would still be there when she returned. After all, he was one of her regulars and had been practising obedience for a while.

It didn't take Ruby long to run down the stairs and into the reception area, still carrying the whip. There she saw one of the girls managing the reception desk and she knew straightaway that Tiffany had gone to sort out whatever problem had arisen.

'Whose room is it?' she demanded.

'Pammy's,' said the girl.

Ruby dashed through the club in the direction of Pammy's room. She arrived to find a man hurling abuse at Tiffany while Pammy stood back from them, wearing no more than a hurt expression, her hand cradling the right side of her face.

'Just look at her, she's fuckin' fat!' hollered the man, waving his arm in Pammy's direction. 'I'm not paying full price for that! I want a reduction or one of the other girls.' He was standing there without his shirt on, but still wearing his trousers as though he'd had a change of heart mid-way through undressing.

'I've told you, no one else is available and we can't have you assaulting our girls so I want you to leave,' said Tiffany.

On hearing Tiffany's words and seeing Pammy's hand on her face, Ruby guessed what had happened. 'Has he hit you?' she asked, incensed.

Before Pammy had chance to speak, the man said, 'It was nothing. She shouldn't have been giving me grief, shouting her mouth off, right up in my fuckin' face.'

'He called me a fat cow!' shouted Pammy, the hurt evident in her tone of voice.

Ruby marched towards the man, pushing Tiffany out of the way and holding up the whip. 'Don't you fuckin' dare assault one of my girls!' she thundered. 'I don't give a shit what your problem is; you never hit one of my girls!'

'Well look at the fuckin' state of her,' said the man but, despite his confrontational words, Ruby could tell that he had become wary at the sight of the whip. 'You don't expect me to pay full rate for that, do you?' he asked almost beseechingly.

'I'm not interested in your bullshit!' yelled Ruby. 'You knew what size she was when you booked her. You're just fuckin' trying it on. For your information, Pammy is one of our most popular girls and you're lucky to spend any fuckin' time with her.'

'Pffft!' hissed the man.

Suddenly Ruby lifted the whip high and sliced it through the air so that it gave out a mighty cracking sound. The man was visibly shocked, his eyes growing wide as he quickly stepped back.

'Right, now are you gonna leave my premises like you've been told or do we have to fuckin' force you out?' she asked.

Despite his apparent concern at the sight of Ruby wielding the whip, the man must have thought he still had a strong argument and seemed to fancy his chances against a bunch of women. 'I'm going nowhere till I get what I came for. What about her?' he asked, nodding at Tiffany. 'Isn't she available?'

Without warning, Ruby brought the whip down swiftly on the man. It struck the top of his arm with several of the tail ends twisting round his body and biting into his back. The man yelled and gripped the top of his arm, instinctively advancing towards Ruby. Then he seemed to think better of it, and stopped where he was, his face a mix of pain and indignation.

Seeing his cowed reaction, Ruby bent to the ground and scooped up his shirt, throwing it at him while still clutching the whip in her other hand. 'Right, now fuck off!' she yelled. 'Unless you want more of the same.'

The man grasped at his shirt and pushed his arms through the sleeves, then grabbed his jacket and ran from the room without even bothering to fasten his shirt buttons. Ruby turned and watched him leave, feeling gratified as she spotted the blood seeping through the back of his shirt.

'And don't fuckin' bother coming back!' she shouted after him before turning to Pammy who had started to put her clothes back on with trembling hands. When Ruby saw the look of shame on Pammy's face it reminded her of how she'd felt as a child when people had looked down on her with a mix of pity and scorn. Her anger at the man was swiftly replaced by sympathy for Pammy.

'Are you two OK?' she asked. Both Tiffany and Pammy said yes even though Ruby could tell by looking at them that they were both shaken. 'Take no notice of that fuckwit!' she said to Pammy. 'We both think you're beautiful and so do lots of the clients too.'

As Tiffany nodded, Pammy managed a half-smile before Ruby said, 'Why don't you take the rest of the night off, Pammy? You've only got one more client booked in so you won't be losing much. And I'll not charge you for your room tonight so you won't be any worse off.'

'OK, thanks,' said Pammy, her voice tiny and shaking.

Ruby knew that, although Pammy had the strength of character common in most of the working girls, that cruel man had touched her sore spot, and she was on the verge of tears. Ordinarily, Pammy let everyone know how proud she was of her ample cleavage and generous curves, but Ruby could now see that it had all been an act.

Ruby knew too well that it didn't take much to undermine your confidence and take you right back to that place of insecurity and inadequacy. After all, it was the very place she had come from as a child when she felt inferior to all the other girls who always had more than her. Ruby crossed the room and put her arm around Pammy. 'Please don't let an arsehole like him get to you, Pammy. You just remember, you're beautiful in your own way.'

Then she and Tiffany left Pammy alone to shed a few private tears before she pulled herself together and shielded her insecurities behind a low-cut dress and a fresh application of makeup.

'You sure you're alright?' Ruby asked Tiffany later that night when her own client had left and she'd joined her partner at the reception desk.

'Yeah, fine now,' said Tiffany. 'I hope Pammy will be OK.'

'She'll be fine. You watch, girl, she'll come bouncing back through that door like nothing happened.'

'What about you?' asked Tiffany.

'I'm OK,' said Ruby. 'I can easily handle a little shit like him.'

'I noticed,' said Tiffany, laughing.

Afterwards, Ruby thought over what she had said to Tiffany about her ability to handle the awkward client and her mind drifted to the problems she'd had to deal with since the club had opened. As well as abusive clients and visits from the police, Ruby had had one of the more popular girls getting too cocky. She'd confronted Ruby, telling her she should be passing more clients her way until Ruby had told her to fuck off and see if she could do any better elsewhere. She'd lost a few clients as a result of the girl leaving but had soon found a replacement and gained new clients.

Yes, she'd had her share of difficulties in running a brothel but nothing major, and certainly nothing as bad as what she'd faced as a young girl working the streets of Manchester. She'd handled all the problems at the club with help from Tiffany, the love of her life. And, despite all the challenges, she still loved her status as manager as much as she had at the outset. It was her life. There was nothing she could think of that she would rather be doing. And she wasn't prepared to have it spoilt by anybody or anything.

40

August 1998

Trina had disliked the man straightaway. He had a superior air about him and, although he wasn't abusive as such, he talked down to her as though she was scum. He told her that he wanted full sex then, as soon as he'd parked the car in a secluded area, he got on with it in a cold, matter of fact way. That didn't bother Trina so much; she knew the drill by now and didn't expect clients to behave lovingly towards her. With clients like this one she detached herself emotionally and hoped for it to be over with as soon as possible.

But this client was a problem. To start with he had difficulty getting an erection. Trina offered to give him his money back and leave it at that but the client was emphatic that they should keep trying. Eventually he managed to perform, but it wasn't for long.

'I think we'd best call it a day,' said Trina.

'Oh no we won't! I haven't come here for nothing,' he said. 'You'll just have to help me out more.'

'That'll cost more then.'

He tutted. 'Just do it!'

But no matter how much Trina tried, it wasn't happening. She was relieved when the man zipped up his trousers and started the car engine, even though he scowled at her as though it was her fault. Trina was also perturbed at the way the man locked all the car doors before they set off.

They returned to Trina's usual spot and the man took out his wallet and flung two notes at her. She looked at the money. 'There's only fifteen pounds here. It's twenty-five for full sex,' she said.

'But it wasn't full sex, was it?' he snapped. 'And as you failed to satisfy me, I think I've been more than generous.'

Trina realised that the man was trying to shift the blame for his own inadequacy. His haughty tone annoyed her and she was tempted to retaliate. But then she remembered that he'd locked the car doors. The crafty bastard!

'Give it here then,' she said, holding out her hand.

Once the man had paid her, he unlocked the car doors and she jumped out onto the pavement. 'Bastard!' she shouted as he drove away. 'It's not my fault you can't fuckin' get it up.'

She continued hurling abuse at the man until his car disappeared into the distance. Even when she'd stopped shouting, she was still angry. *The stuck-up bastard!* It was bad enough that he hadn't paid her the full amount, but then to have the cheek to blame it on her was just too much.

Trina stood at her usual spot for a few minutes more, but the night was drawing on and, if she was honest with herself, she'd had enough. That last encounter had left her full of bitterness about men like him who thought they could treat her in whatever way they liked. And the lack of punters at this time only made her feel more deflated so she decided to call it a night.

As Trina headed angrily for home, she consoled herself by thinking about how she would put tonight's earnings in the hiding place where she had kept her money and other valuables for the last two weeks. Although that had put a stop to Shelley's stealing, she still hadn't paid back the money she owed her.

Then Trina remembered something. The necklace. She had been admiring it before she came out to work but she couldn't remember putting it back in her hiding place. She rushed home, desperately hoping it would still be there when she returned.

Back at the flat, Trina dashed into her bedroom and searched her dressing table for the ruby necklace, but there was no sign of it. She tried not to get too worked up. Perhaps she had put it away after all. But a search of her hiding place confirmed that the necklace had disappeared. She checked the rest of the room to be sure but couldn't find it anywhere. *Oh no!* Her lovely ruby necklace was gone.

Trina's anger of earlier resurfaced but she was also upset. That necklace had been special to her. *How could Shelley just take it?* Her upset was as much about Shelley's betrayal as it was about the necklace. Shelley had known how much the necklace meant to Trina and yet she had still stolen it.

Trina stomped through to Shelley's room determined to find out what had happened to her precious necklace. In a rage she began searching the room, dragging clothing from wardrobes then turning out drawers and tipping the contents untidily over the bed and floor. On top of Shelley's chest of drawers she found a box full of trinkets and she tipped that out but there was no sign of the ruby necklace. She was just about to search under the bed when she heard Shelley entering the bedroom.

'What the hell do you think you're playing at?' shouted Shelley.

This time Trina was too fired up to exercise restraint, unlike their previous confrontation. 'I'm looking for my fuckin' necklace, that's what I'm doing!'

Ignoring Shelley's angry protestations she continued to scour the room, withdrawing a plastic storage box from underneath the bed and slamming it on top of the mattress amongst the clothing and other items. As she removed the lid of the box, Shelley flew across the room and grabbed her arms, trying to stop her. Trina threw her off and riffled through the box while Shelley shouted and cursed.

Trina dragged out several empty containers and slung them across the room. Then she came across a cardboard gift box, the type that housed fancy toiletries, and she shook it. She could hear the sound of something inside and she pulled off the lid. And there, nestled in the decorative tissue paper at the bottom of the box, was Trina's ruby necklace.

'You fuckin' thieving bitch!' she yelled, launching herself at Shelley.

Livid by now, Trina punched and scratched at Shelley while Shelley tried vainly to defend herself.

'Get your fuckin' hands off me!' cried Shelley. 'Or you'll be looking for somewhere else to live.'

Her distraught words brought Trina to her senses and, noticing Shelley's tear-stained face, she stopped hitting her and stepped back. But she was still irate. 'Don't worry. I don't want to stay with a thieving piece of shit like you any longer! As soon as I find somewhere else to live, I'm out of here.'

She glared angrily at Shelley then picked up her necklace and marched from the room. Once she had calmed down a bit, Trina sat on the bed in her own room and thought about the situation she found herself in. Perhaps she had been hasty in telling Shelley she would leave. After all, she had no idea where she would go. But it was done now and she'd have to face the consequences. *Besides*, she thought, *surely it couldn't be as bad as sharing a flat with a thieving junkie.*

41

August 1998

For the next few days the atmosphere between the two girls deteriorated. Where Shelley had once been Trina's object of desire, now she could barely stand to look at her. They only spoke to each other when absolutely necessary and Shelley would often scowl until a stern look from Trina sent her scurrying away, afraid of repercussions.

Trina knew she couldn't carry on like this; she had to get out. So for the last few days she'd spent all her free time in search of somewhere to live. But it wasn't proving easy: the flats were too expensive and taking up a room in a shared house would be awkward, given the hours she kept.

At last she found a flat worth visiting. It wasn't too far away, situated above a shop in Old Trafford, and the rent was affordable so she made an appointment to view it. As she put down the phone to the estate agent, Shelley spoke to her.

'You got a viewing?' she asked.

'Yes, tomorrow afternoon,' Trina replied, surprised at Shelley's apparent interest.

'Will you still be going to work?'

'Yes, I'll go straight from the viewing.'

'OK. Let me know how you go on, won't you?'

Again Trina was surprised. Perhaps Shelley was regretting what she had done and didn't want her to leave after all. But it was too late. Trina knew she couldn't stay somewhere where none of her stuff was safe. And if Shelley's drug addiction was so bad that she was stealing from friends then there was no telling what else she might do to feed her habit. She needed to get out as soon as possible.

The following day Trina got up earlier than usual, eager to visit the flat before going off to work. As soon as she was ready, she jumped in a taxi and gave the driver the address. Although it was only five minutes away, Trina wasn't familiar with the area.

When she arrived, she got out of the cab and looked at the row of shops where the flat was situated. There was a bookmaker, off-license, hairdressers, two fast food outlets, and a newsagent on the corner. Although it wasn't yet evening, a small group of youngsters were already gathered outside the newsagents and they eyed her suspiciously as she looked up and down the row for the door number that was written on the small piece of paper she clutched.

Trina was relieved to find the number on a door next to the hairdressers. Before knocking, she looked up at the building. It was constructed from red brick and looked old, with a dormer window on the roof above each shop. The window frame above the hairdressers was painted white and she could see even from here that the paint was cracked and peeling. There was also a green patch of mould running from the gutter down to the sign above the hairdresser's shop, which spelt out 'Kuts Above' in large, faded red lettering.

Trina knocked on the door and was greeted by an estate agent. He was a young man with an effortless charm and an ingratiating smile, and Trina felt that his pleasant demeanour was perhaps overcompensating for something. She nodded politely and managed a faint smile but once inside the flat Trina understood what that something was.

The state of the exterior had acted as a precursor to the interior, which didn't get any better. Straightaway Trina noticed a musty smell as she followed the estate agent into the property, and it was far worse than the slightly musty odour she had detected the first time she visited Shelley's flat. She looked down the hallway, noticing that it was painted an insipid shade of pale blue with an old carpet that was bunched in parts and frayed in others.

In the living room somebody had made an attempt at brightness through the flowery curtains and papered walls. Unfortunately, that had been some time ago. The curtains were mustard coloured with sage-green leaves on the flowers and the paper wasn't just peeling; it actually had a hole which ran through to the plaster. On the floor beneath the hole Trina could see a tiny pile where the plaster had dropped onto the bare floorboards.

The state of the kitchen was just as Trina had anticipated; cupboards hanging at different levels with a hinge missing from one of them. In one corner was a stainless-steel sink unit, which was tarnished, and stained with what looked like paint. Trina couldn't think why as the flat didn't look as if it had been painted for decades. And the floor was covered in dusty, faded lino.

While he led her around the drab flat, the estate agent chatted away about its potential, and its proximity to bus routes and shopping facilities. Trina zoned out; her interest was already waning. Then he mentioned the bills, which were to be paid in addition to the rent. In her naivety Trina hadn't realised that the bills would have to be charged separately and with this revelation she quickly made up her mind.

'I don't want it,' she said abruptly.

'But you haven't seen the bedroom and bathroom yet,' said the estate agent. 'The bedroom's a good size.'

'I've seen enough, thanks, and I don't want it.'

The estate agent looked put-out, his smile now replaced with a grimace. 'Fair enough but I think you're making a huge mistake. You don't see many rental properties coming on the market at this price and it does have a lot of potential. You just need to see beyond the outdated décor.'

Trina was becoming irritated by the man's persistence. 'I said I don't want it. It needs too much work.'

She turned away from him and made her way along the hall and down the stairs, leaving the estate agent babbling away about the flat's supposed merits. Trina was disappointed and she couldn't wait to get away from the place. She had got her hopes up, anticipating that the flat would provide an escape from the tense situation with Shelley. But, unfortunately, it wasn't to be and Trina went to work that evening worried about her future living arrangements.

★

It was in the early hours of the morning when Trina returned home from work. As soon as she walked inside the flat, she knew something wasn't right. It was eerily quiet and the living room door had been left ajar as well as some of the other doors. But instead of hearing sound coming from the rooms, there was nothing. *Perhaps Shelley was already in bed*, she thought, but as she walked into the hall her footsteps seemed to echo.

Trina pushed open the living room door and was shocked at what she saw. Her breath caught in her throat and she instinctively covered her mouth with her hand. The room was practically bare. All the high-end furniture and electrical equipment had gone, including the TV. The only furniture that remained was the two battered old armchairs. Even the new cushions and television stand Trina had bought were missing.

Around the room were scattered letters with empty envelopes lying close by. It looked as if someone had been pulling them out of the envelopes then discarding any that didn't seem important. A bunch of newspapers and magazines, previously stacked at the side of the TV, were also scattered all over the floor.

Trina stepped further inside, taking in the state of the place. It felt hollow, the sound of her movements reverberating off the walls. But the heating was still on and the warmth felt at odds with the starkness of the room.

She dashed through the flat calling Shelley's name, but it was soon apparent that Shelley was no longer there. The kitchen was also half empty, most of the cupboard doors left open, although some basic pots and pans were still there and a few tins of food. Shelley had even had the cheek to leave a sink full of dirty pots!

Inside Shelley's bedroom it was the same story; anything of value was gone and the remaining items were discarded on the floor. Then a thought hit Trina with startling clarity. What about her own room? What if Shelley had found her hiding place? She rushed through the flat and over to the chest of drawers where she had hidden her valuables on the floor beneath the bottom drawer. But she was disturbed to find that all the drawers had been wrenched out and slung on the bed.

She raced over to the empty chest and looked inside, but there was nothing there. Everything was gone. Her jewellery. Her money. And the ruby necklace she loved so much. 'Fuck you, Shelley!' she howled as she tried to come to terms with what her one-time friend had done to her.

Then Trina collapsed onto the bed and sobbed as she hammered her fists into the mattress in frustration. 'Just wait till I get my fuckin' hands on that thieving little bitch!' she yelled, knowing that she would rather be pummelling Shelley's face than the mattress.

Shelley had evidently been planning this for some time, deliberately waiting till she knew Trina was going to be out for a while. Then she'd rushed through the flat grabbing anything of value and leaving anything that didn't matter to her.

No wonder she was so interested in Trina's viewing. It wasn't because she didn't want her to leave: it was because she knew Trina would be out of the flat for longer than usual, giving her time to empty the place of all the valuables.

Trina continued sobbing for some time as this realisation hit her. She felt betrayed, and by someone who she'd once thought so much of.

Once she was over the initial shock Trina thought about the wider implications. How the hell was she going to keep this place going on her own as well as keeping herself fed and clothed? And what if Shelley still owed rent? How was she going to pay that back?

She thought briefly about returning home but knew it wasn't what she wanted. Then she thought ironically about one of her mother's favourite phrases, *Be careful what you wish for, child*. Well, she'd certainly wished to have her own place. But not like this. Shelley had hurt her deeply and Trina knew she was unlikely to ever see her again. Neither would she recoup the money Shelley had taken or her precious ruby necklace.

42

October 1998

Trina was exhausted when she got up at midday. It was some weeks after Shelley's disappearance and was the fifth night in a row that she'd worked. Although she hadn't got to sleep till the early hours, Trina wanted to do a bit of cleaning before she went to work and then grab some shopping.

Ideally she would have liked to have taken the night off but it wasn't possible. Ever since Shelley had left, Trina had been putting in extra hours to ensure she earnt enough to live on.

Shelley's absence had been a revelation. When the landlord came to collect the rent, Trina discovered that not only had Shelley not paid the arrears but she'd also racked up a further month's rent. It meant there was a thousand pounds owing altogether. At first the landlord was hostile towards Trina, but when she'd explained the situation with Shelley and offered to pay extra each month towards the arrears, he had mellowed. Trina thought it was perhaps because she had paid something towards the arrears previously and he recognised her willingness to sort things out.

As if the rent arrears weren't bad enough, Trina also found out that most of the other bills on the flat were behind too. So, not only did she have to pay all the bills and her own living costs but she also had to catch up with the debts Shelley had left and replace a lot of the furniture and other items Shelley had taken.

Having all of these problems made her realise how difficult it must have been for her mother to run a home and provide for four children. And she was beginning to realise just how much she missed her mother and brothers. The few chores she'd had to do when she had been at home seemed nothing in comparison to having to run her own place and meet all the bills. But she couldn't go back home now; her pride wouldn't let her admit that she'd been foolish to leave.

Because of all the financial demands Trina was working extra hours, and she was finding it difficult. There wasn't as much custom in early evening or towards the end of the night so she had to find new places in which to solicit.

The more Trina had to work, the more she grew to detest what she did for a living; having to have sex with repulsive, smelly men who talked down to her and treated her roughly. And she felt resentful towards Shelley who hadn't told her any of this when she had enticed her into prostitution, probably so she'd have someone to help with the bills.

That night when Trina arrived at her usual spot, it took a whole half hour until she got her first customer. The night was chilly. Trina was wearing a short skirt to show off her long, toned legs and a bomber jacket with the zipper half open, revealing her cleavage. Her clothing didn't protect her very well from the cold weather and she was glad to get inside the stranger's car and warm her frozen thighs.

When the man brought her back, Trina asked him to drop her further up the road. She knew she wouldn't get much custom in her usual spot at this time in the evening so she wanted to stand nearer the centre of the red-light district where it was a bit busier. The other girls wouldn't like it, but she'd just have to take her chances.

Trina hadn't been there long when a hard-looking, petite blonde got out of a car and approached her. 'You here again?' she asked. 'I thought I'd fuckin' told you to hop it the other night.'

Trina scrutinised the girl who was so thin and frail looking that a gust of wind could easily have carried her away. There was no way she was going to let a skinny cow like this one intimidate her. Besides, she had to be where it was busy; she needed the money.

'And I told you to stick it,' she said. 'I've just as much fuckin' right to stand here as you have!'

'Oh, have you?' said the blonde. 'We'll soon fuckin' see about that!'

Trina ignored her and for a few minutes they competed for custom. Trina won the battle and she smiled smugly at the girl as her client sped away with her sitting in the passenger seat of his car. As Trina got down to business, she shrugged off the girl's threat.

It wasn't until she returned to the spot and the customer had driven away that the girl returned. But this time she wasn't alone. Trina gulped as she sized up the girl's friends. There were three of them and they were all substantially bigger than the blonde. Not only that, but they were carrying baseball bats. As she looked at the hostile expression on the face of the petite blonde, and saw her friends close in behind her, Trina knew she had a problem.

'This is her, the cheeky bitch!' said the blonde, pointing Trina out to a big girl with mousy hair, coarse features and a heavy, aggressive stride.

The big girl looked vaguely recognisable and as she stepped forward Trina guessed that she must have been their leader. Trina barely had a chance to register the appearances of the other girls as the leader sped towards her, yelling abuse and waving her baseball bat.

'It's OK, I'll go, I'll go,' yelled Trina, instinctively raising her arms above her head for protection.

But there was no time to escape or to talk her way out of things. Before she knew it, the girls had crowded round her and were beating her with their weapons. Trina felt the stinging blows to her arms, legs and back. Unable to dodge them, she crouched low to protect most of her body from the vicious attack. But she still felt the heavy impact of the baseball bats as each agonising strike sent waves of pain shooting through her.

Trina howled and pleaded with the girls to leave her alone. Her head was face down with her arms covering it and, although she couldn't see much, she could sense everything. Trina knew there was no point in fighting back; she was no match for four baseball bats, and raising her arms would just leave her more exposed. While the savage beating was taking place, Trina also felt a hand snaking through her pockets. Her heart plummeted as they reached inside her jacket and pulled out her cash.

Although the hiding was over in a couple of minutes, it seemed to last forever. Just as Trina felt she couldn't take any more she heard the sound of screeching tyres and the girls fled.

She remained crouched on the ground, her arms still trying to protect her head and face, afraid that the assault wasn't finished. Trina shuddered as she heard footsteps approaching. Then her sore and tender back stiffened as she prepared for another blow. But instead she heard the gruff sound of a man's voice.

'You alright, love?'

She looked up to see the imperfect features of a stranger hovering over her. Behind him was a car parked on the edge of the pavement, the lights still on and the driver's door open. She guessed he was a punter who had been kerb crawling. Feeling vulnerable, Trina got unsteadily to her feet while the man helped to support her.

'Jesus, they've given you a good going over, haven't they?' said the man.

Trina shrugged off his attentions, physically removing his hands from under her arms where he had been holding her. Then she straightened herself up.

'Yeah, but I'm OK.'

'You don't look it, love. Come on, let me drive you home.'

But Trina didn't trust him. People didn't do you favours for nothing in her world. 'No, I'm fine. I can get myself home. I don't live far.'

Trina backed away from the man then turned and walked off, feeling his eyes still on her for several seconds. Then she heard the sound of the man walking away followed by the slamming of a car door. She felt relieved. The unwanted attention from a stranger had put her on edge at a time when she was already feeling so defenceless.

She'd tried her best to remain upright as the man watched her but once she knew he was out of the way she gave in to the intense pain. She could feel it all over her body, even her face which she'd tried so hard to protect, and her nose was pumping blood. As she hobbled away, she became aware of more and more bruised and tender areas on her body. It felt as though each part of her was being hammered like a set of drums reaching a crescendo; the throbbing beat rapid and frenzied.

Trina felt sore, defeated and humiliated. It brought to mind that other time she'd been attacked when only a child, and she subconsciously fingered the scar on her cheek. Feeling the sting of a bruise she fought hard to contain her tears, silently cursing the cruelty of the girls and of those who had marked her once before.

When Trina reached home and examined her injuries, she was shocked. Her arms, legs and back were a mass of bruises. There was also a bruise on her left cheek in the same place as her scar and a cut on her wrist where a particularly hard blow had broken the skin. A trickle of blood was still coming from her nose.

The sight shook her and she could no longer hold back her tears. Hating herself for being so weak, she sat down on the edge of the bed and gave in to her emotions. Feeling sorry for herself as well as angry with the girls, she wondered desperately where she would go from here.

But her self-pity didn't last long because Trina was a fighter. She knew she couldn't go back to working the same patch. There was too much risk of running into the vicious bunch of girls again and, although Trina felt afraid, she tried not to admit it to herself. Instead, she reasoned that too many bruises were bad for business and losing her earnings just didn't make financial sense.

Trina therefore decided to try a new patch altogether. She'd heard mixed reports about Manchester. Aytoun Street was a good place to try from what she'd been told so maybe she would start there. She knew there would still be risks but there was no way she was going to leave herself so vulnerable again.

Trina had already had enough of troublesome clients even before the attack by the other prostitutes and she wasn't prepared to take shit from anyone any more. So she'd do what she should have done a long time ago and make sure she carried a weapon. And as anger from tonight's attack gripped her, Trina knew that, if necessary, she would be prepared to use it.

43

December 1998

It was during Trina's second night on Aytoun Street that she noticed another young girl watching her. She was obviously a street girl; her provocative clothing and gaudy makeup gave her away. Trina immediately became wary, thoughts of her beating at the hands of the group of prostitutes never far from her mind.

Trina weighed up her chances if things should turn nasty. The girl was only of average height so Trina wasn't worried about her. But what if she had friends nearby?

When the girl walked over Trina braced herself for an encounter. 'You new to this patch?' she asked.

'Yeah,' said Trina.

'What's your name?' she asked.

Trina whispered her name, remembering Shelley's rules never to let a client know her real name.

'Is that what the clients call you?' asked the girl.

'No, it's my real name but they don't know that.'

'I'm Laura,' said the other girl, 'but the clients don't know that either. You got a pimp?' she asked.

'No!' said Trina.

'You're joking, aren't you? You can't work this patch and not have a pimp. It's way too fuckin' dangerous.'

'I've managed up to now,' said Trina with her usual bravado.

'I know someone you could work for,' said Laura. 'He well looks after us. I can introduce you if you like.'

Trina thought for a moment. It would mean having even less money to herself and she didn't really like the idea of giving some of her earnings to a man. But then she reflected back on her beating at the hands of the other prostitutes and the difficult clients she'd had to deal with. She was tempted by Laura's suggestion but didn't know how she'd manage financially.

'I can't afford one. I'm already in the shit with money.'

'How come?'

'My flatmate pissed off and left me in a load of debt.'

'Really? Does that mean you've got a room to spare?' asked Laura.

'Yeah.'

'Where?'

'Whalley Range.'

'Oh, yeah. Well, it looks like it's your lucky day then cos I'm looking for somewhere to live. How much are you charging?'

'Half the rent of four hundred a month plus half the bills.'

Trina wished she hadn't said anything. After all, she'd only just met this girl and didn't know anything about her. But, there again, she was desperate. Although she'd been working long hours, she still hadn't paid off all the debts or replaced all the things Shelley had taken. Laura seemed alright, and she was certainly a lot friendlier than the prostitutes she'd met in Whalley Range. And, surely, she couldn't be any worse than Shelley?

'OK,' she said. 'Do you want to come and see it? Oh, and you'd have to buy your own food as well.'

'Sure. Is tomorrow OK?'

'Yeah, about three o'clock.'

'OK. Do you want to meet my pimp as well?'

'Yeah, could do.'

'OK, I tell you what, you give me the address of your place. I'll come round about half four or five and then take you to the Rose and Crown about six o'clock. A lot of us meet in there before we go to work and my pimp's always there. I'll take you over to him.'

'OK,' said Trina, managing a smile. This girl didn't seem too bad after all.

It was the following night and Trina and Laura were on their way to the Rose and Crown. Laura had already visited Trina's flat and, after showing her round, they had both decided that Laura would become Trina's new flatmate.

Trina had taken to Laura straightaway. She had a friendly, down to earth way about her and was easy to get along with. Trina could tell that, despite Laura having been on the game for a few months, she was still naïve in many ways. Having stayed on her friend's sofas for the past few months she didn't know much about running her own place and was still getting used to the adult world just like Trina was. Trina also realised that she had a far more dominant personality than Laura and she somehow felt that living with her wasn't going to be a problem.

They soon arrived at the Rose and Crown and Trina followed Laura inside. It was an old pub with dated furniture and an interesting mix of customers, who Trina's Aunty Tamara would have referred to as 'characters'. It also smelt of cannabis. Trina recognised the peculiar odour from some of her clients who smoked it. But none of that bothered her. She was used to this type of pub as she'd been to a few in Whalley Range, which had a similar clientele.

As soon as they got inside, Laura strode up to the bar where she joined a tall, skinny guy. 'Hi, Gilly. I've got someone to introduce you to,' she said, an ingratiating smile on her face. 'This is Trina and she'd like to come and work with us.'

Trina wished Laura hadn't have said that. It put her in a difficult position straightaway as she hadn't made her decision yet.

Gilly surveyed Trina from head to toe and she became conscious of his eyes roaming from her face to her breasts and then her thighs before travelling back up her body and finally making eye contact.

'Nice,' he said. 'What you having to drink, Trina?'

Trina replied abruptly, 'Lager.'

She had taken an instant dislike to this man. His cocky attitude. The way he looked at her. The way he spoke. And his smug good looks. While he had been inspecting her, she had also been examining him. He was definitely a looker but, even if she'd have been interested in men, he wouldn't have appealed. There was something superior about him.

Although he was dressed scruffily and tried to talk street, his refined accent spoke of a different class and gave away his background.

And the way he looked at her was dismissive. She felt just like a piece of meat for sale and he made no attempt to hide the fact that, in his eyes, that's exactly what she was. As soon as the drinks were served, he grabbed his own and left the girls' drinks on the bar for them to fetch.

'Come on. We'll go and sit at a table and have a chat,' he said, matter-of-factly.

Then, once Trina had joined him, he laid out the rules: what she should charge, how much she would earn, the hours she was expected to work and so on. Trina listened, but didn't take it all in. There was a lot of information and Gilly was whizzing through it too fast.

'Oh, and you'll have to change your name,' he said. 'I like my girls to sound exotic. That's why we chose the name Crystal for Laura. So, I think the name of a precious stone would be good, something like Sapphire, Emerald or Ruby. What do you think?'

'Ruby,' Trina answered straightaway, thinking of her precious necklace that Shelley had stolen.

'Nice one,' said Gilly before briefly mentioning his role as protector then holding his hand out for Trina to shake.

'You on board then?' he asked.

Trina hesitated a moment. But then she saw the encouraging smile on the face of her new-found friend and thought about the dangers of the street to a girl of seventeen. And something about the name Ruby drew her in; it made her feel special. She was now part of a group instead of being on her own.

'OK,' she said.

But she'd already decided this wasn't necessarily going to be a permanent arrangement. She'd gone it alone before, but she was nervous at the moment after her recent attack. She hated the thought of having to rely on a man to fight her battles so she'd use Gilly's protection for now and see how it went. Then, if things didn't work out, she'd drop him and go back to working the streets on her own. After all, just because she'd agreed to work for him for now, it didn't mean she had to work for him forever.

44

A few months after the client assault on Pammy, there was another significant visit to the club. This time, the visit involved two men rather than one. Tall, dark, good-looking and just a few years older than her, Ruby recognised them instantly even though she hadn't seen them for years. It was her cousins Josh and Calvin, and the shocked expressions on their faces told Ruby they also recognised her.

Ruby greeted them enthusiastically, pleased not so much at seeing them, but at the fact that she was now in a position of power. She still recalled their putdowns when she was a child and it felt good to be able to show them what she had achieved. Despite the feeling of exasperation that they had always engendered in her, she welcomed them with a smile.

'Hi, long time, no see. How are you two doing?'

'Good,' said Calvin, and Ruby could see that they were still sporting their designer gear and were heavily decked out in expensive-looking jewellery.

Just then a regular client approached the desk. 'Excuse me a minute,' she said to her cousins while she checked the

258

man in on the computer and directed him to the room of the girl he had booked.

Her manner was professional and the man was courteous and friendly towards her. While she was tending to him, she could see her cousins exchange looks, as though they were impressed with her status and the respect she commanded.

Once she had dealt with the man, she turned her attention back to her cousins. 'What are you up to nowadays?' she asked although she already knew the answer. She'd heard the rumours that they were now running a gang and were involved in all sorts of illegal operations.

'This and that,' said Calvin while Josh remained tight-lipped, seemingly embarrassed at being spotted in such a place by a member of his family.

'Good, well it looks as though it's paying off anyway,' she said, curling a finger under one of Calvin's gold chains and lifting it towards her to examine.

'Oh yeah, it always does,' said Calvin. 'Anyway, what about you? Is this your place?'

'Sort of. I'm the manager and I have half the profits. I've just bought my own house too.'

'Really?' asked Josh, his embarrassment temporarily forgotten. 'Where are you living?'

'Altrincham,' said Ruby, smugly.

'Wow! Nice one. And how did you cop for this?' he asked, his eyes taking in his surroundings.

Ruby laughed. 'Probably the same way you copped for all your designer gear and gold. Hustling.'

Her two cousins couldn't resist joining in with her laughter. 'Nice one, cuz,' said Calvin. 'It looks as though you've done well.'

Ruby felt a sense of pride when she thought about all the times her cousins had put her down as a kid and now, here they were, admiring what she had achieved.

'Thanks,' she said. 'It pays anyway, and I enjoy it.'

'How's the family?' asked Calvin.

'Good. Ellis and Jarell have left home now and got their own places. There's only Tyler still at home with my mam.'

'Is she alright?'

'Yeah, fine. Same old, y'know. What about your mam and dad?'

'Yeah, they're great,' said Calvin.

'All this talk of their families suddenly put Ruby on her guard. 'Please don't let any of them know about my job, by the way. I'd hate it to get back to my mam. Y'know what she's like.'

Calvin smiled, cheekily. 'Sure. We wouldn't want any of the oldies knowing what we get up to either.'

'I think they've already got a good idea,' laughed Ruby.

She couldn't help thinking what her mother's reaction would be if she knew she was running a brothel and her two wayward cousins had just called in as customers.

'You ever get any bother?' asked Josh.

Ruby shrugged. 'Sometimes, but it's nothing I can't handle.'

'Must be hard for a woman though,' he commented and Ruby felt that familiar irritation from her childhood at his dismissive attitude.

'I manage OK,' she said. 'Anyway, come on; let me introduce you to the girls.'

'Oh, we're only here to suss the place out,' said Josh, and Calvin looked at him pointedly.

'It's OK,' said Ruby. 'There's no shame in visiting a brothel, y'know. You'd be surprised at the men we get in here, and they're not all seedy old men in anoraks either.'

'Come on then,' said Calvin to Josh. 'What are we waiting for?'

Sometime later when her cousins were ready to leave, they came across to the reception desk to have a few words with Ruby before they went. Calvin had a smile on his face but Josh was looking sheepish.

'We're off now, cuz. See you around some time,' said Calvin.

'Sure, feel free to call in any time. It's no problem,' Ruby replied.

'OK,' said Calvin and, as he turned to go, Josh leant into the desk and said in a low voice. 'If you ever do have any problems, you can always give us a ring. Let me give you my number.'

Ruby remembered her irritation of earlier. There was no way she would have them thinking she needed their help! It was about time they knew she was just as capable as any man.

'No, it's fine,' she said. 'Like I said before, there's nothing I can't handle.'

Overhearing the conversation, Calvin said, 'Come on, cuz, you never know. Besides, even if you don't need any help you can put our numbers in your phone and let us have yours. Then we can always ring and let you know if we're coming by so you can save your best girls for us.'

He grinned lasciviously and Ruby felt a sense of revulsion,

but she passed him a slip of paper and a pen. Business was business, after all. Calvin scribbled both his and Josh's numbers down and passed the paper back to her.

'Cheers,' she said before they said their final goodbyes and left.

After they had gone she reflected on their visit. How times had changed! They were no longer the annoying boys she had grown up with. Instead they seemed to respect her and all she had achieved, although Josh still seemed to think her abilities as a woman were limited. Nevertheless, it was good that they wanted to help her, which was more than they had done when she had been attacked as a child. Perhaps they were growing up at last.

She punched the numbers into her phone; maybe it would be good to keep in touch. They were her cousins when all said and done. And besides, although she was loath to admit it, there might just be a time when she would need them. After all, this was a high-risk business and Ruby knew as well as most that she had been lucky up to now not to encounter any serious problems.

45

April 2011

Ruby greeted Victor with a smile as he walked into the waiting area where she was sat chatting with two of her girls. Today he wasn't here just to discuss business. He was here for a session with Ruby and his face lit up when he noticed that she was already dressed in her dominatrix gear of black rubber catsuit and thigh-high boots.

Ruby's Massage Parlour had now been open for over three and a half years and, although Victor paid occasional visits to the other girls, it was the sessions with Ruby that he enjoyed the most. Ruby knew exactly what she needed to do to satisfy Victor's particular urges and her ability to meet his requirements kept him coming back for more.

Ruby got up from her seat. 'You ready?' she asked.

'I need to have a chat with you first,' he said, his expression grave.

'OK, can't we chat upstairs?' asked Ruby.

'I'm afraid not, no. I wouldn't want anything to distract us from business.'

Victor smiled but it looked forced, unlike his usual eager

expression just before a session. She led him to a spare room, guessing that he had something serious to discuss.

'Well, what is it?' she asked.

Victor came straight to the point. 'We need to start charging the girls more for the rooms so we can maximise profits.'

'But why?'

'Like I've just said, we need to maximise profits.'

Ruby noticed that his whole persona had changed; instead of the meek, subservient man that entered her dungeon, he was forceful and determined, his features rigid, his shoulders back and his chest puffed out. It made her realise how he must appear to others when he was conducting business. 'But we're making enough,' she said.

'Enough isn't what I'm looking for. That's not what business is about.'

'But it'll upset the girls.'

'Never let sentiment cloud your judgement, Ruby. That's one of the first rules of business. I thought you were strong-willed, not someone who the girls can walk all over.'

'I am!' she snapped, insulted at his implication that she was a soft touch.

'Then do as I say. Oh, and I want us to start charging the clients for coffee and tea. Some of them are taking advantage. I've noticed how much we're going through. In fact, the girls will have to pay too.'

'That's ridiculous! And how would I do it anyway? It's not a coin operated machine.'

'For heaven's sake! Use your imagination. Why do you think I put you in charge? Stick some signs up and a box to collect their money, or something. Oh, and make sure the girls know.'

Ruby wasn't happy. 'I don't like this, Victor. It's like you're winding people up for no reason.'

'I've told you, Ruby, it isn't about sentiment, it's about business, and many businesses fail because the owners are too soft with their employees and customers. I thought you were strong, that's why I chose you.'

Ruby wanted to retaliate but the backhanded compliment had floored her. She knew that to continue arguing would make him think she was doing it for the wrong reasons; because of sentiment or whatever. And she needed to prove that she wasn't soft. So, even though the anger was festering inside her, she kept her temper and agreed to his wishes.

When they'd finished their meeting, she led him upstairs and into Ruby's Dungeon where she soon adopted her fierce Mistress Ruby persona. Victor had changed too. Gone was the ruthless businessman and he had once again become the subservient little man who would do anything she demanded. But Ruby was still annoyed; she hadn't forgotten the way he'd spoken down to her and almost forced her to agree to his wishes. Twenty minutes later she had him tied to a stool wearing a gimp mask and chastity device with his hands strapped tightly behind him while she smacked his back with a wooden paddle.

As she increased the strokes of the paddle Ruby could feel Victor's mounting excitement and, after a while, he struggled to grasp his genitals and release his pent-up frustration. But the bonds around his wrists and the metal chastity device prevented him.

Ruby smiled to herself in amusement; she enjoyed this part of the job where she had complete control over the clients and at the moment it was giving her an outlet for her anger. She would time it just right, till the clients felt they could stand it no longer then she would release them from their shackles and allow them to masturbate.

But Victor was nowhere near ready yet, and she still hadn't started with the leather whip. She finished with the paddle, allowing him a few moments to recover while she walked tantalisingly around him and selected a whip from the rack, running it through her fingers while he watched in keen anticipation.

Victor was still struggling, his hands pulling against the bonds that held them tight, and he was murmuring as though he was trying to tell her something. But the gimp mask made his words sound distorted and she couldn't tell what he was trying to say. Ruby didn't care anyway; he deserved to be punished after the way he'd spoken to her. Then he started rocking backwards and forwards, his hands still pulling against the restraints.

'Well, well, Victor. You are excited tonight, aren't you?' she teased as she brought the whip down on his backside.

Victor's rocking became more frantic, and Ruby wondered for a moment whether she had overdone it. Normally she could gauge how far to go by his level of twitchiness but this rocking was a new thing and it unsettled her for a moment. But then she realised she was overreacting. She couldn't have overdone it. She'd hardly got started yet. Usually she would increase the intensity of the lashes till she felt the client had had enough. And with Victor, this would generally take a while.

But as his reaction became more intense, she stopped for a moment, shocked. Ruby realised she had a problem just as Victor's rocking became so frenzied that he lost his balance and keeled over onto his side. Then he tried to bring his knees up to his chest as though he was in pain.

In a panic, Ruby rushed to remove the gimp mask. 'Are you alright, Victor?' she cried.

Victor was struggling to breathe and he couldn't get his words out. He was still trying to prise his hands from the bonds so Ruby untied them. As soon as his hands were freed Victor clutched his chest.

'Oh shit!' muttered Ruby, worried that her temper had perhaps made her go harder on him than she realised.

By the time she suspected that Victor was having a heart attack, it was too late. He was already unconscious.

In her panic, Ruby left Victor where he was, and locked up the dungeon while she dashed to the reception desk to see Tiffany.

'What's wrong?' asked Tiffany, concerned when she saw the alarmed expression on Ruby's face.

'We've got a big fuckin' problem!' said Ruby, panting and looking around to make sure nobody was listening. Pammy was the only girl now sitting in the waiting area and Ruby hoped she couldn't hear as she leant in to Tiffany and whispered. 'It's Victor. I think he's had a heart attack.'

Tiffany was so shocked by what Ruby was telling her that she spoke louder than Ruby would have liked. 'What? You're joking!'

'Shush,' said Ruby, whispering, 'I wish I fuckin' was!'

'So, where is he now? Is he alright?' asked Tiffany.

Ruby shook her head, feeling tears cloud her eyes as she said in a shaky voice. 'I think he's dead. He keeled over. And then he couldn't breathe. Then he stopped breathing altogether. And now, I don't know what the fuck to do!'

Ruby was normally the one in control, but now she was in a total panic about Victor and she was glad she had Tiffany to lean on.

'And where the fuck is he?' Tiffany asked again.

'I've left him upstairs.'

'You're joking! He might need medical attention.'

'I didn't know what the fuck else to do! And I think it's a bit too late for a doctor...' She could feel a sob catch in her throat as she added, 'I think he's dead, Tiff... seriously. What the fuck am I gonna do?'

Tiffany placed a reassuring hand on top of Ruby's. 'OK, let me think,' she said, glancing over Ruby's shoulder to see Pammy walking up to the desk.

'Is everything alright?' she asked.

'Yeah, sure,' said Tiffany, but Ruby gave things away when she burst into tears. 'She's just had a bit of a shock, that's all,' Tiffany added.

'What kind of a shock? Is it something to do with Victor?' asked Pammy who knew Ruby had taken Victor up to her dungeon. 'He hasn't tried to harm you, has he? Because, if he has, me and Tiffany will help you sort him out, Ruby. I don't give a shit if he owns the place. I know you'd do it for any one of us.'

Pammy's compassionate words were only making Ruby more upset so Tiffany spoke for her. 'No, it's nothing like that.'

'Well, what's wrong then? And where's Victor? I didn't see him leave.'

Ruby didn't know whether it was because of Pammy's sympathetic approach, or the fact that she already knew too much but, for whatever reason, she decided to share what had happened.

'It is to do with Victor,' she sobbed while Tiffany flashed her a warning glance. 'I think he's dead, Pammy. And I don't know what the fuck to do!'

'Oh shit!' said Pammy. 'What happened?'

'Heart attack, I think. And now the bloody cops will be all over the place.'

'But it's not your fault, Ruby,' said Pammy. 'He could have gone at any time.'

'The police aren't gonna see it like that though, are they? Especially when they see what I've got upstairs.'

'OK,' said Pammy, managing to stay surprisingly calm in the midst of Ruby and Tiffany's panic. 'Here's what we'll do...'

She leaned conspiratorially towards Ruby and Tiffany but, just at that moment, Rose emerged from her room with a client. Tiffany bid him goodbye while Rose went back to the waiting area, but Ruby remained with her back to them, afraid they would see her tears and wonder what was wrong.

'You stay and manage the desk, Tiffany, so it doesn't look as though anything's wrong,' whispered Pammy. 'Ruby, you come to my room while we have a chat. I'll fill you in on it later, Tiffany.'

At a loss for what else to do, Ruby followed Pammy to her room and listened while she outlined her plan.

46

April 2011

After Pammy had spoken to Ruby about the situation with Victor, she went back to the waiting area and chatted to the other two girls who were now there. She was doing her best to act normal. Meanwhile, Ruby went to join Tiffany at the reception desk and quietly filled her in on their scheme.

But before Ruby had chance to act on Pammy's scheme, Crystal came into the club. She was wearing a grave expression and Ruby guessed that she hadn't come with good news. She watched Crystal as she approached the reception desk looking shifty, her eyes flitting around.

Crystal's lips were clenched tightly, her eyes narrowed, as she took a deep breath and then said. 'I need to have a word with you, Ruby, in private.'

Ruby sighed. 'Is it important, Crystal? Only it's a bit full-on here tonight.'

'Oh yeah,' said Crystal. 'It's something you'll definitely want to know about.'

Ruby turned to Tiffany. 'Will you mind reception while I go and have a word with Crystal?'

'Sure, no problems.'

'Oh, and tell Pammy we'll sort that problem out as soon as I'm back.'

'Come on, we'll find a room that isn't being used,' said Ruby.

As they made their way to the vacant room, Ruby's mind flashed through a few different scenarios. Knowing that Crystal still worked the streets, she wondered if she might have encountered a problem that she needed help with. Her brain hadn't focused on many other possibilities in the short time it took to get there.

Once they were inside and sitting down on the bed Crystal sighed and pursed her already tightened lips. 'It's Gilly. He's got a parole hearing soon. He thinks he's got a good chance of being released cos he's kept his nose clean while he's been inside.'

'Shit!' said Ruby, and her mind flashed back to the look of hatred Gilly had given her on the day he'd been sent down for GBH against Crystal. She knew he'd be released eventually and, if she was honest with herself, she'd been dreading it. Ruby wasn't frightened easily, but there was something evil about Gilly that disturbed even her.

'The thing is,' said Crystal, looking even more ill at ease if that was possible, 'I went to visit him a couple of days ago, and he's still saying he'll get you back for grassing him up.'

Ruby felt a chill but she put on a brave face. 'Will he?' she demanded. 'Well, we'll soon fuckin' see about that! You tell him that if he takes one fuckin' step near me I'll cut off his balls and feed them to him.'

Crystal shifted in her seat. 'OK. I'm just giving you the message,' she said. 'It's not my fault.'

But Ruby's emotions were bubbling up inside her. Fear. Dread. Anger. And, at the moment, some of that anger was directed at Crystal as Ruby thought about how foolish she'd been to stand by Gilly after what he'd done to her.

Ruby got up off the bed they'd been sitting on so that she was now towering over Crystal. 'I don't want that fuckin' head-case anywhere near me. And, if you've got any sense, Crystal, you'll stay the fuck away from him too!'

She stormed out of the room, leaving Crystal with her mouth hanging wide open. Ruby hadn't waited for her response. She knew too well that, no matter what Gilly had done, Crystal would still be foolish enough to be waiting for him when he was back on the outside.

Ruby arrived back at the reception desk, relieved to find that Pammy was the only person now in the waiting area. She watched Crystal walk past on her way out of the club and she and Tiffany said their goodbyes.

'Is everything OK?' asked Tiffany.

Ruby shook her head. 'Not really. I'll tell you later.'

Then, with Crystal gone, Ruby looked over at Pammy and, on receiving her cue from her, Ruby quickly ran to the club's entrance and locked it so no more clients could come inside. She knew they had a window of at least half an hour in which to act before the girls had finished with their clients.

Ruby raced back to the reception desk where Tiffany and Pammy were already waiting for her. 'Ready?' she asked, and they both nodded. 'Right, let's go. And let's hope that nobody comes out of any of those rooms and susses what we're up to.'

The three of them rushed up the stairs and into Ruby's Dungeon. The sight of Victor on the floor, still naked and wearing the chastity device, brought tears to Ruby's eyes. But she contained herself while they did what needed to be done. She could see the look of shock on Tiffany and Pammy's faces and, as she took in the sight of Victor, his flesh already beginning to lose its colour and his features slack, there was now no doubt in her mind that he was dead.

Ruby tried to block out what she was seeing as she removed the chastity device and put Victor's underpants back on. The three of them lifted him and between them they managed to get him downstairs. When they reached the door at the bottom Ruby had a quick look round to make sure the coast was clear. Then they dragged Victor into Pammy's room and plonked him face down on the bed.

Tiffany raced back upstairs to get Victor's clothes while Ruby and Pammy covered his lower half with towels and smeared massage oil over his back.

When Tiffany came back into the room, Ruby said, 'Right, he's ready. Let's do it.'

Then Ruby went back downstairs to unlock the front door of the club while Tiffany took up her place at the reception desk, leaving Pammy in her room with Victor. Within a minute Ruby was seated at the reception desk alongside Tiffany while they waited for Pammy to act.

It was another two minutes and a client had just approached the reception desk when Pammy ran out of her room screaming. 'Oh my God!' she yelled. 'I think Victor's dead.'

'What?' asked Ruby and Tiffany, acting suitably shocked, before running into Pammy's room to inspect the body.

Ruby came running out again. 'Jesus, I think he is!' she shouted. 'What the fuck happened?'

By this time, they had made so much commotion that two of the girls emerged from their rooms with their perturbed clients following behind. Word soon spread and within minutes a crowd of girls and clients had gathered in the reception area, sharing their shock and abhorrence at the way in which their owner had died whilst having a massage from Pammy.

Ruby rang the emergency services and reported what had happened while the clients fled the building, worried about being caught in such a place. She gave all the girls the rest of the night off and stuck a notice on the outside door to let any clients know that they were closed for the evening due to unforeseen tragic circumstances.

That would prevent having clients asking about their various services while the police were there, thought Ruby as she hid the key for her upstairs room somewhere where no one would ever find it, disconnected the phone on the reception desk and waited for the police to arrive.

It was the end of the night. The police had been and gone, and the only people remaining in the club were Ruby, Tiffany and Pammy.

'You sure you'll be alright now?' Pammy asked Ruby as she put her coat on.

'Yeah sure, you get yourself home. Oh, and thanks for everything, Pammy.'

'It's no problem,' said Pammy, with a faint smile. 'You've always looked after us girls and I know you would have done it for any of us.'

Ruby could feel her eyes cloud with tears again but she fought them back. Pammy seemed to realise that Ruby didn't want to give in to tears, and she quickly made her way to the exit, saying, 'If you need anything else, just ask.'

Once she had left, Ruby turned to Tiffany. 'Jesus Christ! I could do with a fuckin' drink after tonight.'

'Me too,' said Tiffany. 'Do you think the police bought our story?'

'I fuckin' hope so...' Then Ruby became pensive before adding, 'It should be OK. Don't forget, they've got evidence from all the other girls who saw Pammy run out of her room in shock, so that should back up what we've told them. And, thank Christ, they didn't ask to look upstairs. Even if they think we're running a brothel, they can't prove it without seeing the dungeon.'

'Looks like we're home and dry then,' said Tiffany.

'Oh, I wouldn't say that.' Ruby spoke ominously. 'We've still got other problems to deal with.'

'What do you mean?'

'I'll tell you when we get home,' said Ruby. 'I've had enough of this place for tonight.'

47

April 2011

When they eventually arrived home from the club it was the early hours of the morning. Ruby and Tiffany were so tired that they tumbled straight into bed and Tiffany was asleep within seconds. But Ruby couldn't settle as thoughts of Victor and Gilly whirled around inside her head.

By the time she had managed to grasp some sleep and woke up to find her partner in the kitchen preparing a late lunch, it seemed that Tiffany had forgotten all about Crystal's visit as all her chat related to the situation surrounding Victor's death. Ruby decided not to mention what Crystal had said unless Tiffany asked, as she didn't want to worry her.

It was a few days later when Tiffany finally broached the subject. They'd just got home from work. It had been a busy night and they decided to have a quick nightcap in the lounge before going to bed.

'You haven't been right for days,' said Tiffany as she poured the drinks. 'Is it about what happened to Victor or is there something else worrying you?'

Ruby sighed. At first she deliberated over how much to tell Tiffany, but after the immense stress of the last few days she decided that she really should confide in her partner. After all, the situation with Gilly might mean Tiffany could be in danger, so it was only fair to warn her.

'Come on, let's sit down so we can talk,' she said, her voice sounding downbeat.

Tiffany picked up on Ruby's glum mood as she followed her to the sofa, her face full of concern.

'Well, for a kick off,' began Ruby, 'now Victor's dead, how the hell are we supposed to keep the club running?'

'Shit, I didn't think of that,' said Tiffany. 'Surely we'll be able to sort something out.'

Ruby didn't reply. Instead she put her head forward and ran her hands through her hair. Then she looked up at Tiffany. 'There's more.'

'Go on,' said Tiffany. 'Is it to do with Crystal's visit? I forgot to ask you about her with everything else that's been going on. How was she anyway?'

'Same as usual,' said Ruby, sounding subdued. Then she cleared her throat. 'She told me something while we were alone... It's Gilly. It looks like he's gonna be released soon.'

'Shit! When?'

'I'm not sure. He's got a parole hearing soon and from what Crystal says, he thinks he'll be released cos he's kept his nose clean while he's been inside. According to her,' Ruby continued, her tone now sharper, 'he's coming for me when he gets out. He wants his revenge for grassing him up.'

'Shit,' said Tiffany, again. 'Why didn't you tell me? When's the hearing?'

'I'm not sure,' said Ruby, ignoring Tiffany's first question. 'I was that bloody worked up when she told me that I didn't think to ask. Plus, I had Victor on my mind. But it's not far off from what she said.'

'Jesus, no wonder you're stressed! I'd be scared too. The guy's a nutcase from what you told me.'

Ruby didn't bother correcting Tiffany's assumption that she was scared; her girlfriend was one of the few people who saw Ruby with her guard down. Instead she said, 'I'm fuckin' angry too. I might have grassed him up, but I had a good reason for it. The man's a fuckin animal! If it hadn't been for me, Crystal would have died in that dingy back alley and there's no way I could let a nutcase like him carry on roaming the streets.

'What really pisses me off though is that Crystal's daft enough to still put up with him after what he's put her through. And no matter how many times I tell her, it doesn't make any fuckin' difference! You'd have thought she'd have taken the chance to get away from him while he was inside. But no, not Crystal.'

When she'd given Ruby chance to finish her rant, Tiffany patted her shoulder and said, 'Eh, you don't know if she will take him back.'

'Oh, I know alright. It was written all over her face.'

Tiffany now ran her hand down Ruby's arm, attempting to comfort her as she said, 'Try not to worry, Rubes. It might be an empty threat.'

'You don't know him. The guy's a fuckin' psycho! And don't forget what he did to Crystal.'

Tiffany frowned. 'Well, at least now you know, you can be prepared for him.'

Ruby didn't reply. She just screwed up her face while she picked at the cushion to the side of her.

'Oh, I forgot to mention,' said Tiffany, changing the subject. 'A letter came for you this morning. I forgot to give it you before we went to work.'

Tiffany got up from the sofa and quickly went to fetch the letter. Ruby felt a pang of guilt about her outburst, knowing that Tiffany was anxious to placate her. When Tiffany returned with the letter and handed it to her Ruby slid her finger under the seal and pulled the letter out.

It was on a solicitor's letter-headed paper and Ruby quickly scanned the contents, curious as to why a solicitor would write to her. By the time she reached the end of the letter a relieved smile replaced her angry look of earlier.

'What is it?' asked Tiffany.

Ruby looked up at her, the smile on her face now wider. 'Good old Victor,' she said. 'He's only gone and left me the massage parlour.'

'Yes!' shouted Tiffany, punching the air with her fist then getting up from the sofa and jumping up and down while cheering.

When Ruby didn't join in with her enthusiasm she sat back down and said, 'Sorry, poor taste. I'm sorry he's dead, but it does get us out of the shit, doesn't it?'

'Yeah,' said Ruby. 'He did right by me. And, d'you know, he might have been weird but I'll miss him in a way. Still, it's a relief to know I'm still in control.'

'Yeah, course it is,' said Tiffany. 'So why don't we celebrate? Maybe we could do something special on our next night off. I'm sure Victor wouldn't have minded.'

Ruby tried to cheer up, not wanting to spoil Tiffany's

happiness, and knowing she was trying to take her mind off things. But it was difficult to relax and share in her girlfriend's joy, not when she knew that a short time from now a violent man would be on the loose and gunning for her.

48

June 2011

Things at Ruby's Massage Parlour had been going fine in the few weeks since Ruby had found out she was the new owner. Because Ruby had always been the face of the club, none of the clients knew things were any different. The girls knew Victor was the previous owner but Ruby wouldn't have expected them to share that knowledge. She had therefore managed to retain all of her clients. This included Ruby's cousins who had become regulars ever since the first time they had walked through the doors.

The only fly in the ointment, as far as Ruby was concerned, was her anxiety regarding Gilly. His parole hearing had now taken place and he had been given a release date, which was fast approaching. Crystal hadn't told her the exact date and, although Ruby had asked her to let her know as soon as he was out, she suspected that Crystal might not bother as her first loyalty was to Gilly.

With Gilly's release imminent, Ruby had become hyper alert and distrustful of any new person who came into the club, wondering if they could be in any way connected to

Gilly. So, when two strangers walked in and started looking around at the girls, Ruby was suspicious straightaway.

They were both dressed in sporty designer gear and baseball caps and, although the weather wasn't particularly warm, they were both wearing tight fitting tee shirts, showing off their muscles.

One of them was below average height and of medium build, his huge biceps overcompensating for his lack of height or frame. He obviously put a lot of hours in at the gym. The other one had the height and frame to match the muscles, standing at over six feet and wearing a beard and a scowl. The smaller man seemed to be the leader of the two and he led the way across the reception area, strutting over to the desk.

'Who's in charge here?' he asked.

'Me,' said Ruby, her back stiffening as she sensed trouble, and got out of her seat.

'Aah, you must be Ruby then.' As he spoke, he turned to his friend and sniggered.

At first his reference to her name unnerved her until Ruby realised that as the brothel was called Ruby's Massage Parlour it was an easy assumption to make. But his next words unsettled her even more.

'So, you're the new owner now old Victor's popped his clogs, are you?'

Ruby bristled. There was no way that was common knowledge, other than amongst the girls. Victor had always taken great care to keep his name out of things. But somehow this guy knew the situation, and it wasn't a good sign.

'That's right,' she said, fixing him with a hard stare.

'Right, well in that case, it's you that we come to for our money now.'

'What are you on about?'

The man tutted and rolled his eyes as though she was being dense. 'We're the security firm for this place. Victor used to pay up regular as clockwork, but we ain't had fuck all since he snuffed it so let's stick to the same arrangement, eh? I don't want you giving us any problems.'

'And what do I get in return?' asked Ruby, flabbergasted at first because, despite her experience as the madam of a brothel, she wasn't very familiar with security firms up to now.

'Our fuckin' protection, of course,' said the smaller man, becoming confrontational. 'If you don't pay it, we won't be able to protect you from any problems, will we?' He looked knowingly across at his friend then sneered before continuing. 'Gangs raiding the premises, ripping the place up, beating up customers, maybe even hurting you and your girls, if you get my drift.'

As he spoke he grabbed hold of Ruby's chin and lifted it. 'Know what I mean, babe?'

Because of her height advantage Ruby soon escaped his clutches, stepping back and squaring her shoulders whilst glaring at him. 'Get off my fuckin' premises!' she yelled. 'How dare you come here and threaten me and my girls!'

There were several girls and two customers sitting in the waiting area and the sound of Ruby's raised voice drew their attention. The small man glanced across, his expression serious, as he realised they'd been sussed. His type of business relied on covert threats without a room full of witnesses. He shifted uncomfortably then scowled at Ruby before lowering his voice and growling at her.

'You'll regret this!' he said. 'We'll be back with our boss to see if he can talk some fuckin' sense into you so you'd better be ready.'

Then he quickly fled the building with his goon following behind.

The threat had bothered Ruby and an hour later she was still jittery when she received a call on her mobile, the sudden ringing making her jump. She looked at the display and saw that the call was from Crystal so she pressed the call receive button.

'Hi, you alright?' asked Crystal once Ruby had answered the phone.

'Yeah fine. Are you OK?'

'Alright...' Then she paused momentarily before saying the next words, 'Ruby, I'm just ringing to let you know that Gilly's being released tomorrow.'

'Shit!' said Ruby who then quickly tried to recover herself as she saw a client approaching the reception desk. 'Crystal, I've got to go,' she said. 'But thanks for letting me know.'

Once Ruby had dealt with the client, her mind switched back to the call from Crystal then to her visit earlier that night, and she felt overcome by dread. The thought that she had been targeted by a protection racket terrified her. From her limited knowledge about them she knew they were bad news and, although she'd seen them off for now, she was worried that they'd soon be back for their money. Then there was Gilly to contend with. He was bad enough on his own without having any other problems.

Ruby would have liked to have confided in Tiffany straightaway. But it was Tiffany's night off and Ruby knew that she would be having some much needed sleep by now. She therefore decided she would tell her about the problems the following day. Even though Ruby was the strong one in the relationship, it always helped to talk things through with her girlfriend who would offer comfort. She daren't tell anyone else; she didn't want to worry the girls with this new threat to the business.

Ruby's anxious thoughts wouldn't go away. For the rest of the night she remained on edge and by the end of her shift she was glad to lock up and go home. But as she made the journey to her luxury home in Altrincham, Ruby still felt anxious and downhearted. After things had been going so well, she couldn't believe that in the space of one night, things had taken such a drastic change for the worse.

49

June 2011

Ruby had been churning things over for days, her mind in so much turmoil that she found it difficult to eat and sleep. She refused to let Tiffany run the reception desk alone in case those guys returned, which meant she had now worked five nights in a row, and she was shattered.

Whenever she was inside the massage parlour she couldn't relax, expecting the thugs to return at any time or even for Gilly to pay a visit. And even when she was at home she wasn't completely at ease. What was to stop any of them finding out where she lived and harming either her or Tiffany?

The sound of Tiffany speaking broke into Ruby's troubled thoughts. 'Rubes, where's those sausages I bought?'

'What sausages?' asked Ruby.

'Y'know, the ones I bought the other day. You were with me when I bought them.'

'I don't know, do I?' Ruby snapped. *I wish my only worry in life was where to find the bloody sausages*, she thought, bitterly. 'Why don't you try looking in the freezer or summat?'

'I have done,' said Tiffany, 'and they're not there.'

Ruby could tell by Tiffany's tone that she was becoming exasperated with her and it wasn't long until Tiffany came to join her on the sofa. 'We can't go on like this y'know, Rubes,' she said, patting Ruby's shoulder in her usual affectionate way.

'What the fuck you talking about?' asked Ruby.

Tiffany pulled her hand away, sat back and glared at Ruby. 'That,' she yelled. 'That's what I'm fuckin' talking about! I know you've got your problems, Ruby, but there's no need to take them out on me and every fucker else.'

Ruby stared back. It was rare for Tiffany to lose her temper and for a moment she was shocked. But her girlfriend's display had done the trick. It had made her realise how difficult she had been to live with for the past few days, and how unfair she was being to her.

She sighed. 'You're right, Tiffany. I shouldn't take it out on you but, to be honest, girl, I'm fuckin' worried sick.'

'I know you are,' said Tiffany, moving forward but stopping short of touching Ruby's shoulder again. 'But we can't go on like this,' she repeated.

'What do you suggest then?' Ruby bit back sarcastically.

'I don't know, Rubes, but something's got to change.'

Tiffany then got up from the sofa and went through to the kitchen, leaving Ruby to ponder over what she had said.

In the end Ruby decided that Tiffany was right; she couldn't go on like this. She needed to take control. After all, she had never let men intimidate her in all her adult life, so why should she start now? Sod the protection racket! They couldn't force her to pay if she didn't want to. Let them do their worst. She carried her own protection anyway and she was prepared to use it if necessary. And, as for Tiffany, she'd do her best to make sure that she didn't let her out of her sight.

If Ruby was going to stand up to these men then she would have to start somewhere, and she'd decided to start with Gilly. He was clearly toying with her, waiting for the right time to take his revenge. But she'd had enough of sweating it out waiting for him to make a move; instead she would go to him.

Ruby felt that there might be a connection between Gilly and the thugs who had entered the massage parlour demanding protection money. It seemed a bit of a coincidence that the men should visit her just as he was due to be released. And there was a chance Gilly might have known about Victor's death if Crystal had blabbed her mouth off to him.

While Ruby had never known Gilly to be involved in protection rackets, she knew he had contacts and she wouldn't put anything past him. He might have sent the men just to scare her as a twisted way to get his revenge. So she intended to end the situation once and for all and have it out with him.

She had timed it so that none of the working girls would be inside the Rose and Crown, arriving after she knew they would be working the streets. It would only complicate matters if Crystal were there. Crystal knew of Gilly's plan for revenge and she might try to calm things down before Ruby had a chance to deliver her message.

When she walked inside the pub Gilly was standing at the bar chatting to his cronies. But Ruby knew she wouldn't confront him in the pub. No, this was better taking place outside, away from prying eyes.

She marched up to him and said, boldly, 'I want a word with you! Outside.'

Ruby strode out of the pub purposefully to the sound of a barrage of questions aimed at Gilly. She also heard Gilly following behind as she had known he would; his ego was too big to stand down a challenge from a woman. Ruby had deliberately chosen a precise location, knowing it would unsettle him. She kept a swift pace as she turned down the side street and into the alleyway. The same alleyway where he had left Crystal for dead.

With her back to him Ruby could sense his hesitation as he realised where they were heading; his footsteps becoming slower and more tentative. Good! Her plan was working. She swivelled round and stopped next to a bin while she watched him hover at the mouth of the alleyway. Then he quickly recovered himself and followed her down, stopping before he reached her. Ruby knew she was taking a risk but she had taken precautions and she was glad to see one of those precautions materialise in the form of Tiffany who emerged at the mouth of the alleyway. Gilly turned round on hearing her footsteps and stopped, trapped between the two women.

He swivelled round to face Ruby again. 'What the fuck's going on?' he demanded.

Ruby slapped her hand angrily on the top of the bin.

'Recognise it, Gilly?' She watched the expression of alarm on his face. 'Yeah, that's right. It's the same fuckin bin where I found Crystal after you'd left her for dead!'

'I didn't leave her for dead, just slapped her around a bit, that's all. She fuckin' asked for it!'

'Just slapped her around a bit?' Ruby mimicked. 'Is that why she was unconscious and covered in blood?' When he didn't reply, she continued. 'Her face was a fuckin' mess, Gilly! You broke her nose and eye socket. And you broke two of her fuckin' ribs. Can you blame me for turning you in to the police?'

'You don't fuckin' grass, no matter what happens,' Gilly countered.

'According to who?' shouted Ruby. 'I don't go by the rules of fuckin' scumbags like you!'

Angry at her words, Gilly rushed at her. But she was ready. Before he had quite reached her Ruby pulled out her knife and flicked out the blade. It caught Gilly on the hand just as he charged into her. Gilly jumped back, squealing.

'You fuckin' bitch!' he yelled, turning to the side, his eyes shifting about, looking at each of the girls in turn and trying to decide his next move.

Tiffany had also taken out the knife that Ruby had told her to carry. She doubted that her girlfriend would have used it, but Gilly didn't know that. He finally stepped towards Tiffany, perhaps deciding that she was the lesser threat. Then, while walking away, he turned his head and issued a parting shot for Ruby.

'You've not fuckin' heard the last of this!' he spat as he struggled to keep a safe distance from Tiffany in the narrow alleyway.

Ruby wished she could have felt relief that it was all over but she was afraid that she had only made things worse. Instead of frightening Gilly off, she had just made him more determined to exact his revenge. And she hadn't even had chance to confront him about the gang intimidation; things had moved too fast. So now, she was none the wiser as to whether Gilly was involved or not. But, regardless of that, she hadn't taken care of either problem.

As Ruby made her way back to the massage parlour with Tiffany, she heard her phone ringing. It wasn't the first time she'd heard it that evening but she'd been too occupied with Gilly to answer. It was a central Manchester number, which looked familiar and she soon realised it was someone ringing her from work. She hit the call receive button and heard the distressed voice of Pammy on the other end.

Ruby immediately felt alarmed, knowing she had left Pammy managing reception while she and Tiffany were out. It was obvious to Ruby that Pammy was worked up. As she tried to speak, her voice was shaking and she was breathing heavily. Considering how calmly Pammy had dealt with the cover up of Victor's death, it must be something bad to make her react like this.

'Ruby, we've been attacked by a bunch of fuckin' gangsters!' she gasped.

'Shit! What happened?'

'They came in here carrying baseball bats and wearing masks. They were asking for you, said you owed them some money. When I said you weren't in and hadn't mentioned any money, they started smashing the place up.'

'You're fuckin' joking! Did you get a look at any of them?' asked Ruby.

'Did I fuck! I told you, they were wearing masks. They've left a fuckin' mess. We were terrified.'

'Shit!' Ruby repeated. 'How many of the girls saw what happened?'

'Just me and Rose.'

'OK. Well listen; keep it to yourself and ask Rose to do the same. I'll make it worth your while. I'll be back in a few minutes.'

'What the fuck's going on, Ruby?'

'They're just a bunch of thugs trying to scare us, Pammy.' Ruby tried to play it down. The last thing she needed was to have the girls panicking and leaving her. 'Don't worry, they've done their worst. That's probably the end of it now.'

'Oh, I don't fuckin' think so,' said Pammy, her voice now shaking with anger as well as fear. 'They left you a message. They're gonna be back to see you.'

'Okaay.' Ruby dragged out the word, stuck for what else to say. Finally, she said, 'I'll chat to you when I get there.' Then she cut the call hoping she would be able to calm Pammy down when she got back.

'What's wrong? What's happened?' asked Tiffany.

Ruby closed her eyes for a moment and breathed in deeply, wishing this wasn't really happening. When she opened her eyes again, Tiffany was still waiting for her reply. 'Things just got a whole lot fuckin' worse, Tiff. Those thugs have been and smashed the place up with baseball bats and told Pammy they'll be back.'

'Oh shit! What are we gonna do?'

'I don't know what the fuck to do!' said Ruby. Then

she looked pointedly at Tiffany and grabbed hold of her hand. 'I'm fuckin' scared, Tiff. These are bad bastards we're dealing with.'

Tiffany stared back at Ruby, her eyes wide with fear and her mouth agape. She didn't say anything but her expression said it all; if Ruby was scared and didn't know what to do then things must be bad.

50

June 2011

It was only a day later when the two thugs returned to the club, and the sight of them threw Ruby into a state of panic. She'd just about got the club back in order. The damage had fortunately been minimal, just a dinted coffee table, some broken cups and a picture knocked off the wall. Ruby guessed that it was more of a warning than an intention to inflict any real damage.

Following her previous encounter, the thugs were instantly recognisable from their sporty designer gear, cocky swagger and hard features. But this time they were accompanied by a third man; a man she thought she knew. As he approached the desk she stared hard at him, her heart pounding. Could it be…? No, surely not!

But then he reached the desk and she knew for sure. He still had the same callous features and cruel sneer. As recognition dawned she felt the room sway and she gripped the arms of her chair, thankful that she was sitting down otherwise her legs would have collapsed beneath her.

She realised that he was their leader. He was ruthless

enough to fulfil that role. He'd always been ruthless even as a child. Kyle Gallagher. The savage who had attacked her when she was only ten. And left her with a lifetime of physical and emotional scars.

On seeing her reaction, he grinned smugly. He'd evidently recognised her straightaway. The facial scar was a giveaway.

When he spoke his words were cutting. 'So, Ruby is it now?' He laughed as he addressed his two goons. 'Last time I saw this one she was a scruffy little fucker called Trina.' Then he nodded at the watch she was wearing. 'Love the Rollie by the way.'

'What do you want?' she snapped, trying to disguise her fear with aggression.

But, even as she did so, she was battling with traumatic memories that threatened to overwhelm her. It had been the first time in her life she had known real fear and she tried to fight the feelings of panic that came rushing back. Just like when she was ten, she could feel her constricting throat, rapidly beating heart and shortness of breath as she relived the assault in her mind:

The stinging blows as Kyle and his friends attacked her and the feeling of desperation as she felt her clothing being torn. Her sense of helplessness as she tried ineffectually to defend herself. Begging and pleading with the boys while they sniggered and squealed. Then the knife being plunged into her face and the blood streaming onto her hands.

'You already know the answer,' said Kyle in reply to her question. 'These two explained it to you last time they were here.' The two goons nodded and Kyle continued to speak. 'But, from what they told me, you weren't very nice. And, I've heard that you've had a bit of bother since we last called for our money. Now, if you'd have paid when we asked, you might have been able to avoid that.'

It was obvious to Ruby that they had been responsible for the attack. It was their way of *persuading* her to pay up. But she knew how ruthless Kyle was and she didn't want to risk upsetting him, so Ruby kept her mouth shut while she listened to what he had to say. 'You already owe us a month's protection. Eight hundred quid.'

'I-I don't have that much in the till,' said Ruby. 'The clients pay the girls direct and I just charge for the rooms.'

'In that case, I'll send my men round the rooms and they can collect from your girls instead,' said Kyle, grinning smugly.

'No, don't!' said Ruby.

She looked desperately over at the waiting area, concerned for her girls, and was met by a curious stare from Rose. Ruby flashed a warning glance her way. 'I can get it!'

'Right, well you'd better make it fuckin' quick!' threatened Kyle. 'We'll be back tomorrow night.' He lifted a pen from her desk and pointed it in her face. 'You'd better be fuckin' ready!'

Then he left, taking the pen and his two goons with him. As soon as they were gone, Rose dashed up to reception. 'Is everything alright?' she asked Ruby with an anxious expression on her face.

'Oh, no worries,' said Ruby. 'They were trying it on but I soon sent them packing.'

She could tell Rose wasn't convinced. The terrified expression on Ruby's face was incongruent with her words. She couldn't face any further questions at the moment and in her panicked state she just wanted to flee.

'Rose, please will you man the desk for a few minutes?' she asked, dashing away from the reception area without giving Rose a chance to reply.

Ruby knew where she wanted to be now; somewhere she could be alone. She could have taken the night off, but Tiffany would be at home and she didn't want to alert her. Tiffany had been scared enough about the threat from the gang and Ruby knew that if she told her Kyle was behind it then she would freak out because she knew all about what had happened to Ruby as a child and just how badly it had affected her.

So Ruby headed for her dungeon where nobody else came unless it was pre-arranged. It was the only place where she could guarantee she wouldn't be disturbed.

As soon as she arrived, she collapsed onto the bed, sobbing, her hands covering her face. Her heart was still racing and her head was fuzzy. She pulled her hands away; they were wet with tears. A flashback to that other time struck terror into her. Wet hands; soaked with blood from the gaping wound to her face. Ten years of age and traumatised.

She looked away, trying to refocus her mind. But as she gazed around the room, she was struck by the irony of the place she had chosen as her retreat. The instruments of torture seemed to laugh aloud; each one looming menacingly towards her. In deep torment she threw her face into the pillows and closed her eyes, trying to escape her troubles.

It took a while until she had cried out her anguish and managed to calm herself down. Ruby had to get back to reception. She didn't want to arouse suspicion. Nobody must know about the terrifying threat that hung over them. And Rose would already be suspicious.

Ruby got up off the bed and went into the adjoining bathroom. She stared into the mirror at the pink puffiness around her eyes and noticed how flushed she was before switching on the cold tap and rinsing her face. When her cheeks had cooled she walked down the stairs, locked the door to her dungeon and prepared herself to face Rose.

'Are you OK?' asked Rose, her face still full of concern.

'Yes, sorry about that,' said Ruby. 'I've got a dicky tummy.'

'You sure?' asked Rose, clearly sceptical.

'Yeah, I'll be OK. It's probably the takeaway I had last night.'

'You sure it's not about those guys upsetting you?'

'What guys? Oh, them? Nah. I told you, they're just trying it on. It'd take more than a bunch of drips like them to bother me.'

Her act was convincing, especially coming from someone as strong-willed as Ruby, and Rose soon returned to the waiting area, leaving Ruby to run the reception desk. For the rest of the night Ruby tried to carry on as normal, smiling politely at the customers and sharing banter with the girls. But although she managed to convince them all that everything was fine, the reality was just the opposite.

She knew Kyle and what he was capable of and as Ruby chatted, smiled and laughed at the right times she couldn't belie what she was feeling inside. Kyle's visit had changed everything. As well as sabotaging her business, it had destroyed her peace of mind, and nothing would ever be the same again.

51

July 2011

It was the second time Kyle had called to collect his money and, as she looked across the reception counter at him, Ruby couldn't hide the scowl on her face. She hated him! And she begrudged having to pay her hard-earned money to him in order to buy his so-called protection. The look that he gave her in return told Ruby he was well aware of her resentment.

She was tempted to refuse payment, but the sight of him sent a shudder of fear through her and she felt powerless. Kyle had turned up alone, confident that he didn't even need his goons to elicit fear into her and persuade her to pay up. Ruby reached into the drawer under the reception counter and withdrew an envelope full of cash.

As she reluctantly handed the envelope to him, Kyle grinned smugly. 'Well, things seem to be working out alright don't they?' he asked as he tucked the cash away. 'I take it you've had no trouble?'

'No,' said Ruby.

She wondered if it would make any difference if they

had. The term *protection* was clearly a misnomer. Kyle was here for one reason only and that was his own personal gain. But it didn't stop him going along with the pretence.

'As we've been doing such a good job for you, I think we deserve a little reward for our services,' he said, still wearing a smug grin.

'What?'

'Well, there's no point looking after a sweet shop if you can't help yourself to the candy, is there?'

'No!' yelled Ruby.

'Calm the fuck down!' he hissed, looking around to make sure she hadn't drawn attention to them as he grabbed hold of her hand and squeezed, digging his nails into the soft flesh. 'If I say me and my men can have freebies, then we'll fuckin' have them. We'll be back tomorrow night so you'd better fuckin' line up your best girls because if you don't, this place will go up like a fuckin' inferno.'

Before Ruby had a chance to protest any further, he was gone. This latest threat struck terror into Ruby, her heart pounding as her fear intensified. She knew she'd have to go along with it; she was frightened of what might happen if she didn't. But how could she expect her girls to work for free? They all worked for themselves, charging their own fees and just paying her for the rooms. How could she persuade them not to charge, without raising their suspicions?

In the end she decided on a cover story. She would tell the girls it was an arrangement where the client would pay her as a group booking and she would pay each of the girls their share. It would mean that the free services would actually come out of Ruby's own profits but it was the only way she knew to keep the truth from the girls and, at the same time, keep Kyle and his gang happy.

Ruby had underestimated Rose who had been suspicious of Kyle's men even before they started taking advantage of the services offered by the girls. But now, as she listened to Rose demanding to have a chat with her in a voice that was even more whiny than usual, and stared across the counter at her stony expression, Ruby knew she had trouble. It had only been a few days since Kyle had started his new arrangement and it was already causing problems.

'Do you wanna go and make a cuppa?' Ruby asked Tiffany who was working on reception with her that evening. She could tell as soon as Rose spoke that there was going to be a scene and she preferred it if Tiffany was out of the way. Although Ruby's partner knew about the threat from the gang, she still didn't know about Kyle's involvement or his identity.

'No, it's OK. I'll stay,' said Tiffany, eyeing Rose warily as she continued her spiel.

'I'm telling you, Ruby, this has got to stop. That big bugger already put the shits up Ria the other day, and now I've had that nasty little bastard to contend with. I'm not having any client getting their rocks off by fuckin' slapping me, no matter what your arrangements are with them.'

Ruby knew Rose was talking about the visit by one of Kyle's men a couple of days ago and now this latest incident involving Kyle himself. It didn't surprise her; it sounded like it would be just his style.

'OK, leave it with me, Rose,' she said. 'I'll have a word with him and tell him he's out of order.'

'Out of order? And you think that'll do the trick do you? Well, if you think I'm taking on that nasty little bastard again, you're wrong! And I don't think you should be sending him to any of the other girls either. Y'know, Ria was really shaken up after that big bastard came to see her. You can't have these people manhandling the girls, Ruby. It's not on!'

'Alright, Rose!' Ruby snapped, the stress of the situation getting to her. 'I'll let him know it's not on. Trust me, I'll put a stop to it.'

'That's just it, Ruby. I don't fuckin' trust you! Why are you putting up with this shit from them? Why don't you just fuckin' ban them from the premises?'

Ruby noticed the way Tiffany stared open-mouthed at Rose, shocked that she should challenge her in this way. Nobody challenged Ruby if they knew what was good for them and, as Ruby felt the pressure of expectation, she yelled back at her.

'Don't tell me how to run my fuckin' business!'

But Rose wasn't finished. 'If you ran it properly I wouldn't fuckin' have to!'

Ruby was livid that she was questioning her authority even though Rose was right. But there was nothing Ruby could do; she had no defence. For seconds they stared venomously at each other and, even though Ruby was in the wrong, Rose was the first to back down, softening her tone as she asked, 'What's going on, Ruby? Who *are* these men?'

But Ruby was still fired up, the hopelessness of the

situation getting to her as she snapped, 'You don't need to know!'

'Right,' said Rose. Ruby's harsh words had reignited her fury, but she fought to stay in control of her temper. 'If you won't tell me then I'll have to make my own mind up. I've already got a good idea who they are and there's no way I'm staying in a place that's being controlled by a bunch of fuckin' gangsters.'

'Shush!' urged Ruby, leaving Rose in no doubt that she had guessed right.

'I'm sorry for you, Ruby. I really am. But there's no way I can stay here. And that means Ria will be leaving too. She's a good friend and I'm not leaving her at risk if what I said is true. And I think it is.'

'Suit yourself,' said Ruby, trying to save face.

Rose looked at her and shook her head before walking away. Ruby turned to see that Tiffany's eyes were on her. 'Don't say anything, Tiff, please,' she said, swallowing back an overwhelming surge of emotion. 'I don't think I can take any more tonight.'

But the night became worse and by the end of it they had lost Rose, Ria and another girl called Bianca.

'Shit, Ruby. What are we gonna do?' asked Tiffany.

'There's nothing we can do, girl,' said Ruby in despair. 'We just have to hope we can get replacements and that none of the other girls leave. And, as for Kyle, I'll have a word but I don't think he'll take much notice.'

'Kyle? Who's Kyle?'

Ruby felt her heart lurch. She'd slipped up. 'He… he's the gang leader,' she said.

'And?' asked Tiffany, sensing her panic.

Ruby sighed. Maybe it was time to open up to Tiffany. She didn't want to worry her but, at the same time, she hated keeping her in the dark. She was her partner after all, and they'd always shared everything.

'I know him,' said Ruby. 'Remember when I told you what happened when I was a kid?' she asked, subconsciously fingering her scar.

'Aah! I knew that name rang a bell. It's him, isn't it?'

'Yes,' said Ruby, who then looked down at the countertop, afraid she wouldn't be able to hide her feelings.

Then she felt Tiffany's arm around her shoulder. 'Don't worry, Rubes. You're not alone. We're in this together.'

It was good to have Tiffany's support and Ruby wished she could draw comfort from it. But she felt that, despite Tiffany's brave words, even the two of them were useless against a ruthless man like Kyle. And as she wallowed in her own despair, she realised the hopelessness of her situation.

52

July 2011

Ruby admired the way Tiffany slept soundly no matter what was going on in their world. Perhaps it was because Ruby was the stronger one in the relationship. Maybe Tiffany had this unerring faith in her to come up with a solution no matter what predicament they were dealing with. But that night, as Ruby lay awake going over everything in her head, she was just adding to her worries rather than coming up with a concrete way out of them.

She'd given up on trying to sleep; it was a waste of time. Anxious thoughts were spinning around inside her mind making her head ache and her muscles tense. She was concerned about her future and the future of the club. What if the girls continued to become intimidated and more of them left the club? Word would soon get around and she might end up with no girls at all.

She could try having a word with Kyle but she knew he'd only laugh at her concerns. What if she ended up having to sell the club? What would she and Tiffany do then? She dreaded the thought of having to work the streets again.

Even though selling the club would enable them to pay off the mortgage on the house, they would still have bills to meet, and they'd have to find a way to pay them.

What was the alternative if she ended up having to sell the club? Would she be able to get another building? No, she didn't think so; she remembered how hard it had been to get this one. Besides, Kyle would probably find her again, and where would that leave her?

Her troubled mind switched to her relationship with Tiffany. What if all the stress and pressure proved too much for them and put an end to their relationship? She knew she was getting carried away as her thoughts went round and round in her mind, but she couldn't help it.

And then another worry occurred to her; while all this was going on there was still the danger of reprisals from Gilly. The threat from Kyle and his gang was so huge that Gilly's threat had become miniscule by comparison. But, nevertheless, it was still there.

As well as being anxious, Ruby felt angry at her own powerlessness. Yet again, she was being controlled by men; something she had sworn would never happen. That anger chipped away at her, making her feel even tenser. Somehow, she had to find a way to beat Kyle. She couldn't go on like this.

Eventually Ruby became so exhausted that she fell asleep in the early hours of the morning. She had only slept for just over three hours but it had been enough to enable her brain to relax a little while her subconscious came up with the answers. And, by the time she came to, Ruby had reached a decision about what she had to do to get out of this mess and take back control.

★

Before Ruby had a chance to act on her decision Kyle paid her another visit. It wasn't collection day so she guessed he had come specially to spend some time with one of the girls.

'When's Rose free?' he demanded as soon as he reached the counter.

'She doesn't work here anymore,' said Ruby.

'Shit! She was well fit. Do you know where she's working now? No, scrap that. Why fuckin' pay for it when you can get it for nowt? What about that little Asian girl?'

'You mean Ria?' said Ruby, biting back her irritation. 'She's left as well.'

'Are you fuckin' joking? What the hell's going on in this place?'

Ruby braced herself, dreading his reaction to her reply. But, although she was nervous, she was determined to let him know how his actions were affecting the club. 'They left because you and your men were being too rough with them.'

'You what? Are you fuckin' serious? They're tarts! I'm hardly gonna fuckin' wine and dine 'em, am I?'

Ruby stared at him for a moment, considering her response. There was no point telling him how it was out of order to manhandle a woman no matter what she did for a living. He didn't operate by the same ethical code as everyone else. Wary of winding him up, she decided instead to concentrate on something that *would* concern him; the effect on the club's income.

'We've lost three girls up to now,' she said. 'And they were three of my best; all of them were very popular with the customers. If word gets around, we could lose even more.

Then we'll find it difficult to get replacements too. No girl wants to work in a place where the customers don't treat her right. We might even end up having to shut down and then we would all lose out.'

'Alright, keep your fuckin' hair on!' he blasted.

Ruby knew she'd hit the mark. The potential loss of protection money would bother him as the massage parlour was a big earner. She hoped his concerns would be enough to make him and his gang treat the girls better in future. But, of course, she wouldn't get a verbal commitment from him about it. That wasn't his style.

Despite the effect that her words had had on him, Kyle carried on as though Ruby hadn't raised her concerns. 'Who else have you got?' he demanded.

Ruby went through each of the girls, describing them to him, but he turned down every one.

'Scraping the fuckin' barrel now, aren't you?' he said, scornfully. 'Tell you what, how about you?'

A pang of fear shot through Ruby like a laser beam, making her heart race and her chest feel tight. 'No!' she yelled. Then, realising he might balk at her extreme reaction, she said, 'I don't offer my services, I just manage the girls.'

'Oh, come off it. I'm not stupid! You wouldn't be fuckin' running this place if you hadn't done a bit yourself. Anyway, I've heard all about Ruby's Dungeon.'

'You wouldn't want that. It's a special service for certain customers.'

'How do you know what I fuckin' want?' Then he paused for a moment, grinning arrogantly at her as he sensed her discomfort. 'Nah, you're right,' he added. 'I ain't like those fuckin' weirdos that want to be spanked and all that bollocks. I just want what normal men want. And if you can't get me a decent girl then I'm gonna have to have you.'

'I-I'm busy managing the desk.'

'That's OK. I can come back tomorrow night, but you'd better be fuckin' ready. Cos if you're not, you know what'll happen, don't you? Poof!' As he said the last word, he used his fingers to mime the place going up in flames.

Ruby was relieved to see him walk out of the door. His latest visit had shaken her even more than any other and she dreaded the thought of having to sleep with him. The only consolation was that Tiffany hadn't been on reception that night; if he had chosen her that would have felt even worse.

But, despite that thought, his request to sleep with her had floored Ruby. She knew how violent he was and every time she saw him the traumatic memory of what he had done to her came flooding back. How could she face spending time alone with him when her childhood memories still haunted her so much?

53

July 2011

Ruby was sitting in her lounge with Tiffany, and her cousins, Josh and Calvin. She had called them there for a meeting after updating Tiffany about everything.

'So, come on,' said Josh after they had exchanged small talk. 'We know you haven't called us here for nowt.'

'No I haven't,' said Ruby. 'I'm having a bit of trouble and I'm hoping it's something you can help me with.'

She hated the sound of the words on her tongue. Even though her cousins had offered a long time ago to help her with any bother, it was something she didn't want to do. It made her feel inadequate to have to ask them; she remembered all too well from her childhood what their perception was of her as a female. And now, here she was, living up to their expectations. But, the way things stood, she didn't have any choice but to ask for help. She was out of her depth and knew she couldn't handle Kyle's gang alone.

'What is it?' asked Josh.

'Have you heard of Kyle Gallagher? You might recognise his name from when we were kids.'

The two cousins exchanged looks, their arched eyebrows and furrowed brows showing a mix of surprise and contempt. Calvin was the first to speak, his tone hostile.

'Sure, we know who he is. I don't remember him as a kid though.'

'Has he been giving you bother?' demanded Josh, his voice even sharper than his brother's.

'You could say that,' said Ruby, sardonically. 'He's been taking protection money from us for a while.'

'What the fuck! Why didn't you tell us?' asked Josh.

Ruby shrugged. 'I suppose I didn't want any comeback.'

'Fuck that! Nobody's taking the piss out of my cousin and getting away with it,' threatened Calvin. 'We've got a fuckin' reputation to keep up.'

'There's more,' said Ruby, sighing. 'He's started taking freebies as well and him and his gang are rough with the girls.'

'Yeah,' chipped in Tiffany. 'We've had three of them leave because of it.'

'Really?' asked Josh. Ruby and Tiffany nodded. 'So, you want us to sort them, is that it?'

Before Ruby had chance to respond, Tiffany chipped in again. 'Tell them the latest, Ruby.'

Ruby sighed again, her expression showing her discomfort. 'Kyle wants me to sleep with him.'

'And…' prompted Tiffany.

Ruby shuffled uncomfortably. 'And, it was him and his mates that attacked me when I was a kid. They gave me this scar.' She pointed to her cheek.

'Fuckin' bastard!' shouted Calvin. 'I didn't realise it was the same guy. How come you never told us any of this?'

'I didn't think you'd be interested.'

'Are you fuckin' joking?' raged Josh.

'Well, you did act a bit differently towards me when we were kids.'

Calvin cut in before Josh had chance to respond. 'We can't let the cunt get away with this!'

'Don't worry, he ain't fuckin' getting away with it!' said Josh.

'But they're dangerous,' said Ruby. 'Are you sure you can handle it on your own?'

Calvin sniggered. 'You think they're fuckin' dangerous? You don't know shit! And we won't be on our own. We've got plenty of handy blokes working for us…'

Josh flashed him a warning look to prevent him from giving too much away. 'We can sort it, don't worry about that. I want you to give us as many details as you can; names of the gang members, descriptions, any addresses you might have for them, that sort of thing. Don't worry if you don't have too much on them, we can find out the rest ourselves.'

'OK, but what will you do?' asked Ruby.

'You don't need to know too much,' Josh replied. 'All you need to know is that it'll get sorted. Just leave it with us.'

'Thanks,' said Ruby, her initial reluctance now replaced by relief.

She gave her cousins all the facts she could think of relating to Kyle and his gang and they both listened while Calvin made notes. Although she had dreaded being judged by her cousins because of her weakness, it seemed they had finally grown up. Now, rather than putting her down, their main concern seemed to be in defending her and they had been surprisingly receptive.

'There's something else,' she ventured once she had told them as much as she could relating to Kyle. 'There's another guy who's got it in for me. He hasn't really done anything yet, but he's threatened revenge. I think he's just biding his time, but he might even have sent Kyle's gang round as a way of getting back at me.

'What's his name?' asked Josh.

'Aaron Gill but they call him Gilly.'

'Never heard of him,' said Calvin, 'And if we ain't heard of him then he must be small fry. Is he from Manchester?'

'Yeah. He hangs out in the Rose and Crown. He's a pimp.'

'Why's he after you?' asked Josh, and Ruby told them both what had happened.

'He sounds like a nasty little fucker,' said Josh, 'but Calvin's right, he ain't no big shot. And there's no way he'll be behind Kyle and his gang. Trust me; they don't have anyone pulling their strings. But if you want us to sort this guy out as well, we can.'

'Yeah, I do,' said Ruby. 'Oh, and thanks.'

'No probs, cuz,' said Calvin, ruffling her hair. He turned to Josh. 'Come on, bruv, let's go.' Then he laughed. 'Me and you have got work to do.'

Once they had gone Tiffany took Ruby in her arms. 'Are you OK?' she asked.

Ruby pulled away from her embrace and nodded as she replied. 'I think so.'

'Do you think they'll be able to sort it?'

'Should be able to. I think Josh and Calvin are involved in a lot more than we know about. They didn't seem too bothered about the situation. In fact, they seemed to be looking forward to going up against Kyle's gang. I hope they don't go too far. I should have told them just to warn him off.'

'Do you think they'll be alright?' asked Tiffany.

'I hope so. If owt happened to them I'd never forgive myself. But I don't wanna think about that right now. I'm just keeping my fingers crossed and hoping they can scare Kyle's gang off.'

'Try not to worry, Rubes. After all, it's not as if you had a choice in the matter, is it? And it beats sitting around doing nothing while we wait to see what Kyle's going to do to us next.'

Ruby shuddered. 'Yes, you're right.'

54

July 2011

The following night arrived too quickly and Kyle was soon standing at the reception desk ready for his pre-arranged meeting with Ruby. As she looked at him, she felt a tug of repulsion. There was no way she could go through with this, and the meeting with her cousins had given her the courage to put him off even though she was still fearful of his reaction.

'I'm not doing it,' said Ruby.

'You what?' he asked, glaring at her.

'I can't. I thought I could, but I can't.'

'What the fuck's wrong with you? You're not some innocent fuckin' virgin, y'know. I know for a fact you've had plenty of customers in the past; I've been asking around. And now, just cos you're the fuckin' madam, you think you're too good for the customers.'

Ruby could feel her heart racing and her hands were sweating as she saw the look of fury on his face, but she tried to keep her voice even as she said, 'It's up to me whether I take customers or not, so if I say I don't want to do it then I won't do it.'

Kyle swiped angrily at her, catching the attention of two of her girls and a customer who were in the waiting area, but she dodged away quickly. He then leaned over the reception counter, his head poking forward.

'If it wasn't for the fact that that lot might call the cops, I'd drag you into one of those fuckin' rooms now!' he threatened. 'I'm having no fuckin' tart thinking she's too good for me. You're lucky to get a decent looking bloke after some of the fuckin' weirdos you're used to shaggin' so you'd better have a rethink and fuckin' quick if you know what's good for you. I'll be in touch.'

Then he was gone and Ruby felt her shoulders slump in relief. She saw one of the girls in the waiting area look across at her but she quickly raised her hand palm outwards to stop her from coming over. 'It's OK,' she said. 'Just a troublesome customer, nothing to worry about.'

Ruby looked down at her computer screen, refusing to maintain eye contact with the girl. She'd tried her best to play it down but was worried that if her staff saw the fearful expression on her face, they would realise the threat that Kyle really posed.

While Kyle was busy terrorising Ruby, her cousins were waiting for one of Kyle's gang, Ash, to make his way back home from the pub. It hadn't taken long to find his address; their scary reputation ensured that people were anxious to give them information.

They had hidden behind some bushes near to the house

where he lived, their car parked further away and out of view. The house was only accessible by public footpath and they knew he'd have to pass them on foot once he'd completed the journey by car or taxi. They'd had a tip-off telling them the time he usually arrived home from the pub, and had got there early so they wouldn't miss him. Apparently he didn't usually stay late, often going back early with his girlfriend once he had met with the rest of the gang. But after almost half an hour of waiting they were becoming restless.

As Josh began to wonder whether Ash would arrive home at all that night, his initial adrenalin rush was abating. But when he spotted a man getting out of a car then walking arm in arm with a girl, the rush of adrenalin quickly returned. Ash fit the description they had of him: below average height, slight and only in his early twenties. He must have got a lift home from the pub and was now making his way unsteadily towards them. Although it was still only ten-thirty, he seemed drunk.

'He's there,' he whispered to Calvin. 'But he's not on his own.'

Calvin peered through the bushes. 'You get the girl and I'll take him. It should be a doddle; he's half pissed.'

Josh nodded and pulled the knife from his pocket as they watched Ash stagger up the footpath. As soon as he and the girl passed by, they jumped from the bushes and pounced on them from behind. The girl began to scream but Josh quickly put his hand over her mouth, pulling her close to him and jabbing her in the back with the knife.

'Keep your fuckin' mouth shut, and nowt will happen to you,' he hissed, dragging her into the bushes.

Josh watched as Calvin jumped Ash, wrapping his left arm

around Ash's middle and dragging him towards him while he prodded the knife at his throat. But Ash was surprisingly quick. He aimed a sharp backwards kick at Calvin's calf, his heel painfully connecting with the shin bone. Calvin let out a yell and slackened his hold. It gave Ash chance to pull away. Then he spun round and pulled out his own knife.

Josh felt helpless as he watched what was taking place, his heart pumping fiercely and his hand sweaty against the girl's face. The need to help his brother fought with worry about letting go of the girl. He couldn't let her raise the alarm.

Before he could do anything, Ash charged at Calvin, his drunkenness making him fearless. But it also made him clumsy and, as Calvin sidestepped him, his blade caught the edge of Calvin's arm, grazing his jacket but missing his flesh. With nothing to stop his momentum, Ash keeled over.

Calvin was straight on him, pinning him down where he lay on the ground. As Ash tried to break free Calvin held his knife to the side of his neck. But Ash didn't heed the warning, and continued to put up a fight.

'If you keep still, you little fuck, you'll be alright,' threatened Calvin. 'We're not after you. We just want you to send a message to Kyle.'

But Ash carried on struggling, yelling abuse and wriggling around on the ground.

'Shut the little fucker up!' yelled Josh, as he noticed a light come on in a house further along the footpath.

Calvin grabbed Ash's hair at the back and yanked his head up off the ground. Then Josh noticed one swift moment and Ash lay still. It was only when he saw the blood seep from beneath him that he realised Calvin had slit his throat.

Calvin sprang up, away from the body, as though it was contaminated. And for a moment the brothers remained still, both in shock at what Calvin had done. They had only intended to scare him!

But then the girl noticed the blood too. She became hysterical, fighting to free herself from Josh. He held on tight despite her thrashing about and kicking. Then he felt a sharp pain in his hand as the girl chomped down hard. Josh yelled and pulled his hand away. She was about to make a run for it when Calvin pounced on her so she was trapped between them both. Calvin quickly stepped back and aimed a sharp slap to her cheek, stunning her into silence.

'Shut the fuck up!' he yelled.

The girl remained quiet, her body trembling and tears pouring down her face as she stared helplessly at Ash's prone body. Josh grabbed hold of her arm and hissed into her ear.

'Right, we want you to deliver a message. It's for your boyfriend's leader, Kyle. With the knife still in his hand, he pointed it towards Ash. You tell that fuckin' Kyle that that's a warning. And tell him to leave Ruby's Parlour alone, and anyone who works there, or there'll be worse to come. Do you understand?'

The girl whimpered in response so Calvin grabbed hold of her chin, forcing it upwards till their eyes connected. 'Are you fuckin' listening to what he's saying?' he yelled.

'Yeah,' the girl cried, and Calvin let go of her.

'Right, well you make sure that fuckin' message gets back to Kyle or we'll be back for you. OK?' The girl nodded but the only sound coming from her was a painful whine. 'I said, OK?' Calvin yelled again.

'Yeah,' said the girl, but it sounded more like a plea than an affirmation.

'C'mon, let's go,' said Josh, afraid someone might emerge from the house where the light had been switched on.

He let go of the girl and she slumped to the ground, her legs weak with fear and grief. They left her where she fell, and ran.

55

July 2011

Ruby was on reception with Tiffany when she heard her mobile phone ping. She jumped at the sound, aware that it could be Kyle, but also expecting to hear back from her cousins at any time.

'Who is it?' asked Tiffany as Ruby picked up the phone. She looked as anxious as Ruby felt.

Ruby scanned the text message then showed it to Tiffany.

Your biggest problem has been dealt with. On our way to deal with the other one. We'll be in touch soon.

Even if she didn't have the number stored in her phone as Josh, Ruby would have realised who the text had come from. He was being deliberately cryptic, maybe to cover himself in case of comeback.

Tiffany looked at her knowingly and Ruby nodded back. But although Ruby didn't say anything her thoughts were alive; wondering, speculating, worrying. If Josh had felt the need to cover himself then how bad had things become?

What exactly did *dealt with* mean? And who had been dealt with: Kyle's gang or Gilly? She was anxious to know exactly what had happened.

'Hang on here,' she said to Tiffany. 'I'm giving them a ring. I want to find out more.'

She went inside an unused room for privacy but, despite ringing both of her cousins, she couldn't get a reply. Ruby continued to ring throughout the night but neither of them answered the phone. They were obviously occupied sorting out problem number two.

The night's events had taken Josh by surprise. He didn't like to resort to killing if he could help it; not so much out of compassion for the enemy, who deserved everything they got, but more because it usually resulted in even bigger problems. He knew Kyle wouldn't take the news of Ash's death well so they had to be prepared for comeback from him.

It wasn't as if it was the first time Josh and Calvin had killed; in their line of work it was an occupational hazard. And, even though the death of Ash was still fresh in their minds, they decided to go ahead and deal with Gilly that same night just as they had originally intended. Calvin was already fired up from the incident with Ash anyway and was eager to carry on.

When they arrived at the Rose and Crown they went straight inside, having already discussed how to play it. It was a short while after last orders so they knew there wouldn't be many customers inside the pub, just a few of the regulars. They strode straight up to the bar and soon picked out Gilly from the photograph relating to his court case, which Ruby had shown them.

Josh walked up to him and whispered in his ear. 'We want a word, outside.'

Gilly backed away and looked slyly from one to the other of them. 'No chance! Whatever you've come to say, you can fuckin' say it here.'

Some of the pub's customers became interested in what was happening. 'Everything alright, Gilly?' Josh heard one of them say.

Josh looked at the customers standing at the bar and weighed up his chances. Having decided there was no major threat he sidled up to Gilly and whispered into his ear again. 'What would the landlord think if we smashed this place up because we had beef with you? Then, when we'd done that, we'd haul you out of the pub and kick the shit out of you.'

He watched Gilly's reaction and could tell he was trying to decide what to do for the best, so he added, 'We only want a chat. If you cooperate, we'll leave it at that.'

Gilly looked around then whispered something to the man standing at the other side of him. Josh presumed he'd instructed him to bring help if he didn't return soon but he wasn't worried. The man looked as though a good meal would kill him; he was an obvious junkie, as were the two men standing further along the bar.

They were soon standing in the street that ran down the side of the pub. Gilly stopped before they reached the back alleyway, then turned and asked. 'What d'you want?'

Josh could see the fear in his eyes straightaway and knew this was going to be easy. His first reaction was physical as he grabbed the front of Gilly's hoody and gripped it tightly under his chin, his knuckles pressed against Gilly's windpipe. He could see Calvin hovering to the side of him, keen to get involved.

'I'll tell you what we fuckin' want! We want you to leave Trina alone.'

Gilly made a choking sound so Josh eased the pressure a little, allowing him to speak. 'Trina?'

'Yeah. The girl who owns Ruby's Parlour.'

Gilly's eyes flashed in recognition. 'I haven't fuckin' touched her, mate.'

'No, but you've fuckin' threatened her!' yelled Calvin.

'Only cos she grassed me up!' said Gilly, his pupils now wide with fear. 'But I wasn't gonna touch her, I swear.'

'Are you fuckin' sure about that?' asked Josh, still clutching Gilly's hoody.

'Yeah, cos from what we've heard you're pretty fuckin' handy at beating women up!' said Calvin, his face now up against the side of Gilly's head.

Gilly shifted to one side and Josh released his hold then stepped back, nodding to Calvin who threw the first punch. His fist connected with Gilly's chin, hard enough to make his head smash into the wall behind him, and Gilly let out a yelp.

'Is this what it fuckin' felt like for the girl you beat up?' demanded Josh, sensing Gilly's panicked reaction and nodding at Calvin to hit him again.

Calvin thumped Gilly fiercely around the face and head while Gilly made a feeble attempt to defend himself, holding his hands up till Calvin swiped them away. When Josh spotted blood, he ordered Calvin to stop.

Josh moved in again as Calvin stepped aside. 'That's just

a fuckin' taster,' he said, jabbing his finger in Gilly's bloody face. 'If we hear you've been anywhere near Trina then we'll come back and finish the fuckin' job off!'

'I won't. Honest. I promise,' pleaded Gilly.

Josh turned to Calvin. 'Come on, we're done.'

He'd left the dirty work to Calvin, but Gilly's obsequiousness had annoyed him. Maybe he should have given him a good smacking himself. The guy was a cowardly bastard!

But they'd done what they set out to do and Josh was satisfied that there'd be no repercussions for Ruby. The guy was too shit scared to dare! He and Calvin started to walk away but, as they did so, Josh turned back and caught the expression on Gilly's face. It wasn't just relief; it was conceit, as though he thought he'd got off lightly. And Josh couldn't have that. He had a reputation to protect.

The look of surprise on Gilly's face when he turned back and swiped him was priceless! Josh laid into him, heedless of the blood spatter and Gilly's pleas for mercy. He didn't stop till his energy was spent. By that time Gilly's face resembled a freakish piece of modern art in scarlet hues with pallid undertones.

Josh stood in front of Gilly and scowled at him while he got his breath back. Gilly's mouth was hanging open, the blood pumping from his nose and his bottom lip, and he was whimpering like a baby with tears flowing freely from his eyes. His expression was no longer one of conceit, more of terror and desperation. This time Josh knew they'd done the job right. His deduction was borne out by his brother's amused expression, which he could see out of the corner of his eye.

'Don't you ever dare to fuck with us!' yelled Josh and he was rewarded by Gilly's look of anguish as he drew his head back, anticipating another blow.

Not wanting to be left out of the fun, Calvin jabbed Gilly sharply in the ribs before they left him.

'Did you see the look on the cheeky bastard's face?' Josh complained to his brother.

Calvin smiled widely. 'He ain't fuckin' laughing now, is he?'

Josh chuckled. 'No. Stupid bastard! He could have got off lightly if he'd played it right.'

'What the fuck's wrong with you, bruv? You going soft or what?'

'Like fuck! I'm just knackered and wanted to call it a night. I'm glad we let him have it though. I don't think our Trina will have any more trouble with him. The dickhead shit himself!'

'Yeah, well, he's only good at slapping women around, isn't he?' said Calvin. 'He's out of his fuckin' depth when it comes to dealing with anyone with a pair of balls. Anyway, that's both jobs taken care of now. What's next? Do you wanna go for a drink somewhere? Then we can ring Trina and let her know what's gone down.'

'Nah, there's no rush, is there? It's getting late now and I'm knackered. Let's leave it till the morning,' said Josh and, satisfied with their night's work, they set off for home.

56

July 2011

Ruby watched the last of her girls putting on her coat and walking past reception.

She waved a cheery goodbye to Ruby and Tiffany. 'See you tomorrow.'

'Bye,' they shouted in unison until Ruby turned her attention back to her partner. 'I'll just try giving Josh and Calvin another ring before we go home.'

'OK, but I don't think you'll have any joy at this time of night,' said Tiffany.

Tiffany was right and when her calls rang out unanswered Ruby decided to leave it till the next day. 'Come on, let's get off home.'

They switched off the PC and left everything ready for the following night, then made their way down the stairs. Tiffany walked out of the building first, leaving Ruby to lock up. She was just about to turn the key in the lock when she heard movement behind her and Tiffany let out a scream.

Ruby swivelled around to find Kyle glaring into her face

and clutching a baseball bat. He had brought a gang of men with him, all mean looking and wielding weapons. Her heart raced as she saw one of them grab hold of Tiffany.

Kyle gripped Ruby's arm while snarling at her, 'Open the fuckin' door! You ain't going anywhere.'

Ruby felt the first stirrings of panic, but she brazened it out. 'Let go of my arm then. I can't fuckin' move it!'

He released his grip on her so she could unlock the door. She couldn't escape anyway. Kyle and his men had formed an impenetrable barrier. As she tried to put the key back into the lock her hands were shaking and she found it difficult. Kyle jabbed her in the ribs with the baseball bat.

'Get a fuckin' move on!'

'Alright! I'm trying,' she replied, with an edge of desperation to her voice.

For Ruby the scene was too painfully familiar. Kyle: angry and threatening. And his group of bully boys: equally menacing and dangerous. It took her back to that traumatic event in her childhood. But this time she wasn't alone; she had Tiffany with her. Ruby wished this thought brought her comfort. But it didn't. It made things worse as she dreaded what was about to happen to the two of them.

Eventually she got the door open and Kyle rushed her upstairs, jabbing her in the back with the baseball bat while another of his men stayed with Tiffany and the rest of them raced ahead. By the time Ruby reached the top of the stairs, Kyle's gang were already laying into the place, smashing the furniture up with baseball bats and slicing up the sofas with machetes.

The last attack on the club had been bad enough, but this time it was obvious they were intent on inflicting even more damage. Ruby looked on helplessly, restrained by Kyle's vicious grip on her arm once more, as the gang trashed the club.

'Oh my word!' she yelled. 'You bastards!'

Kyle swiped her across the face and Ruby instinctively retaliated, launching herself at him and sinking her nails into his scalp. But he brought the baseball bat down hard and Ruby screeched as she felt the painful blow. Giving her no chance to defend herself, Kyle brought it down again, and again, each blow more vicious than the last.

Ruby fell to the ground, noticing as she did so that Tiffany was getting a hiding from another of Kyle's men. She could hear her girlfriend's tortured screams as the man set about her with a baseball bat.

'Leave her alone, you bastards!' she shrieked, and she was punished with another savage blow from Kyle.

Eventually he stopped, but his anger was still evident as a stream of abuse spewed from his mouth. 'You fuckin' bitch! Did you honestly think you could get away with taking one of my fuckin' men out? Whore!'

Ruby looked at him, confused as well as terrified. 'I don't know what you're talking about.'

He aimed a sharp kick at her stomach, making her double over in agony. 'You fuckin' liar! I know you sent your bastard cousins. Did you really think they could scare me into leaving you alone?' You must be fuckin' joking!'

As he spoke, he carried on kicking her then resumed with the bat, smashing it down onto her back. Amid the haze of pain and terror Ruby realised what had happened. A feeling of dread circled her senses, overshadowed at the moment by the agony of the attack. Her cousins must have killed a man in reprisal for Kyle's threat to her business. The stupid pair of bastards!

When Kyle had exhausted himself, he stopped the attack and began talking. His tone was still angry, but this time he was managing to hold it more in check. He was now focused on delivering a message rather than just hurling abuse.

'So, your cousins want me to leave you and this place alone, do they? Not a fuckin' chance! In fact, you've just made things a lot fuckin' worse for yourself. From now on you'll do everything I say unless you want to see your girls go missing, one by one.'

Ruby felt the sting of his words as acute as the pain from her battered and bruised body. She knew she couldn't afford to lose any more girls. She'd already lost three of her best thanks to Kyle and his gang. And the thought of what he might do to any of her other girls terrified her.

'OK, OK, I'll do anything you say,' she pleaded.

'Oh, you will! But not now. You look a fuckin' mess!' Ruby became conscious of the blood on her face, which was dripping onto her clothing. 'Get yourself cleaned up and you can ring me tomorrow. I want you to arrange another meeting with me and this time it *will* go ahead. Unless you want to face the consequences.'

'Alright,' said Ruby. 'I'll do it.'

'Right. That'll save you and your club. And when I've finished with you, I'll be arranging to spend some time with your girlfriend too. But that can wait till another night. I want you first. Oh, and as for your cousins, I'll make sure them two cunts are fuckin' dealt with!'

Ruby felt a chill of terror as he glared at her before

summoning his men and leaving her and Tiffany, battered and devastated, amongst the wreckage of their massage parlour.

As soon as they were gone Ruby looked over to where Tiffany lay whimpering. 'Are you OK?' she asked.

'Think so,' cried Tiffany. 'But it fuckin' hurts.'

'Me too.'

Ruby got up off the floor, her body tender and throbbing in places. She went over to her girlfriend.

'Fuck! You're bleeding,' said Tiffany.

'It's OK. It's nothing,' Ruby responded, subconsciously placing her fingers on the bridge of her nose then quickly pulling them away when she felt the sting of a bruise beginning to form.

Ruby was trying to play it down even though she could already feel the blood congealing in her throat. She stuck out her hand and helped Tiffany off the floor then checked her over. Although there was no sign of blood, her face was flushed and already beginning to swell.

'Bastard's hit you in the face,' she murmured, her terror already being replaced by anger. 'Are you sure you're OK?'

Tiffany managed a faint smile. 'Yeah. What about you?'

'Sore,' said Ruby, stroking her tender back. 'But I don't think I've broken anything.'

'Me neither. But it fuckin' hurts.'

'That Kyle's a crafty bastard,' Ruby said. 'He knew just how much pain to inflict without doing any permanent damage. He wants us fit for work so he can carry on earning his fuckin' protection money.'

She dared to examine the waiting area. It was a mess. Her sofas had been split in several places, the foam bursting out of them. The pictures, which she had so carefully selected, had been dragged from the walls. Some of them were broken into pieces, and the coffee machine and planters had been knocked over, their contents leaving a muddy mess on the sumptuous pink carpet. Even the walls had angry gashes down them where the gang had hacked away with their machetes.

As she stared around at the devastation, Ruby could feel tears forming in her eyes. Even though she tried to fight her overwhelming emotion, she couldn't help but cry. Not only had she and Tiffany been left bloody and bruised, but the club had been ravaged too. Unlike the last attack, this one was intended to inflict maximum damage and Ruby knew she'd have to shut up shop for at least a few days while she carried out repairs. It would probably cost a fortune to put right too.

Tiffany walked painfully towards Ruby and gently wrapped her arms around her. For a few tearful minutes they remained wrapped in each other's arms trying to comfort each other as they took in the extent of the damage.

'I can't believe what they've done,' sobbed Tiffany.

'Bastards!' cursed Ruby.

'I heard what he said,' whispered Tiffany as though she was afraid to say the words out loud.

'What about?'

'About you meeting him. And then me.'

Now the immediate danger had passed, Ruby's terror was turning into fury. 'Don't worry, I won't let it get that fuckin' far!'

'What are you gonna do?' asked Tiffany.

'I don't know yet. Shit! I can't believe how far Josh and

Calvin went. I never thought they'd do something like that. What a pair of fuckin' idiots! And now we've got to pick up the pieces. I could have fuckin' told them Kyle would never stand for them killing one of his men.'

Tiffany went to speak, but her words were drowned out as Ruby continued with her rant.

'Just how the fuck did he know they're my cousins, and that you're my girlfriend?' Tiffany shrugged while Ruby carried on speaking. 'I need to ring Josh again. I want to know just what the fuck happened tonight.'

She grabbed her phone and dialled the numbers of both her cousins but there was still no reply. Frustrated, she slung the phone inside her handbag knowing she would have to wait until the following day to find her answers.

Still feeling hyped up, Kyle jumped into the passenger seat of the BMW while one of his gang took to the wheel. He looked back at the other gang members and exchanged high fives.

'Good job, lads,' he said, grinning. 'That should fuckin' show 'em what's what!'

His gang members shared his enthusiasm and for several minutes they offered their input, jeering and laughing about the damage they had inflicted. Their high spirits eventually lulled to an excited murmur and Kyle turned back round to face the road ahead as he became occupied with his own thoughts.

They'd certainly put Ruby in her place for now but he was still furious at the death of Ash. And he knew that, in terms of revenge, this was only the start. By the time he had finished, Ruby and her cousins would wish they'd never fucked with him.

A smile played across his lips as he thought about his forthcoming meeting with Ruby and what he was going to do to her. It would be the ultimate humiliation. He knew her feelings about men; he'd been sure to do his homework. So, what better way to get revenge than to force her to spend a few hours acting out all his depraved desires?

And, after that, he'd move onto her girlfriend. It gave him a sick buzz knowing that the time he spent with Tiffany would hurt Ruby even more than the time he spent with her, especially as Ruby would have already had her turn so she'd know exactly what he had lined up for her girlfriend.

Even then he wouldn't be finished because he still had the cousins to deal with. After what they had done, he knew he wouldn't stop until they were ruined. But that could wait for now. His first target was Ruby and he was looking forward to seeing just how much he could make her squirm.

57

July 2011

'Thank Christ I've got hold of you!' Ruby said into her mobile phone. 'I was trying all yesterday. Why the hell didn't you tell me you'd killed one of Kyle's men?' she asked her cousin, Josh. 'I can't fuckin' believe you'd go that far!'

'We were going to call, but it was late so we decided to hit the sack and ring you today. Why? What's the urgency?'

'What's the urgency? Are you for fuckin' real, Josh? You've killed a man! And Kyle's livid. Him and his gang came to the parlour last night. They smashed the place up and beat me and Tiffany up too.'

'You're fuckin' joking! Are you OK, cuz?'

'Just bruised,' she said, rubbing the painful area on her back, 'but they really shit us up! It was bad, Josh.' She could feel her voice crack with emotion but she tried not to let it show.

'Shit! I'm sorry, Ruby. I honestly thought he'd leave you alone after what we did to that guy.'

'Is that why you killed him?' asked Ruby. Then, before he had chance to respond, she added, 'You don't know him,

Josh. The guy's a fuckin' savage! And, to be honest, I'm shit scared of what he's gonna do next.'

This time Ruby did give in to her feelings. Her fear of reprisals overrode any need to put on a brave front as the worry about her imminent meeting with Kyle hung over her. Then a thought occurred to her. 'What about Gilly? You didn't kill him too, did you?'

'Nah, he was a piece of piss. The guy shit himself as soon as we took him outside the pub. I don't think you'll be having any more trouble from him.'

She let out a weary sigh. At least one of her problems had been dealt with. But then she thought of something else. 'Kyle's threatened to deal with you and Calvin too.'

'I'd like to see him fuckin' try!'

'You don't know what you're dealing with, Josh.'

'No, *you* don't know what you're dealing with. Believe me; we're used to taking care of fuckwits like him. He ain't no big deal! You've gotta do them before they fuckin' do you.'

'Is that why you killed that guy?' Ruby asked again.

She could hear Josh let out a puff of air, as though in irritation. 'Not really, no. We didn't really mean to fuckin' kill him. We were just gonna send out a warning, but the guy wouldn't cooperate so we just fuckin' did what we had to do.'

'Brilliant, well now we're all in the shit!' Ruby fumed. 'Because this won't stop here, Josh, I'm telling you.'

Josh raised his voice to counter Ruby's rage. 'Alright, alright! Shush a minute and listen to what I've got to say.' When Ruby went quiet, he carried on, 'If you really think it's gonna go further, then we've got to fuckin' get to him before he gets to us.'

'No!' said Ruby, shocked.

'Well what's the fuckin' alternative? Wait for him like sitting ducks?'

Ruby knew he had a point but she didn't like to think about how this was going to end. On the other hand, she didn't want Kyle to beat her. 'I don't know,' she said, already considering his suggestion.

'Right, I'll tell you what,' said Josh. 'You have a think about it and let me know when you've made a decision. But, in the meantime, we'll be looking out for him, and if this Kyle or any of his gang tries anything with us, they're fuckin' dead men.'

Ruby was at home and was supposed to be making phone calls to arrange repairs to the club while Tiffany was out shopping for some replacements. Despite their injuries they had decided to get things back to normal as soon as possible. Ruby didn't want to spend time moping around. As she'd told Tiffany, their injuries weren't major so she didn't see why they couldn't crack on with things.

But for Ruby it was also an act of defiance to show Kyle and his gang that they couldn't keep her down for long. Why should she lose money while the club remained shut? There was also the risk of the girls going elsewhere if they had to go too long without working. Besides, Ruby needed a focus to take her mind off things. It wouldn't do her any good to dwell on the vicious attack of the previous night and the ongoing menace from Kyle and his gang.

The problem was that once she'd finished her call with Josh, she couldn't concentrate on anything other than the predicament she was in. Ruby was in torment. She wished her cousins hadn't gone so far by killing one of Kyle's gang. But, even if they'd just given him a warning, would it have been enough? Kyle was so ruthless that she now doubted whether a warning alone would stop him.

But the damage had been done and she was already suffering repercussions. The evil look in Kyle's eyes last night as he had made his threats told her that he would stop at nothing in his quest to punish her and destroy her cousins. She didn't like to dwell on Josh's suggestion because she knew what it entailed and deep down she knew that the only way they would find any peace would be by wiping out Kyle and his gang.

Killing people was so abhorrent to her. If only there was another way! But despite the way she felt, Ruby couldn't come up with any other solution to their problems. As Josh had said, what was the alternative?

Thoughts were going around on a loop inside her head. Eventually, when she'd played them over several times, she pushed them aside, and got back to her phone calls. But disturbing thoughts kept returning: Kyle's threat to deal with her cousins, the terror of last night's attack and her imminent meeting with Kyle all refused to go away. They hovered in the background snarling at her conscious mind like a ferocious beast that wouldn't stay down.

Later that day, Ruby's phone rang and her anxious thoughts took over once more. It was Kyle. He came straight to the point.

'Right, Trina, or is it *Ruby* now?' His tone was arrogant and she hated the way he overemphasised the word Ruby as though scornful of her alter ego. 'I'm giving you a few days to recover, and I think that's more than generous. After all, you got off fuckin' lightly. It's not as if you've got any real injuries. So, let's say Saturday night, nine o'clock. I always like having a good time at the weekend.' He laughed but quickly resumed his hostile tone as he added, 'I want you to be in the club ready and fuckin' waiting for me.'

'But the club won't be ready by then. We've got repairs to do.'

'Do you think I'm fuckin' stupid?' he growled. 'We only smashed up the reception and waiting area. The rest of the rooms weren't fuckin' touched. So, we'll be using one of them. In fact, I'll enjoy seeing our handiwork on my way through the club.'

He sniggered and Ruby felt a stab of irritation, but it was overridden by her abject fear at the sound of his voice.

'So?' he shouted. 'Are you gonna fuckin' be there or do you wanna face more consequences?'

'Yes, I'll be there,' said Ruby, then she quickly cut the call.

For a few seconds she stared at her phone screen. She was sweating and the phone felt slippery in her hands. She put it back inside her handbag, the whole of her body now trembling.

Then she grew annoyed with herself. Why was she letting him get to her in this way? This wasn't who she was. He was only a man after all and, ever since she'd been a child, she'd always stuck up for herself. And now, here she was, letting a sly bastard like Kyle Gallagher beat her.

But it needn't be like that. She had the answers; she just needed to act on them. So she pulled her sweaty phone back out of her handbag and called up Josh's number. She knew now that things had already gone too far. It left her with no choice but to see it through to the end.

58

August 2011

It was two days later and Ruby's cousins had called round to see her and Tiffany.

'You still look fuckin' sore,' said Calvin when Ruby answered the door.

'Could have been worse,' said Ruby, trying to be blasé about the attack.

Once they had settled down in the living room and Tiffany had gone to fix them each a drink, Josh asked, 'How's things going with the club? Will you be able to get it up and running soon?'

'Hopefully,' said Ruby. 'We've managed to get hold of a lot of replacements but we'll have to wait for them to be delivered and I've got someone booked in to repair the walls next week.'

'That's good,' said Josh, looking cautiously at Tiffany as she came into the room carrying drinks.

'It's OK. Tiff knows everything,' said Ruby.

They all knew why he and Calvin were here and, now he knew Tiffany was on board, Josh came straight to the point. 'OK, like I told you on the phone, the plan is to hit the whole gang at once. We've done our homework and know the place they hang out. It's a pub called The Duck in Stockport. They normally go down there at weekends so we think Saturday would be a good night.'

He looked across at Calvin who nodded.

'Saturday?' asked Ruby, the terrifying thought of her upcoming meeting with Kyle sending a chill through her. 'What time?'

'Dunno. We've not decided yet. But we don't wanna make it too early. We wanna make sure they're all there.'

'Good idea,' said Ruby, trying to keep a cap on her fear. 'Why not make it around nine o'clock, nine-thirty?'

'Sure,' said Calvin while Josh nodded his agreement. 'We've heard Kyle's usually in by about half seven, but some of his guys come in a bit later.'

'OK,' said Ruby.

'I hope you realise things are gonna get brutal,' said Josh. 'Are you sure you're up for it, Ruby?'

Ruby looked across at Tiffany, noting the fear in her eyes before she said, 'Yes, I've thought it through and, like you say, there's no alternative. I need them wiped out otherwise they'll make my life a fuckin' misery. But I want no comeback.'

'Don't worry. We'll go in disguise and keep schtum. We always cover our backs. There's no way the police will be able to trace it back to us. Oh, and I wanna make sure you two won't say anything either.'

'Course we won't,' said Ruby.

'You sure?' asked Calvin, looking at Tiffany.

'Yes,' said Tiffany. 'Don't get me wrong, I don't like the

idea of any of this. But, like Ruby says, we've got no choice. It's the only way to get them off our backs.'

'OK, as long as we all understand,' said Josh.

For the next few minutes they made small talk. Ruby didn't add anything more about the proposed attack until Tiffany went into the kitchen to fetch them more drinks then she quickly said to her cousins, 'By the way, Kyle won't be there on Saturday.'

'Why not?' asked Josh.

'Because he'll be with me.'

'What the fuck?' said Calvin.

'Don't worry,' Ruby said. 'Just you take care of the rest of the gang. I'll sort Kyle out myself.'

'You sure you can deal with that, cuz?' asked Josh.

'Oh yeah,' said Ruby, outwardly confident.

Inside she was full of trepidation about what she had to do. But Kyle had tortured her for too long. After going over everything countless times in her head, Ruby had finally decided that she was no longer prepared to let him get away with it. Not only did she need to put a stop to Kyle, but she also wanted to make it clear to him that from now on she was the one in charge.

59

Saturday soon arrived. Ruby had thought about hardly anything other than her forthcoming meeting with Kyle and her cousins' plans to annihilate the rest of his gang. She was trying to quash the feelings of dread that consumed her, but found she couldn't settle to anything.

In the end she decided to visit her mother to take her mind off things while Tiffany was out visiting her own family. She surmised that Tiffany was finding things just as difficult and had therefore decided to go out rather than stay at home, anxiously waiting for the hours to tick by.

Ruby arrived at her mother's house clutching a bunch of flowers with plenty of cash in her purse. She had never got over her feelings of guilt for abandoning her mother when she was struggling and had been making up for it ever since with cash and presents whenever she visited.

When she arrived, there was no answer so she tried the front door handle, relieved to find it was open. She pushed her way inside the house and smiled on hearing the high-pitched, jangling sound of her brother Tyler's games console.

She fondly recalled buying it for him a few years previously and it amused her to think that he still played on it even though he was now well into his twenties.

But the smile slid from her face as soon as she walked into the lounge. Before she even saw her brother she sensed the smell of fear and took in the destruction. She could see that the room had been ransacked and scarlet smeared objects were scattered wantonly about.

Then she saw Tyler. His feet were protruding from the end of the armchair where he was sitting with his back to her. As she walked over to him she could see that his body was slumped over the arm, half-twisted as though he was trying to get up but hadn't made it.

His back was a mass of blood-drenched wounds, and as he lay prone the blood continued to seep, covering the seat and the carpet below. The games control had slipped from his hand and was lying on the floor in a pool of blood. Ruby put her hand to her mouth and yelped like a wounded animal.

The constant, repetitive chime of the games console heightened her distress and drew her attention to the TV. Jolly, animated images flashed across the screen, incongruent with the tragic scene. Ruby shifted her attention from the TV, one thought dominating her mind as she yelled for her mother, praying she had escaped the carnage.

Driven by desperation she fled from the lounge, back into the hall and towards the kitchen. But then she spotted something she had missed on the way in: a faint bloodstain on the wall near the kitchen, and a crimson footprint next to the door, darkening the mid-brown shade of the carpet. She rushed inside the room, dreading what she might find, and spotted her mother straightaway.

Daisy was at the kitchen counter, as she often was, preparing food. Ruby could see the veg, half-chopped in front of her and the aroma of stewed meat infused with her mother's herbs and spices filled the air, the pan bubbling away on the hob. But Daisy hadn't finished the job. She was slumped across the counter, the white plastic chopping board now coloured pink and her own chef's knife protruding from an angry wound in her back. Her hair was matted with the thick blood that clung to it and lacerations covered her head, arms and back.

Ruby dropped to her knees and yelled, 'Mam, no! Oh please no…' She became hysterical as shock and sorrow invaded her body and made her shudder with racking sobs. The sound of her agonised wailing drowned out even the chiming, merry sound of the games console coming from the front room.

She had never felt so bereft. Not since that other time when Kyle had left her wounded and traumatised. And as she took in the brutal scene in front of her, harrowing memories came flooding back once more, adding to her grief.

That other time it was her mother who had come to her rescue. She had always been there for her. *And how have I repaid her?* she thought, in despair: *By abandoning her then leading a life of debauchery and bringing ruthless villains to her door.*

Ruby didn't know how long she remained there, but when she eventually calmed down, she had an overwhelming urge to flee the house. She knew she should have called the police and waited for them to arrive but she couldn't bear to look at her mother's mutilated body any longer. So she dashed to her car and spent a tearful half hour driving around aimlessly, her tortured brain questioning the reason for such a callous and devastating attack.

What sort of person would do such a thing? Kyle? Gilly? Kyle's men? A random stranger?

Ruby's devastation and regret soon turned to fury as she thought about the sick mind behind such a brutal slaughter. And fury drove her on. The more she thought about it, the more she came to the conclusion that she knew exactly who had done this. There was only one person it could have been. And she was determined to get even with him in the most callous way possible.

60

It had to be Kyle. Gilly didn't know where her family lived and, as her cousins had pointed out to her, he was small fry and was too frightened to act out his threats once her cousins had finished with him. But Kyle was another matter; he was a major threat and she knew he was ruthless enough. He was also set on revenge and had made it clear that he would stop at nothing to get it.

The fury was building within Ruby. It was as though a box had been unlocked and an irate devil had jumped out. Her brain had fast-tracked to the angry stage of grief. The stage where it manifests itself in rage at the helplessness and injustice of it all. The stage where you question the world around you and how life can be so cruel. And the stage where you want reparation for your loss.

As Ruby's anger threatened to engulf her, she became increasingly determined that reparation was exactly what she was going to get. Despite her grief she would go ahead with the meeting with Kyle. In fact, the discovery of her slaughtered family strengthened her resolve to meet him.

But she would have to hold it together and channel her anger and sorrow, if she was to see this through.

It was five past nine, thirty seconds later than the last time Ruby had looked at her watch. The bastard was deliberately late! Inside the club it was eerily quiet, despite the music from the nightclub below, as they were still shut for renovations. As she sat behind the counter awaiting his arrival, Ruby could feel her heart thundering within her chest and a sheen of sweat covered her forehead. She gripped a pen in her clammy hands, tapping on the desk in front of her.

When she saw him walk through the door with that usual smug grin on his face, she felt as if her heart had jumped up into her throat and was about to choke her. She swallowed hard and took a deep breath as she looked across the reception area at her adversary.

'You not reopened yet then?' he asked, grinning and peering across at the waiting area, which was still in a state of disrepair.

'No, I'm afraid the thugs who did that left us a lot of fuckin' work to do,' she replied sarcastically.

'Ha, funny!' he commented. 'It'll teach you and your cousins not to fuckin' take the piss in future then, won't it?'

Ruby kept a lid on her emotions. She didn't want this to escalate. Not yet anyway. 'Come on then, let's get this over with,' she said, pretending to search for the keys.

'We'll take Rose's room,' he said, leering. 'Then I can pretend I'm fucking her. She was my first choice after all.'

Ruby could feel her anger rising to the surface again and with it her suppressed tears threatened to spill. Who did this little shit think he was? As if she was bothered about his preferences. Again she kept calm, focusing on her plan.

'Shit!' she said. 'Where did I put those bloody keys? I'm sure they were here a minute ago.' She pretended to search the drawers under the counter then presented a key to him. 'Nah, this is the only one I can find. It's for upstairs.'

'You can get fucked if you think I'm going up there where you take all your fuckin' weirdos.'

'OK, so d'you want to do it here in front of the window where anyone off the street can see?' she asked, satisfied as she saw Kyle mulling it over in his mind. After giving him a few seconds to think about it, she added. 'There is a bed in there as well you know; all the other stuff's behind a screen.'

'Go on then,' he capitulated. 'But no fuckin' funny business. I ain't into all that pervy stuff.'

She walked over to the door to Ruby's Dungeon and unlocked it, then climbed the stairs with Kyle following behind. With each step, trepidation threatened to take hold of her, but she fought to maintain control, ignoring her trembling limbs and racing heart.

Finally, she led him into the room and strode over to the bed where she waited for him to join her. Kyle jumped onto the bed, eager as a puppy, and lay alongside her on the scarlet satin bedding. Then he took in the rest of the room.

'Hang on a minute. Where's the fuckin' screen?' he demanded.

But he was too late. Ruby already had her knife jabbed up against his throat. She looked with satisfaction at the expression of sheer alarm on his face. He had obviously underestimated her. Perhaps he was carrying a weapon, but he hadn't even bothered taking it out, confident of his ability to overpower a feeble woman.

'Right, I want you to get up off the bed, really slowly,' she hissed. 'And don't try anything or I'll slit your fuckin' throat!'

'OK, like that, is it?' he asked.

He was putting on a brave act, but Ruby could see through it by the shock and terror in his eyes. Once he was up off the bed, she walked him across the room, keeping the knife pressed up against his throat till they reached the stocks.

'Get down on the floor!' she ordered.

'You must be fuckin' j—'

But Ruby cut him off, viciously jabbing the knife harder till she drew blood. 'Do as you're fuckin' told!' she snarled. Kyle complied. 'Right, good. Now I want you to put your feet and hands through the holes.'

Kyle looked up at her, his expression venomous. 'You'll fuckin' regret this!' he said.

'Do as you're told!' Ruby yelled. 'Now!'

She jabbed the knife again to let him know she was serious and was relieved when he carried out her command. As soon as she had him in the stocks, she secured them then raced downstairs and locked the entrance. Once she was back in her dungeon, she locked that door too. Ruby didn't want anybody to witness what she was about to do.

61

August 2011

She walked slowly round the stocks, enjoying the thrill of anticipation as she took in the agonised look on his face. They were a perfect choice for confinement, enabling her to see his every facial expression but also leaving his back exposed.

Being careful not to get too close, she bent and searched him, firstly pulling up his shirt then inserting her knife in the gap at the back of his trousers and yanking hard till the material split. She pulled the top half of his trousers away and peered into the space between his groin and the stocks. But there was no weapon concealed there.

'You might have shown a bit more enthusiasm,' she mocked, referring to his flaccid penis. 'Most of my clients would have been really excited by this stage.'

'Fuck you, bitch!' he cursed and she knew he was attempting to cover real fear through his angry outburst.

Next she walked round to the front of the stocks, satisfied when she saw him squirm as she approached his feet. Again she inserted the knife and pulled, this time in the bottom of his trouser legs, each one in turn. There she saw the blade, tucked away inside one of his socks. She grabbed it then made a show of examining it before slowly crossing the room and adding it to her rack of implements.

'Should come in handy,' she said before selecting a bullwhip and walking back to the stocks with a fake smile plastered on her face.

His eyes became wide with alarm. 'Steady,' she said, putting down the whip. 'Not yet. We've got something else to do first.'

She walked behind the stocks again and, without giving him chance to anticipate what she might do, she inserted the knife once more, beneath his shirt, and yanked hard, gratified when she heard him let out a terrified screech. The material gave away easily, dropping limply to each side of his bare back.

Ruby raced round to the front of the stocks again, but Kyle had lowered his gaze to the floor; denying her the pleasure of his misery. She bent down and grabbed his hair then wrenched his head back till his eyes stared up at her. 'Pay attention!' she mocked. 'You don't wanna miss the show, especially when you're the star turn.'

Kyle spat at her venomously. 'You'll fuckin' pay for this, you cunt!'

She let his head drop while she wiped the saliva from her face. 'Oh no!' she said, annoyed. 'You're the one who'll pay.'

Ruby swapped the knife for the bullwhip, glad to see him staring up at her now with terror in his eyes. She had deliberately selected one of the most dangerous whips available and she made a show of running her hand along the sturdy handle down to the tail, which came to a menacing twin point like the tongue of a hissing snake.

Then she was behind him once more with her whip ready. Ruby brought it down swiftly across his back. She could hear him painfully sucking in his breath as the tough leather marked his back and the tail ends curled viciously around the delicate flesh on the sides of his body.

Without giving him chance to recover Ruby brought the whip down repeatedly, harder each time till the flesh pierced and Kyle's tainted blood trailed down his back. At first all she heard was a whimper, but as the strokes became harder, he cried out, then screamed in agony. Ruby kept going till he begged her to stop.

'Had enough?' she asked, walking to the front of him once more. This time he didn't curse, the fear of reprisals too painful to bear. 'Not your scene?' she added. 'What a pity! Some of my clients really enjoy it.'

His face contorted with a mix of fear and anger, but still he didn't speak.

'OK,' said Ruby, revelling in this level of control, despite her grief. 'I'll let you have a break, shall I?' She saw the relief wash over him as his limbs became less taut and the intensity of his gaze softened. 'I need to talk to you anyway.'

She now swapped the whip for the knife and was rewarded by a renewed look of panic in his eyes. 'What the fuck do you want?' he asked, desperately. 'You've had your fun so why don't you just fuckin' let me go?'

'Not half as much fuckin' fun as you've had tonight though!' she raged. She could see the shock in his face now. 'Oh yeah, you didn't think I knew, did you?' she shouted, feeling her distress re-emerge, but channelling it into anger.

'Did it give you a sick kind of kick knowing you were going to see me just after you'd fuckin' annihilated my family?' she demanded, her fury now very real.

Even though she was the one in control, Kyle couldn't resist a smirk at the thought of what he had planned, which only intensified her anger. She jabbed the knife hard into his shoulder till the smirk turned into a grimace.

'What were you planning to do, tell me after you'd fucked me, you sick bastard?' she shouted.

He laughed but it was edged with desperation. It was the only way he could get at her now, and he knew it. But she would beat him with words as well as actions.

Then she dealt him a devastating verbal blow. 'You might like to know that they're not the only ones being annihilated tonight.' His expression told her she had won. 'Yes, that's right.' She made a show of looking at her watch. 'It won't be long now till all of your gang are wiped out.'

'You fuckin' bitch!' he yelled, twisting and pulling at the stocks, despite his pain, in a futile attempt to escape. 'I'll fuckin' kill you for this and your bastard cousins!'

'No, you won't. I call the shots now, and I haven't even started with you yet!'

Ruby moved nearer to him, kneeling on the ground with the knife raised. Then she held it close to his face. She let a few seconds pass, revelling in Kyle's terrorised expression. She was just about to take her next step when she smelt the pungent odour of urine at the same time as it crept along the ground and seeped through the material of her jeans. Kyle had pissed himself.

Ruby felt repulsed, but there was no point in dashing away; her jeans were already sodden. Besides, she was determined to finish this. 'Dirty bastard!' she cursed before pushing the knife further forward till it made contact with his face.

'No!' he yelled, pulling back. 'No, no, please no!'

It was gratifying hearing him plead and seeing his anger and torment at not being able to do anything to save his gang or alter his own fate. But, at the same time, it brought back to her how she had felt all those years ago. Ten years of age, and petrified. She fought back those feelings. It was time to pass them onto him.

'This is how painful it felt, Kyle,' she said, pushing the knife slowly into his cheek till the blood spurted out and Kyle screamed. Then she carved the flesh, slowly, painstakingly, reminding him all the while of what he did to her when she was just a kid.

'It fuckin' hurts, doesn't it?' she said. 'And the hurt doesn't stop when the wound heals. Because then you've got the fuckin' scar and all the pitying looks, and the comments, and the whispers that come with it. Then there's all the time spent trying to cover it with makeup, hoping people will stop noticing it. But they never do,' she said, a scowl forming on her face as she allowed the memories to resurface.

When she had finished, she pulled the knife out and stood back, watching him bleeding and howling in pain and self-pity.

'And now you're probably wondering what it will feel like to go through your life with a scar like that, aren't you?' she asked.

Kyle shook his head, all attempts at macho now abandoned as the tears flooded his cheeks. Then his head tilted to one side. He was growing weak as the blood from his various wounds streamed from him; the pool of urine now reddening as it oozed along the ground.

Ruby grabbed his hair and yanked his head back once more. 'Now you know how it fuckin' feels!'

Despite his fragile state, Kyle began yelling abuse at her once more, then screaming for help. Ruby felt his shrill and strident screams pierce through her ears. A final assault. And Ruby couldn't allow that. She sought the exposed part of his gut, plunging the knife deep into his side and slicing through his vital organs till he was silent. Then she withdrew the knife and watched his body slump against the stocks.

Sudden realisation of what she had done shot through her and Ruby broke down. Her mind was a frantic maelstrom of emotions: grief over her family and devastation at the scene in front of her. Earth-shattering cries escaped from her lips. She was trembling, her heart pulsating and her eyes and nose streaming.

When she'd been in that state for several minutes, Ruby heard her phone ping. The sound cut through her sorrow and brought her to her senses. She lifted the phone and pulled up a message on her screen. Then she stared at the text through tear-filled eyes. It was from her cousin Josh, just four words, but it told her all she needed to know.

The job's been done

It was over.

Acknowledgements

It is so amazing to think that the second book in *The Working Girls* series, *Ruby*, is already out there. The time has passed so quickly since I thought of the idea for this series of books.

Ruby was a tricky one to write due to the dual timelines and I did get myself into a bit of a muddle at one point. Fortunately, feedback from Hannah Smith, my excellent developmental editor, was extremely helpful and she enabled me to get back on track with the novel and make substantial improvements.

Big thanks go to all the staff at Aria. I'd particularly like to mention Hannah Smith, Victoria Joss, Nikky Ward and Laura Palmer who do a lot of work behind the scenes both in terms of publication, and marketing and promotion. Thanks also to my copy editor Claire Rushbrook, and Geo Willis for doing a great job with the proofreading.

I couldn't let the publication of *Ruby* go by without mentioning the wonderful Sarah Ritherdon. She was my original editor who welcomed my ideas for *The Working*

Girls with boundless enthusiasm and was a great source of support and encouragement. I wish her well with her future career.

I would like to take this opportunity to thank the Writers Bureau again for their excellent creative writing course and for featuring me in this years' advertising campaign as one of their success stories.

Thank you to all my dedicated readers for continuing to buy and review my books and to the many of you who have purchased copies of *The Working Girls* series ahead of publication day. Thanks also to the book blogging and book reviewing community who take the time to review books and bring them to the attention of readers.

Last but not least I would like to thank all my family, friends, and friends of friends many of whom both buy my books and recommend them to others. Your continued support has been touching.

Newport Community
358
Learning & Libraries

About Heather Burnside

Heather Burnside previously worked in credit control and accounts until she took a career break to raise two children. After ten years as a stay-at-home mum, she decided to move away from credit control and enrolled on a creative writing course.

She started her writing career twenty years ago when she began to work as a freelance writer while studying for a writing diploma. As part of her studies, Heather wrote the first chapters of her debut novel, *Slur*. During that time she also had many articles published in well-known UK magazines.

Heather later ran a writing services business, but eventually returned to her first novel, *Slur*, which became the first book in *The Riverhill Trilogy*. Heather followed *The Riverhill Trilogy* with *The Manchester Trilogy* then her current series, *The Working Girls*.

You can find out more about the author by signing up to the Heather Burnside mailing list for the latest updates, including details of new releases and book bargains, or by following any of the links below.

Sign up to my mailing list
Heather's readers

Find me on Twitter
https://twitter.com/heatherbwriter

Find me on Facebook
https://www.facebook.com/HeatherBurnsideAuthor/

Visit my website
https://www.heatherburnside.com.

25/2/22

PILLGWENLLY